Promise
Bound

ALSO BY ANNE GREENWOOD BROWN

Lies Beneath

Deep Betrayal

Promise Bound

ANNE GREENWOOD BROWN

delacorte press

Text copyright © 2014 by Anne Greenwood Brown
Jacket art copyright © 2014 by Elena Kalis

All rights reserved. Published in the United States by Delacorte Press, an imprint of Random House Children's Books, a division of Random House LLC, a Penguin Random House Company, New York.

Delacorte Press is a registered trademark and the colophon is a trademark of Random House LLC.

Visit us on the Web! randomhouse.com/teens

Educators and librarians, for a variety of teaching tools, visit us at RHTeachersLibrarians.com

Library of Congress Cataloging-in-Publication Data
Brown, Anne Greenwood.
Promise bound / Anne Greenwood Brown. – First edition.
pages   cm
Sequel to: Deep betrayal.
Summary: "The stakes are high, with many lives at risk, but Calder and Lily must confront the past as well as their darkest impulses if they want a chance at being together" – Provided by publisher.
ISBN 978-0-385-74383-9 (hardback) – ISBN 978-0-385-37129-2 (ebook)
[1. Mermen–Fiction. 2. Mermaids–Fiction. 3. Love–Fiction. 4. Families–Fiction. 5. Superior, Lake–Fiction.]   I. Title.
PZ7.B812742Pr 2014
[Fic]–dc23
2013028765

Printed in the United States of America

10 9 8 7 6 5 4 3 2 1

First Edition

Random House Children's Books supports the First Amendment and celebrates the right to read.

For Sammy, Matt, and Sophie,

who changed my world forever

PROLOGUE

CALDER

Jack Pettit was dead but louder than ever. Pavati might have put an end to his obsessive mission to "out" the merpeople, but it wasn't like we were rid of him. Lily–who had a knack for blaming herself for everything–would never forgive herself for his death, and Gabby Pettit's incessant calls made sure she'd never forget.

Still, Gabby hadn't been the only one affecting Lily's mood. Sometime last August, a slightly incoherent Daniel Catron stumbled back to Bayfield after taking off with Pavati. At the time, none of us knew how successful Pavati's procreation plans had been with Daniel. Just in case our fears were realized, Lily befriended him—counseled him, really—to make sure he understood the consequences of agreeing to father a merchild: namely, the need to raise it for a year and then return the baby, without argument, as soon as it was walking. Lily didn't want her family history to repeat itself. None of us wanted that.

But more than Gabby's persistent questions and Daniel's perpetual obsessing, it was Lily's newly acknowledged mergenetics that grated on my mind. "Tomorrow's Friday," she'd say, announcing the end of every week like an alarm clock going off, breaking my heart with the delicacy of a sledgehammer.

Lily would have liked to swim every day, but the metamorphosis back to legs was still so excruciating for her that a weekly torture session was all she could stomach. Jason swam every day, but I waited out the dry week with Lily, unwilling to leave her behind anymore. When Jason's Friday class was over, we'd all take to the water together, returning at sunrise on Saturday mornings. Lily would make me and Jason leave the water first and go back to the house without her. It wasn't just for modesty; she didn't want us to witness her straining and writhing on the beach.

As soon as we reentered the house, Jason would put on Queen's *Greatest Hits* and turn the volume up to ten. Neither of us confessed to Lily that it was never enough to drown out her screams.

Mrs. Hancock—Carolyn, she wanted me to call her, but

I just couldn't do it, so we settled on Mrs. H—dealt with her anxiety over Lily by fussing over me. Each night she made me a comfortable bed on the family room couch, by the fire. Though I reveled in her motherly attentions, it was painful to watch as she maneuvered her wheelchair around the couch, ineffectively tugging at sheets and denying the need for help.

Being part of the Hancock family was better than I could have ever hoped for. It made me eager to solidify my role in the family, and there was a ring in my duffel bag that gave testament to how ready I was to make the ultimate promise. If only I could find the right time. The right words.

So I guess it was no surprise that, with all these distractions, I barely noticed when summer slipped away and was startled by a yellow leaf that floated past my face and settled gently on my toes. I wanted to leave for the Bahamas as soon as the last Labor Day vacationer had packed his station wagon and grabbed a coffee for the road trip home, but Lily had other ideas.

She wanted to go. I was sure of it. Who wouldn't want to explore that new world I described for her late at night as we whispered together in the hammock—a new world filled with turquoise water, red coral, and conch sandwiches on sugar-sand beaches?

But we were all making sacrifices.

Jason had to stay behind and teach at the college, so Lily and I agreed to suffer through the winter in solidarity. If she had known back in September how hard the winter would be, it might not have been such an obvious choice for her. But she'd never shied away from what was hard, so there was little use in pushing her.

Or maybe I let her have her way because I secretly hoped she'd regain her humanity once winter's brutality made the water easier to resist. I was wrong, of course. Winter's ice didn't take away the lure of the lake for any of us. It only sharpened the barb.

Mrs. H's generous acceptance of her family's new "idiosyncrasies" made it easy for Jason to finally get his act together and stay close to home. For Christmas, she bought us an industrial-sized bubbler, which Jason ran on an extension cord to the end of the dock. It hung in the water and kept a twenty-foot circle from freezing. There, in that miserably frigid reprieve we came to call the Spa, Jason, Lily, and I escaped our drying bodies and burned off the pent-up energy that sizzled in our veins.

This was the pattern of my and Lily's lives: six days of drying, one day of freezing, and the steely gray of winter holding us all in its cold embrace. It felt like a never-ending waiting period. Me, impatiently waiting for Lily to change her mind and catch a red-eye to the Caribbean. Jason, stoically waiting for his class to end so he could escape his human legs. Lily's little sister, Sophie, waiting in wonder to see what *she'd* become. Mrs. H, waiting anxiously to see who'd leave her first.

And then, of course, we were all waiting for Maris and Pavati to return to Bayfield with the spring migration—and, most impatiently, for what Pavati might return *with*. If

Daniel Catron had managed to father a merchild, none of us knew how a baby would factor into our lives, and none of us was really that eager to find out.

Once Lily turned the calendar from April to May, we didn't have much longer to wait.

PART ONE

Listen! you hear the grating roar
Of pebbles which the waves draw back, and fling,
At their return, up the high strand,
Begin, and cease, and then again begin,
With tremulous cadence slow, and bring
The eternal note of sadness in.

—Matthew Arnold, "Dover Beach"

1

LILY

It was happening again. I could tell because everything was in color, as if I were Dorothy leaving Kansas and landing in Oz. My dreams used to be in black-and-white. Not so much lately.

Ever since I started wearing the beach glass pendant once worn by Nadia White, my grandmother and Calder's adopted mermaid mother, my dreams had purpose. I didn't know how it worked, and Calder blamed it all on my overactive imagination, but Nadia directed my dreams.

What was more irritating, she never let me be just a

fly on the wall, watching events unfold. Rather, she made me the star–or herself the star, with me wearing her skin. I could barely tell where Nadia's body left off and mine began. Tonight, as I drifted off to sleep, my body felt foreign once again, like a glove when you're used to wearing mittens. . . .

I am walking up the path to my front door. My grandfather, Tom Hancock, has left the door unlocked, but it's not because he is expecting us . . . me . . . *Nadia.* Whatever.

The lack of invitation does not prevent us from stealing into his warm and tidy house and standing outside his bedroom door. From our position in the hallway, we can hear the bedsprings groan as he turns over. We hear a woman's sigh–like gravel on our heart. We close our eyes to shut off the urge to scream at them both, to rip all the hair from the woman's head. Instead, we climb the narrow staircase, touching the pictures on the wall. At the top, we trail along the dark corridor to the nursery and step inside, inhaling the sweet baby smell. Vanilla and lavender.

The moment is pure as sunlight, tickling our senses, but is interrupted by the creak of a loose floorboard on a stubborn nail. We scurry deeper into the room, holding tight to the wall like a startled crayfish.

"What are you doing, Nadia?" Tom asks, his voice dangerously calm.

My grandfather is just as perfect as Nadia remembered. Young. Broad-shouldered. A rough scruff around his jaw. Good hands.

You should be mine, Nadia thinks. *You should be with me. Not with that plain, mouse-colored woman asleep in your bed.* Instead, we say, "Jason is a year old. He's walking."

"I won't let you take him," Tom says.

"Watch me," we say, suddenly brave, louder than we planned.

He reaches forward—both angry and terrified—and takes two steps closer. "Quiet. Diana is sleeping. She thinks I'm a widower."

We shudder at the thought. If Tom only knew how dead we feel. We say, "What do I care of her?" thankful that our words are strong and clear.

Tom closes the nursery door and turns on a small lamp that barely casts a shadowed glow around the pale blue room. The smell of the lake drifts through the open window. It lends the effect of being underwater. Nadia hopes Jason likes it.

Without planning to move, she and I are gliding across the floor. If the braided rug lies under our feet, we cannot feel it. Our hand, long and tapered, each finger like bleached driftwood, strokes the blond head dreaming in the crib.

Jason. My father.

Tom is close behind us. He winds his fingers through a lock of our hair. "You're so beautiful," he says, and for a second Nadia thinks he has changed his mind, that both he and the baby will be coming with us. Tom's voice drops, low and soothing but still negotiating. We can hear the strategy behind the comfort. His warm hand cups our shoulder. "Find someone else, Nadia. Start another family. Leave Jason with me."

A rush of heat flashes through our body and sparks snap in the dry air. Tom jerks his hand back. He knows better than to touch Nadia now, but not enough to stop explaining. "Please don't take my son," he says.

"Your son? Jason is mine," we say.

Tom's face hardens. His pupils expand until his eyes are black, smoldering things. The anxious fear of defeat burns in our gut, but we do not let our feelings betray us.

"He belongs with me," we say.

"Over my dead body," says the man who used to love us, I mean *her* . . . Nadia.

We keep the feeling of betrayal trapped under the heavy weight of our heart. "Tempting," we say.

He smirks. "You've told me too many of your secrets. I know how to avoid you, if I wish."

We lean into him, a molten and hypnotic pulse building steadily behind our eyes.

He diverts his gaze and crosses the room. "Nice try," he says.

We would have pursued him, but the baby rolls over, cooing sweetly. His cherubic lips purse like the open end of a raspberry. Our heart lurches with longing for him. We lunge, but Tom is quick. He has us by the neck, and he throws us against the wall. The window beside our head rattles in its frame, and we feel the chain slip from our neck, snaking over our bare shoulders before the beach glass pendant hits the floor.

"Don't touch him," Tom warns.

"This isn't over," we say. "You made me a promise."

"Some promises were meant to be broken," he says. "I can't turn my son over to a murderer. I can't let him become one."

"You didn't have a problem with who I was before," we say. "I am not the one who has changed." The sky rumbles with thunder, and the floorboards quake. The tremor races up the wall studs, through the drywall, and along our spine.

"Babies change every love story," he says, and we have no answer because we know he is right. "Now go before I reveal you to the world. I should think that would put a terrible crimp in your hunting patterns."

Fear runs the length of our arms. If he made good on his threat, what would become of Maris? Of Pavati and Tallulah? "You wouldn't."

"Try me."

We swallow hard and call his bluff. "No one would believe you."

"Is that a gamble you're willing to take?" he asks.

We straighten our shoulders. "I want my family to be together."

Tom's face transforms with an expression we cannot read. His colors are sad and worried and laced with . . . hope? It is only a flash, but that brilliant gleam of optimism leaves an unmistakable glow. Hope that we will be together someday? We have to assume our eyes don't deceive us, though Tom is quick to mask the emotion. Still, that glimmer of hope gives us the courage to leave and try again another night.

"Your necklace," Tom says, reaching for the floor.

"Give it to our son," says Nadia, slipping away from me like water through my fingers, leaving me alone in the dream, and then . . .

I woke up in Sophie's room (again), standing over her bed (again), while she released a banshee-like scream that rattled the glass in the windows. Again.

"Oh, for the love of God." I slapped my hand over my little sister's mouth, but she peeled away my fingers and took a swing at me. A pile of books lay open on her bed and a few slipped to the floor. The corner of one just about impaled my foot.

"What's with all the books?" I asked.

Sophie slapped my arm and said, "Lepidoptera." Then she groaned at my blank expression. "I'm studying butter-flies. Now would you please stop sneaking up on me when I'm sleeping? You're going to give me a heart attack."

"Shhh, you're only eleven."

"I don't think that'll matter. What do you want?"

What did I want? For one, I wanted these dreams to stop, because if living in Nadia's head weren't exhausting enough, the chronic sleepwalking was turning me into the walking dead. Calder had told me the legend last summer–that Nadia's pendant held his family's histories–but if Nadia was trying to tell me something with these nightly episodes, she was being way too subtle for me. *Spell it out, Grandma. Then maybe we can both get some rest.*

"Sorry, Soph. Go back to sleep."

"That's it?"

"I said I was sorry. Go back to your butterfly dreams."

Sophie groaned and flipped over. She covered her head with her pillow, mumbling, "You are so weird."

I tiptoed back down the hall, hesitating in the spots where my grandparents' ghosts still lingered along the walls and feeling the deep pit of loneliness that Nadia's absence always left in my stomach.

2

CALDER

Sophie's scream woke me up sometime after midnight. I whipped off the covers and leapt over the back of the couch, heading for the ladderlike stairs that led from the Hancocks' front door to Lily's and Sophie's bedrooms upstairs.

"Trouble sleeping?" I whispered, crawling up the first three steps, careful not to wake Jason and Mrs. H, amazed that they too hadn't heard the scream.

Lily slowly descended the stairs, her feet uncertain. She'd fallen asleep in her clothes, and an oversized cardigan drooped off her right shoulder. "Sleeping fine," she lied as the pallor of mustard-colored anxiety slowly drained from her face.

"You could have fooled me," I said. Maris had called during the day. She and Pavati would be arriving in less than twelve hours. I blamed them for Lily's restlessness.

"It's just freezing up there," she said.

Her hair was a wild tangle of red that gave her a beautifully feral look. I didn't say it out loud, though. She brushed off compliments like a nuisance fly. So instead I watched her finish her slow trip down the stairs.

Lily took my fingers lightly in hers and led me back to the couch. She curled into the indentation I'd left in the cushions and faced the fireplace, where, by now, there was only a faint, flickering glow from the remaining log on the grate.

"Feeling better yet?" I asked, though I could see she was still exhausted from her last transformation.

"Maybe if I swam more often it wouldn't be so bad."

"You don't want to overexert yourself."

"At the very least I don't want to hold you back. Don't wait for me. You should go out tomorrow with Dad. You're looking a little dry." She moved over to make room for me on the couch. I hesitated, looking anxiously toward her parents' bedroom.

"If it's all the same," I said, "I'm happier suffering through with you. Besides, you know how much I love a challenge." And it was true. I was pretty damn impressed with myself. A six-day stretch between transformations! It used to be I'd get the shakes after twenty-four hours. A year ago, three days nearly turned me to chalk. I didn't know if it was a matter of practice, sheer will, creative coping skills, or something more phenomenal than all three put together, but I didn't really care so long as I could be there for Lily. I could see how much she needed me.

"Good," she said, as if she were considering a different challenge altogether, and placed her palm over the pendant around her neck.

"Why don't you just take that thing off?" I asked.

She looked at me miserably. "I would, but I feel uneasy without it. I . . . I think Nadia is trying to communicate with me. Remember that story you told me?"

"No."

"You don't remember?"

"I mean, no, I don't want to hear it. I'm sorry, Lily. I really am. But I don't want to talk about my mother."

She stifled a yawn. "That's fine. I don't really want to talk about her either."

"It's probably your imagination," I said. "And the stress of all the changes you're going through."

"I thought you didn't want to talk about it."

I frowned.

"Okay," said Lily, "then let me rephrase my earlier statement. I don't think Nadia is trying to communicate with me. I *know* she is. It's just that I don't know what she's trying to say. You told me the pendant stores mermaid histories."

"That's just a legend," I said.

"Like the dagger was supposedly part of the legend? Like Maighdean Mara was only a myth?"

"Point taken, but that doesn't mean you don't have an overactive imagination."

Lily avoided the argument and changed the subject. "Gabby called again today," she murmured, tapping the couch cushions for me to lie down.

I added another log to the fire and lay beside her, curling my body around hers, protecting her from a threat that I could feel but couldn't see. Lily pressed her face against my shoulder while the logs crackled in the stone fireplace.

"Did you talk to her this time," I asked, my lips behind her ear, "or did you make her leave another message?"

"I couldn't avoid it anymore. Gabby's pretty persistent."

"Is she enjoying college?"

Lily traced the point of my collarbone with her finger. "That's not what she wanted to talk about."

Yeah. I knew that. Lily rolled onto her back, and the fire cast a warm glow across her face. She closed her eyes, and her lids shimmered like gold leaf in the firelight. This was how I preferred her. Warm. The raspberry-pink glow of happiness melting around the outline of her curves. It had been awhile since I'd seen those colors on her.

Lily sighed, and I kissed her forehead. "So what do I do about Gabby? And Jack?" she asked.

"I've told you. There's nothing anyone can do for Jack."

Nearly half a century as a merman, and I'd never had to deal with this side of things before. It made me uncomfortable to think of all the families who were still searching for children because of what I'd done. The days when I hunted humans to satisfy my emotional appetites seemed like a million years ago. Ever since Lily had fallen–literally–into my life, I'd forgotten what it felt like to be empty, desolate, alone. The need to hunt was forever gone.

Lily rubbed the pendant, her thumb moving methodically over its smooth contours.

As she did so, my eyes watched the ring finger on her left hand, wondering, dreaming. Unbeknownst to her, I'd spent some time over the winter fashioning a ring for her. It wasn't fancy, only braided copper wire and a polished agate. But now that it was finished, I had no idea how to present it to her. I didn't even know what it should mean. Only that I wanted her with me. Always.

I'd told Jason about it over a week ago. I guess I was asking his permission. I'd seen that in the movies, but his reaction didn't make me any braver.

Jason: "Well, what did Lily have to say about it?"

Me: "I haven't said anything to her. I thought it was normal to ask the father first."

Jason: "Son, I appreciate the gesture, don't get me wrong. But this isn't something you should surprise her with. Are you sure? You're both so young."

Me: "Do you think she'd say no?"

Jason: "I think she'd say what's the hurry."

Hurry. The need for hurry glowed in Lily's skin, and in her eyes, and in the light that shone from both. Or rather, the absence of that light. Couldn't Jason see that in his own daughter? Couldn't Sophie, who despite her maintained humanity was more in tune to moods and emotions than any full-blooded mermaid I knew?

Jason: "It doesn't have to be an engagement ring. Why don't you call it a promise ring? They were very popular in my day."

I had to admit, a promise ring fit my mer-sensibilities. In promising myself to Lily—a promise she knew I'd be incapable of breaking—maybe I could restore some of the happiness that last summer's events had stolen from her. I don't know. Maybe I was kidding myself.

As Lily worked the pendant in her fingers, she didn't blink; her thoughts seemed very far away. "We could fake some postcards from Jack," she said, propping herself up on one elbow. "You could go to Canada and send them from there, saying, 'Don't worry about me. I'm hiking through Ontario. I'm fine. Love, Jack.' That sort of thing. I wish I had saved the card he gave me. You could have used it to copy his handwriting. It was messy. That's all I can say about it."

Beneath her oversized cardigan I recognized the Jimi Hendrix T-shirt she'd worn when she confronted Jack, and nearly lost her life.

"I would never go to Canada without you," I said. I waited a few seconds, but she didn't respond. Finally I prompted, "So?"

"So . . . what?" she asked.

"So, if I go to Canada, will you come with me?"

She looked at me with a serious expression. "Do you think postcards would give the Pettits some peace?"

"What more can we offer? Really, Lily, people go missing every day."

"And that's supposed to make me feel better?"

No. Not really. I drew one finger through her hair and

tucked a strand behind her ear. "Why do you have to feel bad about this? It's not your fault what happened to Jack."

"It feels like my fault."

I sighed, trying to be patient. "If it were up to you, everything would be your fault . . . but you didn't answer my question."

"What question?" Pine sap snapped in the fireplace and scattered sparks on the hearth.

"If I go to Canada, will you come with me?"

"Let's just wait and see," she said, kissing the end of my nose as if punctuating a sentence.

3

LILY

When I came down the stairs, I was glad to find Calder awake, too. I didn't want to go back to sleep. I smiled against his chest, remembering the way he half crawled, half climbed the stairs toward me and, when he stood up, how his pajama bottoms hung low on his hips, revealing the line of muscle that made my insides squirm.

His bare chest, broad and scarred with a crisscross of cuts in various stages of healing, expanded with a deep intake of breath. I'd never felt the misery I'd seen in regular mermaids, but his reaction to me—like I was filling some emotional tank—wasn't too hard to understand. I felt the same way.

Calder's body warmed me even more than the fire. I curled into his chest and wrapped one arm around him, pulling my knee up over his leg. He drew me closer, and I inhaled the patchouli-like scent of smoke and incense that perfumed his skin and flooded my mind with memories. He dipped his chin and tipped mine up, kissing me.

"Don't fall asleep," he said. "You need to get back to your room before your dad gets up for a midnight snack."

I smiled at the thought of getting caught, but it barely moved my lips. All I could think of was how stupid I was being. Why had I suggested Canada? I wished I'd never brought it up. Why drag out hope for the Pettits that Jack was alive? It was cruel, really. Irrational thought must be the result of interrupted sleep. Right now, I wanted nothing more than three solid hours of dreamlessness. Was that really so much to ask?

No more, I said soundlessly.

Though Nadia had been dead for over thirty years, I trusted she could hear me. *I'm just so tired. No more dreams.*

"Don't fall asleep," Calder said.

But I counted my breaths like sheep, marking each one with another plea because I knew Nadia had more to say tonight, and just like that, in the silent space between two breaths, the line between our two selves began to blur and blend like cream stirred into coffee. I slipped deeper into the dark well of her mind, my bloodstream cooling and my mind roiling bleak and black until the moment when I lost myself: I am me, and then I am we, and then I am not.

* * *

Nadia swims the shoreline. Her body is a solid sheath of muscle and pink iridescent scales that dazzle the school of fish trailing in her wake. Her mind is a tangled web of fury and grief. Someone has wronged her, and whoever that is, he should be afraid. She emerges from the lake, breaking the silver plane with head and shoulders. Dark rings of water run from her body.

Through her large eyes I see my house. Lichen grows on the shingles. Ah, I understand things now. It has been a long time since Tom Hancock has been here. It has been many years since he took Nadia's son.

I clutch my chest in pain. From Nadia's center, dark anger simmers, then boils like pitch, finally exploding in a bolt of electricity from her eyes and fingertips. The electric charge strikes an enormous willow tree at the shoreline and splits a branch down the length of the trunk, charring it, laying it bare on top of the water. Small green leaves rain down.

A sound of disgust rattles in the back of her throat, and with a great whip of her tail, she drowns the beach in a wave.

The dream drifted effortlessly to a new scene: a very young Maris cowers in the shadow of a sunken log and watches her mother. Nadia feels her eyes on her but does not acknowledge her daughter's presence. Instead, she weaves in and out of caves, scraping her belly and tail along the rock, releasing her grief in a long trail of blood. She sings a lullaby that turns into a dirge.

Then there is a noise, or the feeling of noise: a suction and a sinking. And then again, this time louder and heavier than before. The sound pulls Nadia away from the rocks, and she spies a tiny boy clawing with open fingers for the surface. His jaw slackens as his head falls forward, his body rising as if pulled upward from the shoulders. A tremor of bubbles, and the last bit of air escapes the little boy's nose.

Black heavy curls float around the boy's small face like a dark angel's halo. "Calder!" I call out with a gasp.

I woke with a start. A cool hand rested gently on my shoulder and rocked me back and forth. "Babe, it's time. You've got to get ready."

I scowled at whatever was shaking me. Too rough. Too much. Stop it.

"Babe, it's time to get up."

I opened my eyes, disoriented for a moment, thinking the window was in the wrong place and I was too high off the ground. I gripped the edge of my blanket, hoping to find my place in the texture of its fabric.

"You fell asleep downstairs," Calder said. "I had to carry you up before your parents woke up."

"Oh," I said, slowly recognizing the dead-poet portraits on my bedroom wall and the mountain of clean and dirty laundry on the floor. "Sorry."

"Never a problem."

I could still feel the coolness of Nadia's pulse in the pendant. I rolled over so Calder couldn't see my face. He had an easy enough time reading my emotions without letting him see the worry so plainly on my face.

"You really need to get a good night's sleep," he said. "It's like trying to raise the dead with you."

That's ironic, I thought, covering my head with a pillow. Every time I fell asleep I raised the dead.

He whipped the pillow away and dropped it on the floor. "What's wrong?" His voice was tinged with worry.

I gave him a withering look. "Just a dream."

"Tell me."

I groaned and stared up at the ceiling. "You don't want to hear it."

"Tell me anyway. If you talk about it, the dreams will go away."

Yeah, sure. "Maybe if I talk about it, you'll get pissed off."

"I'll try very hard not to."

I looked over at him and had to grimace at his vain attempt to plaster a patient expression on his face.

"Fine," he said. "Don't tell me. But it's ten o'clock. We should get going soon."

He was right, but it didn't make me want to hurry. Actually, I felt a little sick about what the day held in store. Maris had called the house the day before—which was weird and unsettling in itself—but she didn't have a choice because Calder refused to take her calls when she tried his cell. Maris and Pavati's winter hiatus in New Orleans was over. They were migrating back to Bayfield, and she had called to say they'd be here by noon. The fact that they'd called at all led Calder to one conclusion, but Maris didn't say if Pavati had had a boy or a girl.

4

CALDER

Lily dragged her feet like they were encased in concrete. She'd already changed her outfit three times, making me wait in the hallway outside her room, then flinging the door open for a two-second fashion show. If I didn't react quickly enough, she groaned and slammed the door—opening it again a few minutes later, wearing something completely different.

"I know what you're doing," I said through the door. "You're just stalling. It doesn't matter what you wear."

"If you're making me go, I want to look good!" she yelled back.

"For what? For whom? It's Maris and Pavati, for God's sake."

"Exactly!"

I still didn't get it, but when she whipped the door open to outfit number five (yellow leg warmers, a green corduroy miniskirt, and a Sgt. Pepper's Lonely Hearts Club Band T-shirt), I was quick to say, "Perfect. I love it. Now can we go?"

"Fine," she said, stomping down the stairs to the kitchen. "But I don't see why we have to. If there's really a baby, it's Danny's problem. Not yours. And definitely not mine." She opened the refrigerator and drank milk straight from the carton.

"Because I don't trust Daniel Catron to make good on his parental obligations," I said, holding out the phone to her. "And since when did you turn into such an animal?"

"What do you mean?"

I gestured at the milk carton still at her mouth. "As for Daniel, I want to make sure he takes responsibility for the baby, and I want to make sure he gives it back when it's time. It's a long summer, and for a big lake, it can sometimes feel awfully small. If he bails on Pavati, we'll all pay the price somehow. You should call him."

She looked at the phone for a second longer, then took it from me. "You really think Pavati has a baby?"

"Let's just be prepared, okay? If she does, she's going to want to hand it off as soon as she gets here."

"So much for motherly affection," Lily muttered.

"It's not that." I didn't bother to explain. Lily had never

experienced the normal desolation of the mermaid mind or the incessant need to medicate with human emotion. Whether that was because of her Half nature, or because I was the balm to her that she was to me, I didn't know. It didn't really matter. I was only too grateful for her immunity, and I hated to bring up anything that might make her think of it, like how a landlocked baby would interfere with Pavati's hunting schedule.

"Whatever," Lily said. She slid open her phone and hit Daniel Catron's number on speed dial. When he picked up, Lily switched to speaker (though I could have heard him clearly enough without it), and laid the phone on the kitchen counter.

"She's back?" Daniel asked, not even bothering with hello.

"Just about," Lily said. "You need to be at the pier by noon."

There were a few beats of silence, then Daniel whispered, "You've got to help me. My God, what was I thinking?"

Lily looked at me with an expression of restrained exasperation, then said, "Danny, *you* told me you had a plan. *You* said you had this all figured out. For crying out loud, you've had *over ten months.*"

Of course the kid had no plan. Give him another ten months and he'd still have nothing. *Hey, Mom and Dad. Yeah, I know I'm only nineteen, but I thought it would be a good résumé builder to raise my mermaid child for a year. I hear college admissions boards are always looking for unique extracurricular activities.* . . . I didn't know who'd thought this through less: Daniel or Pavati. I could only imagine the conversation between my

30

sisters in the car ride up, especially with a wailing infant in the backseat. Maris had to be *loving* that.

I pulled myself up onto the kitchen counter and turned on the faucet. The warm water calmed my mind as I ran my hand through it.

"Of course I have a plan," I heard Daniel say. "It's just that the time went quicker than I thought it would. No one in Cornucopia even knows I have a girlfriend."

"You *don't* have a girlfriend," Lily said. "I'm telling you, keep it up with the girlfriend talk and you're going to end up dead, just like Jack Pettit. In fact, if Pavati doesn't take you down, I might. So knock it off."

There was another prolonged moment of silence on the other end. Although Daniel had once prematurely assumed Lily was a mermaid, he was now fully informed when it came to the Hancock family. I knew Lily was bluffing when she talked about murder, but Daniel had every reason to take her at her word. She was strong, and he knew she could do enough damage to make her point.

Daniel whispered, "I haven't said anything to anyone."

I butted into the conversation, speaking only to Lily but loud enough for Daniel to hear. "Tell him he should have thought about the consequences before he took off with Pavati."

Lily waved at me to shut up.

Daniel groaned. "How was I supposed to say no to her? You can't imagine how amaz–"

"Spare me the gruesome details!" I yelled, and Lily rolled her eyes. She'd heard Daniel's account of his mermaid hookup at least a dozen times. She agreed with me that Daniel Catron had been a supreme idiot, but she assured me it was only a symptom of Pavati-itis, and that he hadn't always been so dense.

I was going to need more convincing. As it stood, I gave Daniel three months. By that time, I was pretty sure he'd either stick the baby with us, or he'd go in search of Pavati. And even an idiot knew how that would work out.

"Be at the fishing pier in fifteen minutes," Lily said again. "You *are* coming, right?"

There was silence on the other end. I mouthed his unspoken answer to Lily: *Nope.*

She scooped up my car keys from the kitchen counter and tossed them to me, saying, "You better be there, Daniel Catron, or so help me." Then she hung up. He would be a fool not to show.

But just as I expected, when Lily and I got to the fishing pier, there was no sign of Daniel. The adjacent playground was abandoned, save for one mother and her toddler, who was climbing a pink and blue dragon made out of old semitruck tires. We walked to the pier and took our places alongside the splintered rail, leaning against it, smelling the fresh clarity of springtime in the air. We all needed a new beginning.

I took Lily's hand and absentmindedly rubbed my thumb over her ring finger. If she'd only be convinced to set up a new home, with me, somewhere else, far away . . . Lily squeezed my hand, and for a second, I had an unfamiliar flash of optimism.

But then she fidgeted and worry darkened the small bit of human light that still radiated from her body. I was thankful for even that glimmer of her humanity. I clung to it as it clung to her.

"He'll come," I said, hoping my reassurance would refresh her aura to its former raspberry glow.

"What time is it?" she asked.

"Twelve oh two."

She turned away from me and walked to the swing set, taking a seat in one of the black rubber slings. She hung there, barely swaying, picking at a loose thread on her leg warmers.

"Do you think this is going to work out?" she asked as I came up behind her.

"Are you asking me if I think Daniel Catron can raise a baby for a year, or are you asking me if I think there will be a problem at the end of the year?"

"Both."

I sat down on the ground in front of her swing and picked up a handful of wood chips. "From what I know of Daniel Catron, he wants Pavati. Nothing more. I'm more concerned about him not showing up than I am about him not giving the baby back next spring. When Tom Hancock . . . when your grandfather refused to return your dad, that was unheard of. At least, I should say Mother never expected it. Daniel seems like the least likely candidate to . . . well . . . shall we call it 'pull a Hancock'?"

"What time is it now?" she asked.

Before I could answer, a blue VW Bug wheeled into one of the many empty parking spots, and Daniel jumped out, slamming the door behind him. "I don't even have a car seat," he moaned. "I think I'm supposed to have one of those."

"Would you settle down?" I said, chucking a wood chip in his direction. "Just tell people you found the baby on the side of the road. No one will expect you to have the necessary baby equipment."

Daniel's face brightened at my suggestion.

"He's kidding," Lily said.

"No, I'm not."

She rolled her eyes at me. "If Danny says he found a baby on the side of the road, someone's going to call social services. That's not exactly ideal."

"Can't I just keep the baby at your house?" Daniel asked Lily.

Lily paled. "First of all, *I'm* not going to do anything with the baby. This is all on you. Second of all, what about my mom?"

"*Your* mom at least has a clue about all of this mermaid stuff," Danny said.

"No way. My mom is in no shape to be raising a baby."

"Think of it as babysitting," Daniel pressed.

"At seven dollars an hour? For a year?" Lily whipped out her phone and did the calculation. "That's . . . sixty-one thousand three hundred twenty dollars. Cough it up. I get paid in advance."

"Be serious," Daniel said.

"I couldn't be more serious," Lily said. "I'm eighteen. If I wanted a baby, I could get married and have one of my own."

A flash fire of adrenaline burned through my body, and

I quickly looked away. As much time as I'd spent thinking about a future with Lily, a family of our own had never occurred to me. That wasn't supposed to be possible for mermen, but then again . . . Lily was living proof that that bit of mermaid canon law was seriously flawed. The mere possibility of having a baby with Lily made my insides crawl with a combination of anticipation and terror.

"Oh my God," Daniel said, "if my parents find out about this, they'll kill me."

I picked myself up off the ground and brushed the dirt and wood chips from my pants. "Agreed. And I think we can also agree that if you screw this up, *they* will, too." I gestured toward the parking lot, and Lily and Daniel both turned to look. "Figure it out quick, lover boy. Maris and Pavati just pulled up."

Even at this distance I could read Maris's and Pavati's faces through the windshield. Their jaws were set, their lips tight. My money was on them sharing my anxiety about history repeating itself.

A new voice boomed through the tense silence. "They here yet?" Jason asked, striding toward us from the parking lot, his view of Maris and Pavati blocked by blue shrink-wrapped sailboats on drydock.

"Dad!" Lily cried out. "What are you doing here?"

"I thought it was about time I met my sisters. I was never able to hear them in the lake." He turned toward me. "You said that was probably because I'd never heard their voices on land. Time to fix that, wouldn't you say?"

Lily looked at me in panic.

"Maybe you're right," I said, as I studied Maris and Pavati for a second longer. "And it's always good to have the numbers."

"You don't think they're dangerous anymore, do you?" asked Jason. "To us, anyway."

I could only speculate based on my years of living with Maris and Pavati, but I felt confident in my answer. "Lily fulfilled your family's promise to my mother, and Jack paid the price for Tallulah's death. So, no. I don't think they're a danger to you or Lily anymore."

But I turned to Daniel less certainly. "You, on the other hand . . . Word of advice, Daniel: Make it quick. The last time we saw them they were severely weakened. They're at full physical strength now, but their emotional tanks are getting low. Don't get any closer to the water than you are right now. They need you alive for the baby's sake, but you don't want to pose any unnecessary temptation. This should be a quick handoff; then get out of here."

5

LILY

So Calder didn't think Maris and Pavati were a danger to me and Dad anymore? It was nice to know there was at least one perk to my transformation. Besides, they were my aunts, my father's sisters. I knew what Calder would say about that: they always *had* been, and that hadn't stopped their murderous intentions. But still, now that they weren't trying to kill Dad, or me, now that we knew they weren't behind the nightmare of last summer, they couldn't be *so* bad.

Maris and Pavati climbed gracefully out of a silver sedan–Maris in faded jeans and a black tank top; Pavati in a pink floral dress that was thin enough for her long, toned legs to show through when the sun hit it right. Okay. Truth was, they still gave me the creeps. Especially now when they looked so healthy. I could only imagine at what cost.

Danny let out a long, low whistle and when I glanced over his blue eyes were sparkling. "Have you ever seen anyone so beautiful?" he said to my dad, then caught me staring him down.

"You're not going to throw yourself at Pavati," I said. "You're going to stand by me and man up. She's not going to have much time for you anyway. Her focus is going to be on giving you the baby and getting herself in the lake. Don't take it personally."

"I thought you said you didn't know anything about this," Danny said.

"Shut up and be quiet," I said. "And while we're at it, get that lovesick-puppy expression off your face, or so help me, I'm going to slap you."

He swallowed hard. "Right. No puppies."

Pavati reached into the backseat of the sedan and straightened up, holding a massive bundle of fuzzy blue blankets. Somewhere from inside the jumble, I heard a tiny mewing sound. Intuitively, I squeezed Danny's hand to hold him in place. Dad placed his hand on my shoulder, while Calder— despite his earlier assurances—moved one shoulder in front of mine in a defensive posture.

Maris and Pavati strode toward us. Pavati kept her pointy elbows slightly ahead of Maris's arms, as if positioning herself as the new leader of their small band, but Maris did not look resigned to a subservient rank. Seeing the controlled hostility in their expressions, my back stiffened out of habit. I searched their faces to see if the malice was directed toward any one of us, but that did not appear to be the case.

Maris and Pavati had both returned to their natural beauty. Gone was the emaciated, graying look that Jack Pettit had forced upon them. They were both well fed, emotionally and physically. I could see that clearly in the shimmer of light at the corners of their mouths, and in the buoyant way they walked. Maris's white-blond hair shone in the sun, and Pavati's thick chocolaty curls bounced against her shoulders. Their arms were soft and supple, and their collarbones no longer jutted out in dangerous angles. They showed no sign of memory or distress about what had transpired here only ten months ago.

The mermaid sisters broke into matching smiles of serenity that gave me a creepy-crawly feeling up the backs of my legs. Danny's hand softened in mine, and I dug in my nails.

"Thank you for coming," Maris said. Her eyes were hard and all on my dad.

"It's so good to see you," Pavati said, looking first at me, and then glancing quickly at Danny, who sucked in his breath at her brief acknowledgment. Neither Maris nor Pavati spoke to Calder.

I wasn't sure what to say. Their greeting seemed genuine, yet Calder's guarded posture made me suspicious of the pleasantries. I did my best not to make eye contact with either of them, unless I should succumb to unwanted hypnosis.

Maris said, "Jason Hancock, I presume?"

"Maris," he replied.

She looked him up and down. "You look old."

Pavati held out the pile of blue blankets like she was offering a serving tray in a banquet hall. I elbowed Danny, and he reached out tentatively. I could practically feel his mind's wheels turning, trying to think of the perfect thing to say. I spoke so he wouldn't.

"Blue blankets," I said. "Does this mean—"

Pavati nodded, her pride apparent. "The most beautiful boy."

Only then did I realize how much I'd hoped it was a girl. Our fear of history repeating itself seemed even more justified with a boy.

Danny held the bundle awkwardly, uncertain if he was doing it right, and I peeled back the blanket, revealing a small cherubic face. The baby had dark hair and caramel-colored skin, just like his parents, and when he opened his eyes to blink at the sun, they were the same brilliant blue as Danny's. A thick fringe of black lashes lay softly against his cheeks. His lips pouted into the shape of a berry.

An image of Nadia leaning over my infant father flashed in my head as Danny curled his body to shield Pavati's baby from the sun.

"You will take care of him," Pavati said, touching the baby under the chin, while a curl of trepidation wormed its way into my stomach.

Danny nodded. "Will you visit?"

"Maybe." Pavati looked out at the lake, her hands trembling.

"You look good, Lily," Maris said, and when I steeled myself to look at her I saw that her eyes, too, were on the water. "How did the winter go? I was concerned you three might not make it."

She was concerned? I didn't know what to make of that.

"It was no picnic," Dad said.

This time it was Maris's turn to laugh. "I can't imagine." She touched my dad's arm lightly, and both he and Calder braced against it.

She said to Dad and me, "I am glad you both came to the pier today. If we're going to be sharing the lake, it's about time we got to know each other better."

"Um . . . yeah," I said. "We should hang out sometime." And Maris laughed again. Weird.

"Sophie is well?" Pavati asked. "Has she . . . ?"

"No," I said. My shoulders relaxed at her question. "She's still the same little girl as before."

"I see how it is," Pavati said as she drew her conclusion: the consequence of a merman father was that the gene did not pass down to all the heirs. I didn't know if she was right. Only time would tell.

Pavati looked anxiously at the lake. "Now, Maris?"

"Yes," Maris said. "If you'll excuse us, Lily. Jason." Dad's name still sounded hard for her to say. She didn't acknowledge Calder or Danny at all. "We need to go." Maris headed for the trees, but despite her own apparent eagerness, Pavati held back.

Calder and Dad headed toward the parking lot.

"Already?" Danny asked, looking up from the baby's face. "But you just—"

Pavati's eyes grew glossy, then thick with tears that she refused to let fall. She dropped a quick kiss onto the baby's forehead without a word to Danny. To me, she said, "You got my letter?"

"I did," I whispered, casting a nervous glance in Calder's direction. He had to be listening, even from his distance.

"And?" Pavati asked.

I shook my head infinitesimally. Just my luck she'd bring that up with Calder in earshot.

"We'll talk later," she said, and with that she followed Maris into the trees. I pulled at Danny's arm. He didn't need to watch them stripping down. In fact, I was pretty sure that would be a really bad idea.

"Wait," Danny called out to Pavati. "You didn't tell me his name."

"Come on," I said, tugging harder on his elbow, pulling him in Calder's direction. "We can figure all that out later."

"He needs to have a name," Danny said.

There were two clean splashes as Maris and Pavati entered the lake, their migration complete. Danny and I turned at the sound. We watched for some last sign of them, but the lake had returned to a glassy sheet.

"Come on," I said. "Let's go back to our house."

Danny fumbled the bundle of blankets as he readjusted his grip. Calder hit the horn lightly and I waved at him to be patient.

"You okay?" Dad asked. He had his car door open and

he stood just inside it, with one arm resting on the roof. "You want me to take the baby?"

Danny sighed and looked down at the face of his sleeping son. "No. I'm okay for now. He's"–Danny swallowed hard, his Adam's apple bobbing–"he's mine. I've got him."

6

CALDER

As I drove back to the Hancock house with Lily in the passenger seat, I watched Daniel Catron's car in my rearview mirror. What speed was he going? Fifteen miles an hour? I slowed down so I didn't get too far ahead of him. The kid was twitchy, and he made me nervous. Was he slowing down again? The boy had slipped into protective father mode more easily than I had feared.

Lily played with her pendant, rolling it around in her fingers as she stared out the window. She said, "Y'know, Maris wasn't actually that bad. Is it possible you've misjudged her all these years?"

At first I thought Lily was joking and I laughed out loud, but she kept her serious expression, so I had to level her with reason. "Maybe you've forgotten. She used your little sister as bait, knocked me unconscious, trapped me in a fishing net, had Tallulah lure you to your death, then made us risk our lives by going into Copper Falls."

"Okay, okay, I get it," she said.

"Don't tell me I've misjudged her."

"But still," Lily persisted. "It *is* possible she's changed."

"You're generous to a fault," I said.

"Maris said she wants us all to share the lake in peace."

I pulled into the Hancocks' driveway and parked in Jason's usual spot. Daniel pulled in beside us. "Only because she knows you, me, and Jason aren't competition."

"Competition?" Lily asked.

Why hadn't I kept my mouth shut? I looked down at my hands, still on the steering wheel, and said, "We won't interfere with her hunting schedule. She won't have to factor us in when she figures out the pacing and rationing for the summer."

"Oh," Lily said, because what more could she say.

I turned to face her, taking in her innocent expression. Her gray eyes, now tinted with silver. Her auburn hair fanned out across her shoulders. She still looked so very human. Her transformation hadn't brought on many mer-characteristics: no silver ring around her neck, no ability to see emotion, no electrical impulse. She couldn't even breathe underwater, though she could now hold her breath for nearly an hour. The thought that she might not escape the worst of our traits–that she might one day feel the need to hunt–filled me with dread.

I couldn't help but ask, "Are you going to tell me about the letter?"

She blinked. "What letter?"

Fine. We could do this later. I kicked open my door and got out. Lily followed. Jason pulled in behind us, and once the driveway dust settled, Daniel got out of his car with the baby. He handed Lily a folded piece of paper.

"What's this?" she asked, unfolding it.

"It was tucked inside the blankets," Daniel said. "It fell out when I put him in the car."

I looked over Lily's shoulder and read the note aloud: "Ambuj. Born from the water."

Daniel said, "I know, right?"

"I don't get it," Lily said. "What's that supposed to mean?"

Daniel took the note back and shoved it in his jeans pocket. "I think it's what Pavati wants to name the baby. We talked about it back when . . . ," Daniel faded off. "Pavati's father was from India. Ambuj must be Hindu or something for 'born from the water,' but how does someone walk around Bayfield with a name like that?"

"He won't be walking around here for long," Lily reminded him. She bent down and tugged at her leg warmers. "As soon as he's walking, he's out of here. Got it?" She held out her arms and Daniel passed her the baby. Lily looked good holding him. Very natural. I liked it.

The front door opened and Sophie wheeled Mrs. H onto the porch. "Is that who I think it is?" Mrs. H asked, her voice lighter and more gleeful than any of ours had been. Of course we'd let her in on the Daniel-Pavati situation months ago.

There was no point in secrets anymore. Now that her husband and her daughter broke into tails on a regular basis, Mrs. H had raised her bar when it came to weird. Sophie had been right about her all along. Mrs. H was stronger than her wheelchair let on.

"Is it a boy or a girl?" she asked.

"Boy," Daniel said.

"Oh, bring him here. Bring him here!" she exclaimed. Lily climbed the porch steps and tried to place the baby in her mother's arms, but Mrs. H declined, saying, "Oh, no. You hold him. I'll just look from here. Isn't he darling, such a sweet baby." She looked up at Daniel. "What did your parents say?"

Daniel shifted his feet and Lily raised both eyebrows at him as if to say, *See what an idiot you are?* Her expression made me choke back a laugh, and Daniel shot me an irritated look.

"I haven't exactly told them yet," Daniel said, as Lily handed the baby back to him. "I'm going to be staying at my cousin's apartment in Washburn. She's been deployed to Afghanistan for the next eighteen months, and she's letting me stay rent-free so long as I keep the place up. My parents are just glad to have me finally move out."

"Oh, dear," said Mrs. H. "A baby isn't something you can just drop on your parents."

I turned her wheelchair around and pushed her back through the door while Lily trailed us into the house.

"Yeah," Daniel said uneasily, following us inside. "I don't think this is something I can ease them into either. My brothers, too. Better they don't know."

"You can't be expected to hide a baby for twelve months," Jason said.

"Jason's right," Mrs. H said. "Maybe you should leave him here with us."

"Mom!" Lily exclaimed, stopping our progression into the family room with her hand placed firmly on the armrest of the chair.

"No!" Sophie said.

Mrs. H looked at both of her daughters with surprise and disappointment. "Who better to take care of him than us? We've already got three under this roof."

"Absolutely not," Lily said.

"Excuse me," said Mrs. H, "who's in charge around here?"

The baby squirmed, stretched, and let out a rhythmic pulsing cry.

Sophie scowled at him. "It's not fair," she said. "He's just a baby. He'll be swimming in a year and at the rate I'm going he'll beat me."

Daniel balanced the baby against his shoulder and tapped its back uncertainly.

"You don't know that," I said, putting my arm around Sophie. She curled into my side and hugged me around the waist. It was good to have a sister again.

"Danny can take care of his own baby," Lily said.

"Of course he can," said Mrs. H. "I'm sorry. I didn't mean to imply you couldn't." The red-faced infant cried and arched its back stiffly. Daniel switched it to his other shoulder, but the baby only screamed louder.

"What have you named him?" Mrs. H asked, wringing her hands with worry at the way Daniel handled his son.

"Pavati likes Ambuj," Daniel said, "but I don't know."

Lily left us where we'd all stopped just inside the front door, went into the living room, and opened her laptop.

"What are you doing?" Jason asked.

"Baby-name website," Lily answered, tapping furiously at the keys. "How about a French name like the rest of your family, Danny?"

I pulled up a chair and sat beside Lily as she scrolled through an unending list of alphabetical boy names, stopping at the *M*'s. I touched the screen. "Mortimer?"

Sophie snorted and Lily smiled.

"It says it's French for 'still water,'" I said. What was wrong with Mortimer? "That sounds peaceful. We could use some peace about now."

"I've only had two years of French," Daniel said, "but doesn't that mean 'dead water'?"

Lily frowned at the screen. "Then how about Moses? 'Pulled from the water.'"

Daniel shook his head. "I don't know."

"Marlowe?" Lily asked. "That means 'from the hill by the lake.' You live on a hill by a lake."

"Hey, you kids," said Mrs. H, "can we find this baby something to eat? He's famished."

Daniel shot Mrs. H an anxious look. Of course he hadn't thought about food. Lily scrolled back to the top of the alphabet. "What about 'Adrian'?" she asked. "It's French, but it means 'from the Adriatic Sea.'"

Daniel came to stand behind Lily's shoulder and read the screen. "Pavati might like that. The Adriatic's in the Middle East, isn't it?"

"Not exactly," I said, remembering one of my first winters as part of the White family—Mother had taken us on a Mediterranean tour. Lots of cruise ships.

"But it's close, right?" Daniel asked.

"Sure," I said. "Closer than here at least."

"Adrian's a good compromise," Daniel said. "I'll tell Pavati tomorrow."

Lily's hands went rigid on the keyboard, and she and I exchanged a panicked glance before looking up at Daniel. I didn't like the direction this was going. Lily spun her chair around and stood up. "What do you mean, 'tomorrow'?"

"Lily's right," I said, raising my voice to be heard over the baby's wailing. "It's not a good idea. And anyway . . . how would you intend to do that?"

Daniel shrugged. "It wouldn't hurt Adrian to dip his toes in the lake just for a little bit. Pavati should smell him, right? She might not need to see me, but she'll want to see the baby, and I'll take what I can get. However I can get it."

The sad droop of Daniel's eyes touched a chord of empathy within me, but Lily said, "Don't be pathetic."

That hurt. Daniel might be an idiot when it came to a lot of things, but, in that second, I understood him better than I ever had. If I were in Daniel's place, if Lily and I were ever separated, I knew I would do anything to be with her again. Anything. And just like Daniel said, I knew *I* would take *Lily* any way I could get her. I'd thought she felt the same way about me.

Lily's phone buzzed, and she picked it up to check the text. "Ugh. It's Gabby again. She's on her way over."

"Then get rid of the baby," Sophie said.

"Adrian," Danny said.

Sophie rolled her eyes. "Whatever!" she shouted over the baby's cries.

"Sophie's right," I said. "No need to have to explain a baby; we've got enough lies to feed Gabby as it is."

Lily agreed with me. "I'll tell her to meet me at Big Mo's instead." She typed out her message to Gabby, then slid her phone shut.

"Let's get this baby fed," Mrs. H said. "Jason, I've got some things saved up in the top cupboard just in case. You'll have to get them down for me."

"In case?" Sophie said, following her dad into the kitchen. "In case of what?"

Mrs. H didn't answer.

"Mom, where's my fleece?" Lily asked.

"Really? It's pretty warm today," said Mrs. H.

"I'm actually feeling a little cold."

"Oh, honey, I hope you're not coming down with something. We've got a baby in the house."

Lily sighed and dug around in the closet by the front door. She wrestled a black-and-white houndstooth trench coat off a hanger and slipped it on over the band T-shirt and miniskirt.

"Ugh," said Sophie. "You're not going to go out in public

like that, are you? Can't you at least leave those leg sweaters at home?"

"I'm cold," Lily said.

"Do you want me to come with you?" I asked. "I can help."

Lily paused for a second, and I could see her answer before she said it. "I've got this." Then she smiled apologetically and was out the door.

7

LILY

Oh, man. I have to say, I didn't mind escaping my house for
the afternoon. Not one bit. Danny didn't seem to be in any
hurry to take his crying baby home, and I'm sorry, I felt bad
leaving Calder behind—but not that bad. Seriously, an hour
or two of lying to Gabby and getting her persistent telephone
calls behind me sounded like a retreat.

I pulled up to Big Mo's and parked the car at the curb,
idling, just to get my story straight. No, I hadn't seen Jack, or
heard from him, or heard anything newsy about him. It was
just like I'd told her before: the last time I saw him was last

July when he loaned me their boat and, no, he never mentioned leaving town.

"You know Jack," I practiced, testing out the tone of my voice, "he's impulsive. He probably has no idea how worried you are."

I caught my reflection in the rearview mirror. One of the side effects of my mermaid transformation: my eyes looked awesome–not just plain gray but almost silver when the light hit right. Kind of like Maris's, I thought, though Calder had never acknowledged the similarity. Actually, he spent a lot of time trying to make me forget about my Half nature. I didn't blame him for that.

"And," I said, continuing my rehearsal for the Gabby Show, "Jack's always had a flair for self-pity. He probably imagines you're all thinking 'good riddance.'" I dug in my purse for my best red lipstick and traced my upper lip with a perfect V. The trick to lying, I'd learned, was to keep the story simple, and to avoid retelling it as much as possible. Get asked about any details, plead forgetfulness because that's where you tripped up.

I exhaled and got out of the car. When I came through the door to Big Mo's, Gabby was already at the hostess station waiting for me. Her face told me she was surprised I actually showed up. She gave me a halfhearted hug, the one-armed kind where your bodies don't touch. When she pulled back, she looked past my shoulder like she really didn't want to have this conversation either.

There are some people who you can go without seeing for a year, and then as soon as you reconnect, it's like you picked up where you left off. No beats missed. Gabby was not going to be one of those people.

"We've got a table at the back," she said, turning.

We? I could feel my feet following, but my brain was scrambling for the door. I rounded the soft-drink dispenser and I was like, *Oh, no no no no.* This is not happening. I could lie about Jack to Gabby all day, every day, and twice on Sundays, but to her parents?

"Thanks for joining us, Lily. It's nice to see you again," said Mr. Pettit. Mrs. Pettit, whom I'd met only once, smiled weakly at me. She looked much older than her husband. Dark purple circles hung heavily under her eyes. She was a thin woman, thinner than I remembered, and her salt-and-pepper hair fell unevenly across her shoulders.

Gabby slid over to the far side of the booth and waited for me to sit, though for a second I couldn't remember how.

I counted out three heartbeats, then sat down gingerly as if the vinyl booth had been stuffed with shards of glass. I wouldn't offer anything. If they wanted to talk about Jack, they'd have to pull it out of me with needle-nose pliers.

"We already ordered," Mr. Pettit said. "I hope you're okay with pepperoni."

My lips tightened against my teeth in a smile that probably looked more like a grimace, and I dug around in my purse for my phone. There was already one text from Calder:

Gabby got you in a headlock yet? Need any help?

Hell's bells. For a second I thought about texting back: Ambushed! It couldn't hurt to even up the numbers some, but Mr. Pettit was already talking.

"How's the house holding up?" Mr. Pettit ran a handyman business, and he'd brought our house back to livable condition after we first arrived a year ago.

"Good, good. No leaks yet," I said.

Mr. Pettit chuckled, and Mrs. Pettit stared at the table where her plate would go. I looked at Gabby to see if her expression would explain why I'd been brought into this family get-together, but her face was as blank as her mother's.

"I had lunch with your dad a couple months ago," Mr. Pettit said, stabbing at his ice water with a straw.

"Oh yeah?" I said. Mr. Pettit's small talk was starting to feel like slow-drip water torture. Maybe if I took control of the conversation . . . "He's really loving teaching at the college, and Mom's doing great up here, so it turned out not to be such a horrible move after all. At first I thought–"

"Your dad tells me you put off college this year. How's that going for you?"

Okay. So much for small talk. I hadn't rehearsed my answers to questions that focused on me. Best to play it off. I shrugged and picked up my water. Hopefully no one noticed the ice trembling in the glass. "I decided to wait a year. No biggie."

"'No biggie,'" said Mrs. Pettit. I think it might have been the first time I'd ever heard her voice. Unlike Gabby's usual self-assured tone and Mr. Pettit's steady inflection, Mrs. Pettit's voice was small and weak. "Excuse me," she said, and she got up quickly and headed for the ladies' room.

"Um," I said. "Did I say something wrong?"

"It's not your fault," said Mr. Pettit.

"That's what Jack always used to say when Mom got on him about putting off school," Gabby said. " 'No biggie.' That's what he'd say."

"Oh," I said with a tight throat. "Lots of people wait a year."

"Are you working, then?" Mr. Pettit asked.

"No, I'm–"

"That's why I asked Gabby to invite you out," Mr. Pettit said.

Gabby looked up from the table and stared me hard in the eyes. For a second, I wondered if confessing the truth about Jack would be a good thing for them. Maybe they should know that their son had been behind the murders last summer and that, in the end, Pavati–the object of his obsession–had to destroy him. But no. I wouldn't poison their memories of their son, and I wouldn't add to their guilt. They'd only blame themselves for not having listened to Jack when he talked about mermaids.

Besides, beyond any of this, I was personally invested in our family secret. Mermaids would remain the lake's best-kept secret. I'd lie like the best of them. My family's safety depended on it.

"My mom's taking antidepressants now," Gabby said.

"Gabby," Mr. Pettit scolded.

"Lily should know how Jack's disappearance is affecting us."

Here we go. "You lost me," I said. "I thought we were talking about my education."

"We're afraid for you," Mr. Pettit said.

I raised my eyebrows. *Afraid? For me?* Their concern was unexpected. I pulled my straw from its paper sheath.

"We don't want you to go missing, too," Gabby said. "Do you have any idea how freaked out I was when you didn't take my calls?"

"Oh! Well, that's really very sweet, but I–" I twisted the paper wrapping around and around my finger like a ring, but I twisted it too tight and the paper snapped. "I'm fine. I'm sorry for not calling you back sooner."

"Yeah, well, sometimes people just need someone to listen," Gabby said, her voice tapering off on the last word.

"You're right. I should have picked up."

"It's just a little odd, don't you think?" Mr. Pettit said, leaning across the table toward me. "First Jack. Now you. Two kids, with everything going for them, good students, good kids with a plan for their futures, then all of a sudden they just . . . stop. No ambition, no plan, content just to stick close to the lake. What do your parents think about all this?"

I shrugged.

"We've got our theories on what happened to Jack, Lily, but we're hoping you can shed some light on the situation."

"I'm not sure what you mean by theories, Mr. Pettit."

"Oh, come on, Lily," Gabby said. "Sometimes you can be pretty dense. My dad's been trolling the shoreline every day since the ice melted."

I waited. Dense was the best defense I had.

"My wife is hoping Jack's joined up with some brainwashing cult, which I know sounds ridiculous, but she watches a lot of TV, and it's a much better option than the conclusion I've drawn."

I waited.

Mr. Pettit folded his hands in front of him as if in prayer. "It's pretty obvious. Jack's dead. The same person got him who killed that other kid, and then Brady and Chief Eaton. I don't see any way around that." He looked up at me then, and I shifted uncomfortably in my seat.

"I doubt that," I said. Out of the corner of my eye I could see Gabby studying me closely, but Mr. Pettit's expression brightened just a little.

"I was hoping you'd say that," he said. "Lily, I was really hoping you'd have something, some little insight that would tell me I was wrong."

"Me?" I asked, turning to Gabby.

"I know you and Jack weren't exactly friends," Gabby said, "but Jack would say—"

"You remember how he was acting at the end?" asked Mr. Pettit, as if he was still making excuses for his son. "With all the mermaid talk?"

"I remember," I said, swallowing hard.

"We had some pretty horrible fights about it. Jack would say things like, 'Why can't you believe me like Lily does?' or, 'If you don't believe me, ask Lily Hancock.'"

"What my dad's trying to say, Lily, is if there's some other explanation for what's happened to Jack, we'd all like to hear it."

"Why do you doubt he's dead?" asked Mr. Pettit, the whites of his eyes turning pink, then shiny with a thin sheet of tears.

I twisted my hands under the table, hoping to work out my discomfort in one part of my body while keeping my face as calm as possible. "For one, no body," I said. "All the others were found on shore."

The waitress returned, setting a large greasy pizza between us. No one ate.

"And if Jack was involved in a secret mermaid cult, I'm pretty sure he was its only member."

Mr. Pettit almost smiled.

Then, in a moment of panic, I grabbed on to the postcard ruse I'd suggested to Calder earlier. "I'm sorry . . . I would have said something sooner if I'd known he hadn't been in touch with you, but . . ." I hesitated, putting the finishing touches on my deceit. "I just assumed . . ."

"Assumed what?" asked Mrs. Pettit, returning to the table, her eyelids swollen and her face newly washed. She smoothed her skirt and sat down next to her husband again.

"I just assumed he'd sent you a postcard, too."

"Lily?" Gabby asked, grabbing my wrist.

"Yeah . . ." *Shoot. Why didn't I just keep my mouth shut?* "I got something in the mail a few weeks ago," I said, plastering my face with my best apologetic look.

Mr. and Mrs. Pettit sat like granite statues, not blinking.

"You got a postcard from Jack," Gabby said, testing out the sound of the words and tightening her grip on my arm. "Why didn't you tell us right away?"

"See!" said Mrs. Pettit. "I knew Jack wasn't dead. I could feel it in my bones. A mother knows these things."

"Margaret," said Mr. Pettit, putting up his hand. "Let's not get ahead of ourselves."

"I thought Jack might turn to you," said Mrs. Pettit. "I thought maybe he was too mad at us to call home, but I thought maybe . . . Oh, Martin, I told you he wasn't dead."

"Let's see it," said Gabby, holding out her hand, palm up.

"See what?" I asked. My hands felt cold and clammy under the table, and I tensed my muscles against the shiver that ran across my shoulders. Did the air-conditioning just kick into overdrive?

"The postcard, of course."

"Oh. I didn't bring it with me."

"We can go to your house, then," Mrs. Pettit said. "It would mean a lot to me to see it."

"We can't," I said. "It got . . . accidentally . . . thrown away."

"You threw away a postcard from Jack?" Gabby asked, her voice going up an octave. The diners around us stopped eating and turned to look.

I said, "Well, *I* didn't. Of course I wouldn't have done that. Sophie just didn't realize what it was." Great. Now I was throwing Sophie under the proverbial bus.

"Well, you can get it back, can't you?" Mr. Pettit asked.

"I don't think so."

Mrs. Pettit started to cry. "I can't do this again," she said, and Mr. Pettit drew her in, holding her against his shoulder while she shook silently.

Do what again? I thought. Gabby's jaw tightened, and her cheeks bloomed red.

"I'm sorry. I really am," I said. "But the postcard didn't say anything." I was a terrible, horrible, despicable person. I wish I'd never come. "The card was blank, except for a J. It had a photo of Winnipeg on the front. I think all he wanted was to let me know he was okay, without letting anyone get close enough to drag him home."

"A 'J.' That's all?" Gabby asked.

"Honest truth."

"You promise?" Gabby asked.

"That sounds like Jack," said Mr. Pettit, nodding his head.

I leaned across the table toward Mrs. Pettit. "If I get any more, I'll bring them to your house right away." I would, too. I'd make up a dozen fake postcards. I'd despise myself, but at least I'd keep hope alive for this poor woman. She was so thin and fragile, she looked like she could snap in the wind.

Mr. Pettit reached across the table toward me, his hand in a fist, and rapped the table with his knuckles. "We know you will. You have no idea what a relief this is. I'm going to take your mother home," he said to Gabby. "You girls stay and eat." He threw a twenty on the table.

After Mr. and Mrs. Pettit left, Gabby and I sat in silence, staring at the cooling pizza. A full minute passed before Gabby said, "I'm not mad at you."

I couldn't look at her. "You're not?"

"First you had me scared when you didn't take my calls; then you had me mad when you showed up here like there was nothing wrong. But I'm not mad anymore. You're a good person, Lily."

I reached for my glass of water, my hand shaking. "How's that?"

"What you did for my parents . . . lying like that . . . that was a really nice thing to do. Because you and I both know what happened to Jack."

I miscalculated the glass's distance and knocked it over, making a huge puddle on the table. "I don't know what you're talking about," I said, laying my palms flat in the water.

Gabby pulled her purse into her lap and dug around inside, eventually pulling out a dagger, its handle decorated in beach glass and copper wire, the same dagger Calder had pulled from the mud at the base of Copper Falls. Sheshebens's dagger.

I hadn't seen the ancient artifact since the day Calder and I had gone looking for Maighdean Mara and found her stony corpse. I could hear the dagger's faint but familiar hum vibrating off the Formica table. I tried not to react, but I couldn't take my eyes off it.

"I found it in our boat after Jack went missing," Gabby said. "Do you know anything about this?"

"What is it?" I asked, feigning ignorance. "It's beautiful." I reached for it, and Gabby snatched it back and returned it to her purse.

"Jack's dead," Gabby said. "I think someone killed him. With this."

8

CALDER

Daniel wasn't in any hurry to leave the Hancocks' house. In fact, Mrs. H asked me and Jason to add another leaf to the dinner table so there'd be room for Daniel to stay. As it turned out, Mrs. H was more prepared for Adrian's arrival than any of us. Not only did she have bottles and formula in the kitchen, she directed Jason to get a cardboard box out of the front hall closet, in which there were several plastic shopping bags full of diapers, blankets, and toys.

"Seriously? You got all this stuff for me?" Daniel asked.

"We'll call it a baby shower," Mrs. H said, "although it's not a very good one. It's a shame your mother can't be here, but I understand how things are. Feel free to bring Adrian over whenever you want."

"Don't take that too literally," I said, defending Lily's position in her absence.

"Calder's kidding," said Mrs. H.

"No, he's not," Sophie said.

"I'm not raising you to be rude," said Mrs. H.

I glanced at Sophie, who was chewing on the inside of her cheek. She threw me a look that said, *Back me up, please.*

I checked my phone. Somehow I'd got it in my head that Gabby was going to corner Lily, and she'd be desperate for me to feed her one of my long-practiced lies. But so far, not a word.

"Calder's right," Jason said. "It's not good getting too attached."

I got up and walked to the kitchen window. The sounds of Mrs. H's cooing adoration drifted past me, through the open window, and out across the yard toward the lake. Daniel came up behind me.

"Do you think she's out there?" he asked.

"Of course not. She went to meet Gabby."

"Not Lily. Dude, not everything is about Lily. I'm talking about Pavati. Do you think she's out there?"

I considered that. Pavati might be listening. She'd probably be anxious and keeping watch until she was confident Daniel was comfortable with the baby. "Yes, she is."

"Then why doesn't she come up to the house?"

I turned toward Daniel, furrowing my brow. "She's. Not. Human."

Daniel smirked. "She can look pretty human to me."

"She's an animal."

Daniel wiggled his eyebrows at me suggestively, but that wasn't the kind of "animal" I was talking about.

"It's a charade," I said. "She studies how to act. She lives on the periphery. But she's never going to come up, ring the doorbell, and make a freaking house call."

"You did," Daniel said.

"Those were completely different circumstances, and not something I'm proud of. I'm different now. Pavati is the same as she ever was, and she won't change. You should stay away. Don't do anything cute."

"Why's that?"

"Right now, the way you light up when you even talk about Pavati, you'll be a greater temptation to her than anyone else she encounters on the lake, and it's early in the season. Not a lot of boaters or swimmers. You'd be about the only option."

"She'd never hurt me. She needs me to take care of Adrian."

I looked over my shoulder at Mrs. H. She was tickling the baby, who lay on the couch, tucked tightly into the corner. I said, "I'm sure there'd be someone to replace you if need be."

Daniel swallowed hard. He bowed his head and wrung his hands, working the knuckles. "Will you talk to Pavati for me? See how things stand between us?"

I returned my gaze to the lake. "Yeah. Yeah, I'll do that. Besides . . . there's something I want to talk to her about, too."

LILY

I didn't have to worry about an argument with Gabby over her theory that someone had killed Jack with an ancient artifact. When I stared at her openmouthed, without an admission, she practically crawled over me to get out of the booth, then stormed out of the restaurant.

After she left, I remained in the booth for a few more minutes, trying to comprehend what Gabby's possession of the dagger might mean. I couldn't believe Calder would have done something so careless as to leave the dagger on Jack's boat, but the way I left him that day, well, it was possible he hadn't been thinking clearly.

Actually, clear thoughts were hard to come by these days. I needed the water. I needed to swim. I could work out what to do about Gabby, if only I had a chance to clear my mind.

I raced home and skidded the car into the driveway, kicking up dust and gravel. The late-afternoon air evaporated the beads of nervous sweat from my face and neck as I ran to the lake, pulled off my leg warmers, and waded in. Technically I was supposed to wait until Friday, but I couldn't. I just couldn't.

I needed the calm the water would bring—even if I had to endure the back-to-human transformation earlier than planned. Plus, it would be nice to be alone. Funny—I'd swum alone plenty before my first transformation, back when Calder and Dad were gone on their perpetual training days, but never again. Calder was ever-vigilant since I'd made the change, even before Maris and Pavati came back. It was like he was watching for me to have a nervous breakdown or something. It didn't matter how many times I told him how right I felt when I was in the water, how happy I was to be fully me, the me I was born to be. All he could ever see was the pain that followed.

Besides the beauty of being in my mermaid form, the fantastic speed, or even the pain, the hardest thing to get used to was the lack of privacy. Every Friday I was sometimes entertained, but mostly irritated, by the cacophony of thoughts that flooded Dad's and Calder's minds. Calder's thoughts could be downright lustful, though he'd try to catch himself before the shocking images drifted on the current toward me or, God forbid, Dad, who (no surprise) became quite the chaperone.

Now that the ice had melted, I'd be privy to Maris's and Pavati's thoughts, too—just as I had been last summer. We were family, whether Calder liked it or not. As he'd once explained, we were beads on a bracelet—strung together—sometimes sliding together, sometimes sliding apart. Despite the apparent improvement in mer-relations, Calder warned me to stay clear—that Maris and Pavati were unpredictable at best, dangerous at worst. I knew that, but my need to swim trumped any risk they might pose.

I walked toward the privacy of the willow tree—I could almost smell the charred trunk from my dream—and dropped my clothes onto its fallen branch that reached twenty feet across the shallows. Standing naked amid the budding foliage, I held my arms out wide, reveling in the wind, the lake air tingling my nose, and the sunlight and shadow dappling my skin.

I walked in—waist deep—and made a shallow dive. The explosion of pent-up energy was nearly instantaneous. How I wished the transformation back to legs could be as quick. I relaxed into my new form and swam straight north toward Red Cliff.

I reached forward with both arms and pulled myself through the water, my raspberry-pink tail undulating rhythmically behind me, pushing me. I wasn't in a hurry. I wasn't going anywhere special.

I squinted through the water, unable to navigate by sight and smell like Calder did. But I could hear just as well, and there was an unexpected vibration in the water.

I reached out with my mind to see who it was, catching muffled sounds, then the familiar clipped tone of Maris White.

"Good afternoon," she said with a smirk. *"I didn't expect to see you again so soon."*

CALDER

I stepped out onto the Hancocks' front porch, surprised to see Lily's car parked in the driveway. Reflexively, I looked back at the house, as if she were inside and I'd somehow missed her return. But I knew better. And so did she. So what the hell was she thinking?

When I got to the dock and searched the lake, there was no sign of Lily. Neither was there any sign of Pavati. I crossed my arms over my head and pulled my T-shirt up and off, dropping it on the dry deck boards. Still nothing. No one. Not even a ripple. I pushed my shorts down to my ankles and stepped out.

"Where are you going, Calder?"

"Gah!" I cried, covering myself while Sophie giggled from her bedroom window. Clearly living with the Hancocks had caused me to lose my touch for being discreet. I dove and sliced the water before Sophie saw more than she should.

It had been a long time since I'd swum alone. I tried to remember, and decided it had been that day at Square Lake–the first time I saw Lily since my escape and her exile. Ever since then, I'd either been with Jason, or Lily, or both. The quiet was a nice change, though I couldn't help but consider the inconvenience of no longer being able to hear my former sisters' thoughts in the water.

My instincts told me Pavati would be close–north of the ferry line, south of Basswood, and somewhere in the space between Madeline and the mainland. It wasn't long before I heard the tinny sound of bracelets sliding along an arm.

Pavati must have felt my disturbance in the water, because she swam directly toward me, smiling in greeting. I was fairly sure she was, out of habit, trying to communicate, but I couldn't hear anything. She frowned at my nonresponse and pointed to the surface. I followed her up, and we broke through the rough chop. The white-capped waves slapped against my face.

"Calder," she said, her face melting into a familiar, dangerously compelling smile.

I looked past her shoulder to avoid getting pulled in by her hypnotic skills. They were better than mine, but I knew her tricks. Perhaps she'd forgotten.

She laid her hand gently against my cheek, but I took her wrist between my forefinger and thumb and lowered it back into the water.

She clicked her tongue. "Fine. I guess I understand why you're still bitter."

My eyes twitched in her direction, but then I looked away again.

"What can you tell me about my baby?" she asked, circling me, letting her delicate fluke breach the surface and catch the sun in dazzling cobalt blue. "Is Ambuj settled in with his father?"

"Daniel Catron," I said, reminding her of his name, "is calling the baby Adrian."

"Hmm. I suppose that will do." She continued to circle. "No, I like it. Tell him I like it."

"I will, but I want you to tell me something."

"Anything," she said. Her whole demeanor softened, her eyes dimming from violet to lavender. Why the generosity? What did she want from me? There had to be some selfish motivation behind her smile.

"Tell me about the letter you sent Lily," I said, cracking

my tail like a whip to keep up with her as she continued to circle.

Pavati's mouth pulled into a close-lipped smile. "She didn't tell you herself?"

"She's been keeping a few secrets lately."

Pavati turned to swim away, but I caught her before she dove.

She looked down at my hand, circling her wrist and said, "Well, who am I to–"

"Pavati." I glared at her.

"Fine. If you insist. Maris is jealous of . . . Adrian."

"Jealous?" I asked. "Wha–Why?"

"Now that I'm a mother, she thinks I'll take over as head of the family."

"That's what you want?"

"Actually, it never occurred to me until I caught her thinking about it. She tried to scramble her thoughts right away, but it was too late. And . . . well . . . would that be so terrible?"

"Pavati, the letter?"

Pavati led me to a quiet cove, where the spring runoff had cut an inlet into the Basswood shore. She pulled herself up onto a semisubmerged rock and tipped her head back to soak up the sun. I stayed out deeper, growing more impatient with her delay.

"The letter?" I asked again.

"I'm getting to that." Pavati reached down and picked off bits of plant life that were stuck to her scales, flicking them onto the rock.

A low growl rumbled in my chest, and she rolled her

eyes as she squeezed the water from her hair. "I sent Lily a letter after the New Year. I suggested to her that Jason, and you, and she might join me. Stage a coup, if you will. Actually, I was hoping Sophie might have changed by now, too."

"I thought you liked Sophie."

Pavati shot me a scandalized look. "I do! What's that supposed to mean?"

"Only that the change hasn't been good to Lily. It hasn't come easy and it doesn't show any signs of getting better. I'm surprised you'd want to put the little girl through that kind of pain."

"I didn't know."

I believed her, and even though I knew better, it warmed me to her. "Did Lily ever respond?"

"Why don't you ask her?"

"Pavati, I don't have the patience for this."

"No. She hasn't. Not yet."

Thank God. At least Lily wasn't keeping too many secrets. If she had promised to join Pavati, I'd have more serious problems than Daniel. "We're not going to join you, Pavati."

"Things would be different if I were the matriarch."

"Not so different."

"You don't know that."

"Getting knocked unconscious has not hurt my short-term memory. Lily may be able to forgive, but it's still not something I've mastered."

"That's what I'm talking about," Pavati said. "Do you think any of that would have happened if I'd been heading up this family? Do you think any of us would have endured those decades of hatred, searching for Hancock, taking down all those misidentified souls?"

"It would have been the same. A promise was a promise. So long as Maris had us believing one had been broken—"

Pavati slid off the rock and swam toward me, coming up under my chin, her lips nearly brushing against mine.

I made a noise at the back of my throat to show my revulsion and turned away. She grabbed my shoulders before I could leave. "I'm begging you, Calder. I can't raise my child under Maris. Look what a mess she made of your life. You've never been whole."

I pushed her away to gain some distance. "Leave Lily alone."

She shook her head. "I can't promise that."

"What is Daniel's place in this?"

"I don't understand."

"Will you keep him?" I asked.

"What? Commit? Take a husband?" She laughed. "Oh . . . I see! This isn't about me, is it? You're wondering about you and Lily. Marriage is not for our kind, Calder. Don't go trying to impose human foolishness on me. Or yourself. That's always been your downfall. You're not human."

"I used to be. I'm trying to be. And Lily still is."

"You think?"

"And I didn't say anything about marriage." I'd always known there was no mermaid equivalency to marriage, although in many ways we were better suited for it than any other species. We held our vows sacred.

"If we were to join you," I said, "who would be left to keep an eye on Daniel? To make sure he returned Adrian next spring? Don't you want some assurance? Leave me and the Hancocks alone, and we'll do you that favor. You'll have Adrian back, on schedule."

"But if Maris is still in charge of this family, is that really what's best for him?"

"You can't mean to leave the baby with Daniel forever? The boy is clueless. He doesn't know which end to kiss and which end to wipe."

"If you're sure Daniel has no interest in being a father, then your decision should be easy. He doesn't need watching. Join me. Lily and Jason will follow. We'll be four strong against Maris. In another year, we'll be five."

"And if you're wrong and Daniel becomes a liability?"

She shrugged. "It will be my score to settle. I won't put it on the rest of my family like Maris did. You and Lily can live your life however you want. Even if you mean to marry her." The corners of her mouth twitched with amusement. "Like I said. Easy."

She made a persuasive argument, but still . . . "There's one thing I know for sure, Pavati. There's too much history between us and none of it was ever easy."

LILY

Maris. Just my luck. I flipped around and tore off in the opposite direction. *Oh,* I thought, *Calder will not like this. Or Dad.*

Maris was having the same thoughts, but unlike me, she

was enjoying them. Plus, she seemed to be enjoying the pursuit. I tried to read her thoughts while hiding my own. I was surprised to find she was making no attempt at hiding hers. Maris's mind was still a new frontier for me. Clearly, she had no more need or intention to hurt Dad. In fact, she was supremely curious about him. *What color is his tail? How fast is he?* And most of all: would he join her before Pavati staked her claim? *If I had first dibs on the Hancocks,* she thought, not caring that I heard, *that would make all the difference.*

So Maris knew that Pavati had asked me to join her? At least that was one secret I wasn't going to have to keep from her, because as fast as I was, Maris kept up easily. In fact, it didn't seem like she was exerting much effort at all.

The consequence of being a Half, Maris thought, answering my frustration. Within seconds she was even with me, swimming in tandem. I wouldn't look at her and pretended she wasn't there, which made me feel ridiculous.

Darting in and out of sea caves, making abrupt turns around boulders, I raced through the underwater topography, but Maris matched my every move. Worse, she mocked every confused and nervous rattle of my mind. She took sadistic pleasure in the discomfort she caused, so I stopped. If I couldn't outrun her, why go along for the ride?

Maris pulled up, too, and held her arms out to me, palms up. Her pale hair floated around her face like an angel's. *"Peace,"* she said, which was about the last word I expected her to say. When I stared at her openmouthed, she repeated the word as a question, clear and bell-like in my mind.

The green beach glass pendant hung low around my

neck. Maris stared at it for a few heavy seconds before looking up to meet my gaze. *"Does it work?"* she asked. *"Have you heard our stories? What does Calder say about it?"*

I hesitated. *"He'd rather I didn't wear it."*

"That's because it contains stories that he doesn't want you to hear." Maris took my hands in a firm grip, lacing her fingers through mine. She pulled back the veil, revealing even more of her thoughts and inviting me in. I knew it wasn't going to be a picnic. By the way Maris's thoughts twitched, I could tell not even she enjoyed the workings of her mind. I winced as I slogged through her memories—it was like treading in molten tar. Maris almost seemed sympathetic.

I focused on the one memory Maris was most insistent I see:

Nadia was tucking her four children into the nest she'd made in a small rocky cave on the banks of Basswood Island. She cushioned the cave with leaves and moss. "Quiet down, now," she told them. "Calder, quit pestering your sisters. I won't tell you a story until it's quiet in here."

"Calder, be quiet," said a young Maris, her pale lank hair clinging to her face. Pavati and Tallulah giggled and cuddled into each other. Nadia moved over to find her place between Tallulah and Calder. He fit his warm hand into hers.

Satisfied, Nadia began. "Once upon a time—"

"When the world was new," Calder added. She squeezed his hand. (Or maybe Maris squeezed mine. I could hardly tell where reality ended and this vision began.)

"The lake was warm with the love of the great Maighdean

Mara. From her came the first of our people—three young maids—and do you know their names?"

"Odahingum," said Maris, "whose name means 'rippling water.'"

"And Namid," said Pavati. "'Star dancer.'"

"Do you know the third, Tallulah?"

Tallulah covered her face with her hands.

"No? The third was Sheshebens, which means 'small duck.'"

"Why weren't there any boys?" Calder asked.

"The boys came later," Nadia said. "Many centuries passed, and the world changed. Maighdean Mara worried about the future of her family. She decided to give each of her daughters a gift. A gift that—should they ever leave her—they could show her upon their return, and she would recognize them as her own.

"To Odahingum she gave an iron chariot to travel the lake and survey the boundaries of their kingdom; to Namid she gave a pendant to wear above her heart to store the histories of our people; and to Sheshebens she gave a small copper-handled dagger that she herself had decorated with beach glass."

I broke away from Maris's grasp. *"I already know this story,"* I said.

"My mother told you?" She seemed both excited and offended at the prospect.

"Calder did."

Her face fell. *"I have to know. Does the necklace work at all?*

78

Does my mother speak to you through Namid's pendant?" Maris asked, staring at the necklace with such longing, I could feel the intensity in my own heart.

"I'm not exactly sure what's happening."

Maris nodded, then looked away. If we weren't under-water, I would have sworn she was crying. *"Does she ever mention me?"* she asked, her thoughts choking on the last word. *"Is she proud of me? Does she understand I've done the best I could? That I did my best to do what she asked? That I tried my best to keep this family together?"*

"I'm sure she understands," I said, but I felt the tug at my heart. Because I knew that Nadia wanted much, much more.

9

CALDER

Just as the last vibrations of Pavati faded away, fingernails raked down my back. I wheeled around to defend myself against an attack, but it was only Lily, accusing me through the water.

"Ha! Scared you!" she said.

"I thought you were Maris."

Lily laughed guiltily. *"That* would *be scary. But I'm glad you took my advice and came out without me."*

"Apparently I didn't. You shouldn't be out here alone."

"I'm not alone," she said. A serpentine current pulled at

her hair. She wasn't swimming in her usual band T-shirt, and my stomach leapt into my throat. How many times had I seen my sisters naked without any thought of it? This was a first for Lily.

She eyed me speculatively. I didn't know what to do. Or how to react. All I could manage to say was, *"I see you've given up on modesty. No band T-shirt?"* I tried not to let the internal eye roll show on my face. I was pretty sure—if she hadn't caught me by surprise—I could have come up with something much smoother.

"It started to feel kind of silly. Especially since I thought I was alone."

"Do you want me to leave?" I asked.

She shrugged, and that ambivalent gesture hurt more than a yes.

"We should go back," I said, trying not to show the wound she'd inflicted. *"Your mom will have dinner ready soon."*

Lily coiled around my chest and squeezed to show me how strong she was getting. For a second, I was too transfixed by the bright pink flash of her new body to respond. Man, she was beautiful.

Once more, she pulled her fingers across the width of my chest, only this time gently, like the brush of long grass, circling me as if I were prey, laughing at my confusion. I'd never seen Lily so overtly flirtatious. We should swim without Jason more often.

When her fingertips reached my right shoulder, she circled, skimming them across my back, then over my left shoulder, until she was facing me again. I caught a flash of smile. Her behavior reminded me of Pavati's, and I was both tempted to lunge at her and to hold her at bay for my own protection. But when she darted away from me—so fast I had to trail her thoughts to follow—I opted for the former. A second later, I lost the connection.

"Where are you?" I called out to a silent lake.

"Right here." She grabbed my ribs from behind.

"Man, you are getting seriously good at quieting your thoughts," I thought, half impressed, half offended. *"I can barely hear you at all."*

"Can you hear me now?"

"Loud and clear." I pulled her into my arms and we spiraled together into deeper water. I felt the pulse of her belly against mine, basked in the images that flickered through her mind. Her thoughts were fleeting, like a slide show running too quickly. Some of them were so beautiful I tried to cling to them, to reinforce them with my own: the two of us together. Forever.

But one of those slides worried me more than Maris ever could. Lily hoped I wouldn't notice it, but she wasn't quick enough to shield me from an image of myself in a car, leaving Bayfield, without her in the passenger seat.

"Lily, there's something I want to ask you."

"Later," she said. *"You and I need to talk about a certain dagger, and how it ended up in Gabby Pettit's purse."*

If she meant to distract me, it worked. I could feel the blood draining from my face. *"What?"*

Lily raised her eyebrows, then darted toward shore.

As was our habit, I left the water first. My clothes were

where I'd shed them—but now neatly folded—on the dock. Lily's were wind-tangled in the willow branches.

"Do you want me to wait with you?" I asked, but she shook her head. Despite my persistent requests to hold her hand through her painful transformation, she always made me leave her behind, to suffer alone. It was the worst part of my week.

Reluctantly, I entered the sleeping house. Mrs. H had left us dinner, wrapped in foil, but I didn't touch it. Instead, I climbed the stairs to Lily's bedroom.

I flipped on the lamp in the hopes of finding a sweatshirt easily. She was going to need it when she came in. The room was in its usual state of disaster, so I didn't find what I'd come for. Instead, I found Lily's journal, *MY SCRIBBLINGS (Vol. 3),* half tucked under her bed.

I hesitated. A muffled scream and crackling *pop* came from the beach. I took a flinching step toward the book, then stopped. She'd kill me if I read it. I couldn't invade her privacy like this. But still . . . Maybe she'd written something about Pavati. Maybe she had started to write a response to Pavati's letter. No. What was I thinking? It was wrong. But maybe if I picked the journal up, something would fall out. Accidentally.

I crossed the room and picked the journal up, holding it in both hands. What secrets did Lily keep inside? What new poems had she written? I held the spiral binding and shook the notebook three times. A black-and-white magazine clipping of a woman in a formal gown slipped from the pages and fluttered to the floor. But nothing else. I won't deny I was disappointed.

I sat down on the bed. After a few seconds, I turned back the corner of the cover and peeked inside. It was a whole page covered in *Lily Hancock-White, Lily White, Mrs. Calder White*. Over and over again in curling, flower-laden cursive writing. It made me laugh out loud. At least I wasn't the only one dreaming about our future.

10

LILY

I watched with envy as Calder pulled himself into the shallows, curled into a fetal position, then extended with a giant popping sound. The pain I knew too well was evident on his face; he grit his teeth, and the veins in his neck strained under his smooth skin, but he was so well practiced that no sound escaped his lips. In less than a minute he was fully human, pushing himself to standing, rivulets of water snaking their way over his scarred shoulders. The muscles in his arms and legs bounced involuntarily, still in the throes of aftershock. He kept his back to me as he found his clothes on the dock.

When he was dressed, he turned around with an expression that showed more pain than anything I'd just witnessed. "Do you want me to wait with you?" he asked, but he knew my answer even before I shook my head.

He nodded and walked up to the house, head bowed. After the front door shut behind him, he reappeared in the kitchen, closed the window, and drew the curtains. I took a deep breath, exhaling slowly. Then another. With my jaw set, I swam as close to shore as I could, then pulled myself onto the sand with my hands. I did as I'd seen Calder do, curling into a ball, pulling all my energy to the center, letting it stew there until I felt it hit a boiling point, then extended straight as a board.

I couldn't do it like Calder did it. A scream raced up my throat and I smothered it in the crook of my elbow. I bit down on my arm to choke off the next scream and panted through my teeth. When my lungs were empty, I sucked in the air that cut like razors across my lungs, giving me nothing more than the ability to scream again.

It was fifteen minutes of this torture—like giving birth to myself—before I regained my legs and found my clothes tangled in the willow branches. I hobbled up the dark porch steps, clinging to the railing for support. I entered the house as silently as I could, camouflaging the sound of my wet footsteps in Dad's gentle snores. I climbed the stairs on all fours, and when I got to the top, noticed my bedroom lamp was on and that someone was moving in front of it, casting strange shadows down the hallway.

I braced myself against the wall and then—when I reached it—my doorframe. "What are you doing, Calder?"

Calder threw *MY SCRIBBLINGS* on the bed and ran to hold me up as my legs buckled. "You got all the way up here by yourself? You should have called me to help. Oh, God, you're bleeding." He wiped the blood off my shoulder, then pulled a sweatshirt down over my head and body.

"I didn't want to wake anyone," I said. "Were you reading my journal?"

"No. Of course not. I was getting you something warm to put on, and I knocked it off your dresser."

Liar. "I didn't leave it on my dresser." *Jeez, what did he read?*

"Well, someone put it there. Probably your mom trying to clean up this pigsty." He braced me as he walked me closer to the bed. "Have you been writing any new poetry?"

"Not much." I picked up my journal and buried it in my underwear drawer.

"Lily, can I ask you something?"

I closed my eyes and exhaled, turning away from him. "Not now, Calder. I'm really tired."

"Just one thing."

"What?"

"Are you planning something behind my back?"

My bedding was a jumbled mess. I straightened the blankets as if I cared how things looked. "Like what?"

"Are you planning something with Pavati? Are you going to join her? Permanently? In the lake?"

"Not without you. Although I wish you'd . . ." I almost said, *Consider it.* But as much as I hated the idea that I was the cause of his severed family relations, I couldn't put that on him. After all he'd been through, I couldn't guilt him into it. Instead, I said, "I would never do that without you."

He traced the shadows under my eyes with his thumbs, then reached behind my neck. My muscles tightened as he undid the clasp that held the pendant around my neck.

"No," I said, grabbing his wrists. His eyes gazed into mine, and . . . reluctantly . . . I released my grasp. He laid the pendant gently on my bedside table. I couldn't take my eyes off it, only inches away and yet so distant.

"Just for a while," he said. "You'll sleep better."

"You'll stay with me?"

"Just for a little bit. Until you fall asleep. I don't want your dad to get the wrong idea."

We crawled into bed, and Calder pulled the covers up tight around my chin. I pressed my back against his chest; he pulled his knees up behind mine until we fit together like puzzle pieces. He kissed my hair. I waited for him to fall asleep.

The clock slowly changed its digital numbers as Calder's body—just as slowly—grew warmer and heavier behind me. When the weight of his arm was too much to bear, I rolled out from under it and waited to see if he'd notice me missing.

His face was smooth and guiltless. Maybe he really had been cleaning my room, but still, I pulled out *MY SCRIB-BLINGS* to see what he might have read.

I flipped through the pages, finally stopping at a Tennyson poem I'd copied down in an attempt to memorize it. A couple of the lines had hit me hard at the time, and I'd circled them in red ink.

So draw him home to those that mourn
In vain; a favourable speed

Ruffle thy mirror'd mast, and lead
Thro' prosperous floods his holy urn.
My Arthur, whom I shall not see
Till all my widow'd race be run;
(Dear as the mother to the son,)
More than my brothers are to me.
—Tennyson, *In Memoriam*, IX

Those circled lines echoed things Nadia had shown me in my dreams, though I couldn't quite piece it together. Just when I thought I could grab on to a coherent thought, it evaporated like the dream itself. I dropped my journal on the floor and fastened Nadia's pendant back around my neck. A piece of me was missing when I wasn't wearing it. I knew it would bring on the dreams, but I couldn't sleep without it. And I was so very, very tired . . .

It has been many years since I last saw Tom Hancock, yet I still watch the vacant house, the dark windows, the rotting dock. Grass grows high in the yard and tangles in the wind. A wild and hungry vine steals along the porch railings, threatening to someday overtake it all. If the place crumbles to the ground, it won't be too soon for me.

I leave the reminder of all I have lost and swim aimlessly for hours, traversing the great expanse of Gitche Gumee, which burns colder than ever.

I ignore the dull pallor of my scales, the fragile transparency of my fluke—thin as last year's spiderwebs. When I surface again, a familiar silhouette perches, knees pulled to chin, atop a rock that sits at the point where the waves meet the sand. The faint hint of sunken footprints marks the path to her perch.

The Thin Woman, as I have come to think of her, is at her post again, staring out across the lake. Even as the years have passed and her face has aged, even though her body has softened, there has always been something thin about her.

We have never spoken–the Thin Woman and I. In part because she is so focused on the one she seeks that I am as invisible to her as the boats that sail through her field of vision, or the butterfly that lands on her knee.

But mainly it's because I am to blame for her pain. And I don't know how to repent.

Still, I know the Thin Woman because I know loss. Perhaps that's what makes me brave. Before I can change my mind, I set foot on the mainland and steal a white terry bathrobe from her clothesline. It hangs on my body like an empty sail.

"Mind if I sit?" I ask.

She looks up, her eyes unfocused, still not really seeing me. Too many seconds pass before she sidles to her right, offering me a place beside her on the rock. Waves crash at its base, sending spindrift into the air. The sky is a hazy yellow. It's been a dry summer. There's a forest fire somewhere in the provinces.

It takes me a second to find the right muscles to sit like her–humanlike, contorting my body into stiff right angles: ankles, knees, waist. Now we sit in silence, both of us staring at the water, which makes it impossible for me to look directly into her eyes and project the message I want so much to send.

Finally I say, "Beautiful."

"Yes," she says.

"And lonely," I say.

"Yes." A silver tear bobs at the corner of her eye before falling into her hair. I take her fingers in mine, and she startles at my touch.

"How old would he be?" I ask. I have lost track.

She flashes with anger. How dare I intrude on her grief? But she regains her composure and says, "He'd be eighteen today."

Eighteen, I think. I'm surprised so many summers have passed. It's easy to forget how the cold lake slows our bodies' aging. In reality, Calder has matured to no more than eight human years.

The woman says, "I lost my boy fifteen years ago. I know he's gone, but I can't let myself believe it—even after all this time. I can still feel him in my bones. To my very center, I can feel him breathing."

I nod, wondering how I can make this right. "I'm sure he's a beautiful boy," I say, "and that every day he makes you proud."

The woman's face is granite hard. Her eyes are storm gray. "Who are you? You have no right."

I keep my eyes on a pair of black-speckled loons beyond the breakers. One dives. The other follows. "I lost my son, too. He's out there . . . somewhere . . . and I am very proud of him. I still hope he will come back to me. Perhaps, someday, your son will, too."

The Thin Woman groans. "What is hope?"

"A mother's sustenance," I say. "If it were in my power to bring him back to you, I would."

She smiles wanly, touches the terry loops of the bathrobe I am wearing, then looks curiously at my face. "If it were in anyone's power to bring him back," she says, "I'd be home making a birthday cake. It's not nice to taunt me with impossible promises."

I don't know why I do it. Perhaps it's because I want the same promise in return. But before I can think things through clearly, I hear myself say, "If it is ever in my power, I promise to send him back."

A wave crashes onto the rock, soaking Nadia and the Thin Woman. When the water subsides, decades have passed. Nadia is now with Calder. He looks twelve or thirteen. His arms are long and sinewy, with the strange angularity of new adolescence.

Through Nadia's eyes, I watch the pale legs of swimmers kicking furiously for shore. Maris pulls one from their ranks. Calder reaches out and holds Nadia's hand.

Nadia says, "Calder, when it is time, when you know it's time, you need to go home."

"But you're my home," he says. His dark hair covers his eyes, and he pushes it aside to watch the bubbles rising from Maris's wake.

"I'm speaking of your first mother. No matter what happens to me, you must go home."

He seems to be only half-listening, watching Maris snake away with her prey. "I don't want to."

"Someday, someone who loves you will show you how. When it's time. And when you're ready." Before she finishes, the vague lilt of a lullaby slowly filters through my consciousness:

The child-starved heart; the hands wrung dry, o'er the waves Mick Elroy cries.

With a ragged gasp I was back in my own body . . . awake . . . pajamas clinging to my sweat-drenched skin, the pendant sizzling on my chest. Calder was still asleep in my bed.

His arms and legs were a tangled mess with mine, as if there were extra limbs that no one knew what to do with. He looked beautiful. Not much different than the little boy in my dream. Sweet. And sensitive. And motherless.

I loved him. I didn't want to do it, but I knew what Nadia wanted me to do.

11

CALDER

As I regained consciousness, I laid my hand flat on Lily's mattress, feeling the cool smoothness of the cotton sheets, slowly focusing on the void Lily's absence left. I was alone in her bed?

"Damn it!" How had I let myself fall asleep? How had I not woken up? How could I betray Jason and Mrs. H's trust like this? They had to know. It had to be obvious the sofa bed had gone untouched. I cursed under my breath. Now I was trapped in Lily's room with no inconspicuous means of escape. I considered the window.

Through it, the morning sun hit the wall where Lily had plastered a series of dead poet portraits she'd copied out of a book. Some of the tape had come loose and the portraits curled at the corners. One dangled perilously from its top right corner, threatening to fall to the floor with the slightest disturbance.

"Lily," I whispered, but there was no answer. Downstairs, pots and pans clanked against the kitchen stove. Queen blared from the stereo. Sophie sang along in the living room. Someone was running the water in the upstairs bathroom.

"Lily?" I called, only slightly louder. "Are you up here?"

There was still no answer, except for more clanking in the kitchen. I sat up in bed, relieved for a second to see Lily standing in the doorway.

"I feel kinda funny," she said, her eyes glossy. "I . . . I . . ." Her back arched, and her knees buckled as she clung to the molding around the doorframe. I leapt from the bed in time to catch her before she hit the floor.

"Whoa, Lily. Your skin's all clammy. Are you all right?"

"It's nothing."

"Tell me." I wiped my hand across her forehead, brushing back the hair that stuck to her face.

"I know what Nadia wants," she said, her voice full of apology.

"That's enough. No more talk about this."

Lily shook her head and started to cry. I lifted her off her feet and cradled her in my arms. The back of her neck was sticky against my arm. I laid her in bed and pulled up the sheet.

"You stay here," I told her. "I'm going to go out and come back through the front door." She turned over, and I retucked the blankets around her tighter. I kissed her hair. A red strawberry of heat burned in the center of her pale cheek. "Back in a minute."

I opened the window and threw one leg over the sash, then the other. The porch roof felt rough and wet under my bare feet, almost like the shoreline itself. It gave me pause–a hesitation I couldn't afford–because just as I turned to close the window, Jason opened Lily's bedroom door, saying, "You up, hon?" I caught his eye in the split second before I jumped to the ground, feeling his disappointment in every inch of my fall.

I ran.

Twenty minutes later, still barefoot and now hungry, I opened the door to the only sanctuary I'd ever known in town, and the only thing open this early. Bells jangled as I entered the Blue Moon Café. Mrs. Boyd stuck her head out of her office, and I dropped into a lime-green chair.

Mrs. Boyd's face lit up in a way that felt out of place with how I was feeling. "Good Lord, Calder, you're a mess. Have you been running for your life?"

"Maybe," I said with a huff.

She wetted a towel in the sink and came to sit in front of me. She wiped the sweat off my face and mumbled, "You're not even wearing shoes."

"Lots of people run barefoot," I said.

"Sure. Kenyan marathoners maybe. Is someone giving you trouble?"

"Actually, I think I make enough on my own."

"That's a good boy," she said, pinching my cheek hard. Her wrist smelled like citrus, and it brought a flash of memory I couldn't place. Lily maybe? Or something with Tallulah? "This town could use a little drama now and then." Mrs. Boyd slapped the towel over my head and returned to the counter. "Can I make you something? Coffee? Get you a muffin? I have some warm ones just out of the oven."

"Yeah. Sounds great."

She sighed. "I miss you around here. Lily, too. How's she doing?"

"She's fighting a bug."

"That girl is always sick. You deserve someone with a stronger constitution."

I pinched my lips together to keep from saying too much. First, I doubted such a girl existed. She'd be a fearsome creature. Second, I didn't deserve Lily, or anyone else for that matter. The disappointed look on Jason's face as I crept out of Lily's bedroom . . . Well, it still burned like salt in an open wound.

Mrs. Boyd set my double espresso on the counter. She still knew what I liked. I walked up to get it.

"Tell you what," she said, taking my face between her hands. It was such an unexpected gesture. I didn't want to offend her by pulling back, but I felt awkward and strange being held like that by my former boss. "You come down to visit me more often, and I'll help you find a girl who can keep up with you. Maybe another barefoot runner, hmm? In fact, there's a new girl working the ferry this summer. She grew up on the island. You two could be cute together."

I took her wrists and lowered her hands to the counter as politely as I could. "I promise I'll come down and visit, but for now how about a box of muffins instead of a setup? I think I owe the Hancocks a peace offering."

"Oh, now we're getting somewhere. What happened?"

"Just a misunderstanding."

"Then you'll want the chocolate chunk. They make the best apologies."

I understand some people complain about washing dishes. Not me. Since coming to live with the Hancocks, washing dishes had become my favorite task. Not only was it amazingly normal and . . . human, but with as much time as I was spending out of the lake, keeping my hands in the warm water had a calming effect on my nerves. It was a perfect way to end a day, or start a day if it started a little bumpy. Like this one.

Jason and I found ourselves doing dishes together. I washed. He dried. Neither of us spoke about that morning.

Sun streamed through the windows, reflecting off the stainless steel surfaces of the newly remodeled kitchen. A watercolor self-portrait, signed *By Lily, age 5,* hung in a red frame under the cabinets. The real Lily slept upstairs in her bed. I hoped her early sojourn into the lake hadn't made her too sick.

After several minutes of strained silence, I said, "It wasn't what it looked like."

Jason took a sudsy plate from me and wiped it off. "If there was nothing to feel guilty about, why jump out the window?"

When he said it like that, I could see how incriminating it looked. "We just fell asleep. It won't happen again."

The corners of Jason's mouth pulled up. "I was nineteen once, too," he said. "Just try to be a little more discreet. For Carolyn's benefit, at least."

I rinsed the plate I was holding and handed it to Jason. We repeated this exercise a few more times, then he said, "Lily asked me something the other night that caught me off guard." His towel was getting too wet to do much good, and he placed a slightly damp plate in the cupboard.

"Yeah?"

"She asked me if I would ever join up with your sisters," Jason said, clearly selecting his words with care to see how I'd react. He opened a drawer and took out a dry towel. "Have you two ever talked about that?"

"They're your sisters. Not mine," I said. "And no. We haven't."

Jason raised his eyebrows, calling me out on my lie.

"Fine," I said, sighing heavily. "Pavati brought it up to Lily in a letter, but it's out of the question. We're not having some big, happy family reunion. And whatever Pavati wants, she's not going to make Lily her designated party planner."

Mrs. H wheeled herself into the kitchen. "Someone's planning a party?" she asked, looking first at her husband and then at me. Mrs. H's smile made my stomach flip-flop. Sometimes I thought it was the glimpses of Lily I saw in her: the way her eyes crinkled when she teased me, or the way she chewed her lip when she was working out a problem.

Jason dried his hands and folded his arms over his chest. "I was asking Calder about reuniting with his sisters."

"Your sisters," I said again. The plate slipped from my hands and landed in the dishwater, sloshing the counter.

"No!" cried Sophie, running from the living room to the kitchen. "Not yet! Not without me."

"You're not really planning on leaving, are you?" asked Mrs. H.

I leaned my back against the counter. "We're not leaving. None of us. I won't let that happen. Ever."

Mrs. H's shoulders relaxed. "Good. Don't scare me like that."

"Of course we wouldn't leave you," Jason said. "But a reunion doesn't mean leaving home. I'd like to hear more about this." He returned to the sink, putting both his hands in the sudsy water, and exhaled. "It could be a good thing. Maybe Pavati's right."

"She's not," I said.

Jason shook his head and kept his eyes on the sink, ignoring me and his wife and daughter. "Lily told me what life was like for you before you came to live with us."

"Lily doesn't know everything," I said.

"I know they put you through hell. I know none of that would have happened if I'd been a part of the family from the very beginning."

I couldn't argue with that. "A reunion doesn't change the past. I'm not going back."

"It could be different," Jason said.

Mrs. H wheeled closer. "Jason, don't pressure him."

"Yeah, Dad," said Sophie.

"Different issues," I said. "Same sisters. You've met them now. Did they give you a warm reception? Make you feel all good inside?" I was practically choking on my sarcasm, but Jason was patient with me, and he deflected my hostility with something he knew I couldn't contest.

"I'm worried about Lily's transformations. They're taking too much out of her. If she stayed in the water long term, she might get some strength back."

We all turned at the sound of the staircase treads creaking.

"Look who's up," said Mrs. H, her voice unnaturally gleeful as Lily limped slowly into the kitchen. Her face was still so pale, the scattering of freckles on the bridge of her nose seemed to float above her skin.

"You look like hell," I said.

"Thanks. I feel like hell." She leaned against the counter. "I think I'm coming down with something." Lily took one of the clean glasses and filled it with water. She drank it down quickly, then refilled it.

Jason said, "Calder and I were just talking about–"

"Not now," I said.

Lily finished her second glass of water, then said, gasping, "Talking about what?"

"I was thinking maybe it would be healthier for you to be in the water for longer stretches. Pain avoidance might let you build up your strength. And maybe we could test out a new arrangement with Maris and Pavati."

Lily looked at him with surprise, and then to me with a question.

I shook my head. "Your transformations are getting better all the time. Joining up with Maris and Pavati–that is not pain avoidance. Trust me."

Jason furrowed his brow at me. "Honestly, Calder, isn't it remotely possible that things have changed? They trusted us with the baby."

Why was this so hard for them to understand? I pinched the bridge of my nose. "Clearly they'll trust any idiot with the baby. It's not like they have a whole lot of choice in the matter, and can you consider–at least consider–the possibility that I'm right about this? Nearly half a century of living with them has to count for something."

Jason's head snapped up and he looked back and forth between me and Lily. "Excuse me?"

"What does that mean?" Sophie asked.

Lily stood up straighter and took a step toward her father. "Dad. Settle down."

"What's this?" Jason asked again, a vein bulging down the middle of his forehead.

"Calder," Lily said, her eyes begging me not to say anything more. "Don't."

"You're my age?" Jason asked, taking two steps toward me.

I backed away, holding my hands up, palms out, and Lily stepped between me and her dad. "No. No. Of course not," I said. "Not really."

Mrs. H wheeled out of my way so I wouldn't step on her.

"Dad, it's not like that," Lily said. "Not at all."

"And you're with *my* little girl?" Jason stormed.

"Hold up," I said. "Let me explain."

"I'd like to hear you try!"

"I would, too," said Mrs. H, rolling around me, but she sounded more curious than mad.

We were now all standing in a circle, like a huddle in a football game no one was going to win. It had been awhile since I'd felt like an outsider in the Hancock house. I didn't like it.

"I'm nineteen," I said. "In every single sense of the word . . . except the calendar."

"I don't understand," Mrs. H said. "How does that work?"

"The lake," Lily said, and I exhaled, thankful for her help. "It slows down the aging process."

"I've matured to nineteen," I said. "Physically, mentally . . . You can't think of this in a human way. You've only had a year, Jason. You haven't noticed your own delay yet. You probably won't for another dozen years; then you'll look around and see the difference. You age one year to every three on the calendar."

"Like dog years in reverse," Lily said, quoting me from a year ago, and I knew she was remembering the first day I revealed my true self to her—the best day of my life; the first day in a long, long time that I felt almost human.

Jason stared at me, openmouthed. "What about Carolyn?" *Mrs. H?* "Oh."

Out-aging a mate wasn't something I'd dealt with before, and now that Lily had changed, it wasn't something I ever had to worry about.

The same wasn't true for Jason. Mrs. H would out-age him. Over the next twenty-five years, he'd age only eight. By the time Mrs. H was seventy, he'd look barely fifty. And the disparity would continue to grow.

"Why didn't you tell me?" Jason asked.

"I didn't think that—"

Then Jason looked up, a new light in his eyes. "Wait a second. You say it slows the body down?"

Lily slipped her fingers into mine as we both felt Jason's tension dissipate.

"What about MS?" Jason asked. "Could it slow that down? Could it cure Carolyn?"

Mrs. H looked at him, eyebrows raised. "Jason?"

"If Carolyn were changed . . ."

"No," I said. "You can't be serious."

"If she were changed . . . could it save her?" Jason asked again, his intensity growing.

There was a hushed awe in the kitchen as the Hancocks considered the possibility. Lily looked at me, silently asking if it was possible. I waited for one of them to acknowledge the elephant in the room. I didn't want to say what I was thinking. I hoped they wouldn't make me because I didn't want to hurt Mrs. H like that. But the fact of the matter was, the lake slowed things down, it didn't change the past. Mrs. H was in a wheelchair. If she was changed, could she even swim?

Fortunately, I had other reasons to say no.

"It's too big a risk," I said to Lily. "To make the change, you know your mom's heart would first have to be stopped."

To Jason I said, "And it doesn't always work. It's more likely to kill her than save her. Plus . . ."

"Plus what?" Jason asked.

104

"Plus, you're forgetting one little thing," I said.

The Hancocks all waited silently.

I sighed with exasperation at their hopefulness and turned to face Mrs. H. "Even if the lake could cure you, even if there was no risk of death, mermen can't change anyone." I turned back to Lily. "Remember? And being a Half, you don't have any electrical charge. So drop it. It's impossible. We're not talking about this anymore."

Their faces fell. They knew I was right. "I'm sorry. I wish I could help you," I said to Mrs. H, and to Jason I said, "And if I haven't already said so, I'm sorry about this morning, too."

12

LILY

Calder looked embarrassed, or ashamed, or something. I wish I could read his emotions like he read mine. Then maybe I would have known how to say the right thing. Mom, however, knew that he didn't need us to say anything. She took his hand and gave it a little squeeze, without any words at all, and I could see it was exactly the right thing to do. That simple gesture made all the difference in Calder. He straightened his shoulders.

"I really wish I could help," he said again, giving Mom that look that always made me wonder if he was thinking about his own mother—somewhere . . . out there. . . .

"I know," Mom said. "We'll figure something out. Why don't you come out back and sit with me, Calder. I'll paint you."

A flicker of a smile crossed Calder's lips, and he turned her wheelchair and pushed her out of the kitchen and toward the back porch, which was now more of an art studio, covered in canvases, drop cloths, and hard, crusty paint tubes squeezed dry.

As I watched him leave and saw how much he wanted to stay a part of my family, the cold fear of what I had to do washed through me. Nadia was never going to rest until her promise to Calder's birth mother was fulfilled. And as long as Nadia wasn't resting, she wouldn't let me, either. Misery loved company after all. The problem was, I had no idea how to convince Calder of any of this, and it broke my heart to think how hard I was going to try.

My cell phone vibrated on the counter behind me, skittering toward the edge. *Buzz, buzz, buzz.* I ignored it. It was probably Gabby, and I wasn't in the mood. The phone buzzed again as I watched Calder practicing funny poses for Mom.

"Are you going to get that?" Dad asked.

"No."

Dad picked it up and looked at the screen. "It's Daniel."

I glanced over. Oh, brother.

"Do you think he needs help?"

Calder was doing Rodin's *The Thinker,* fist on forehead. "No doubt," I said.

Buzz.

"Lily, I think you should answer it."

"Not now."

Dad cleared his throat in a way that told me he was losing patience. "I thought you and Calder agreed to keep an eye on the Daniel situation."

"Ugh, Dad. Keeping an eye on Danny is not the same thing as bailing him out of every little jam."

The phone rang again, only this time it was the home phone ringing. Dad and I exchanged a look. Danny wasn't going to give up.

"Fine," I said, reaching for the receiver. "What?" I said to Danny.

"I need your help," he said in a rush.

I turned to watch Calder's portrait sitting. Now he was doing the *Karate Kid* stork pose. "Make it quick, Danny. I'm busy."

"It's my brothers."

Calder glanced my way and gave me a shy smile.

"I'll be right over," I said, hanging up the phone so hard it rebounded and fell to the floor

Danny's cousin's duplex was in Washburn and located on the north side of Memorial Park. Sided with pale green Masonite, and with a salt-and-pepper shingled roof, the building didn't seem quite centered on its foundation. Danny had the upstairs unit.

When I got to the top step, I knocked. The door cracked open an inch, stopped by the security chain. Danny peered out.

"Oh good, it's you." He closed the door, and I heard the

chain fall loose. He opened the door again, and I walked into a tiny kitchen. It smelled like coffee and bacon grease. "My brothers will be here any minute. I didn't know what to do. Thanks for coming."

"I'm not sure what you expect me to do," I said.

I'd met Danny's brothers, Christian and Bernard, once before–back when I was searching for Maighdean Mara. Daniel's family was descended from a long line of Maighdean Mara devotees, and they were some of the few humans still in the know about modern mermaids, but they weren't exactly our biggest fans. In fact, I didn't see how my presence was going to make this any better.

In the room off the kitchen I could see a wooden crib with chipped paint. Adrian lay on a fleece blanket trimmed in blue satin, staring up at a goldfish mobile. I raised my eyebrows at Danny. "Well, aren't we domestic?"

"I hit a garage sale in White River this morning. I didn't think anyone would recognize me there."

I walked into the nursery and cranked the mobile, making it turn, the fish slowly spinning. The tune "Under the Sea" from Disney's *The Little Mermaid* lilted from the tinny speaker. I snorted.

"I couldn't help myself," he said.

It reminded me of my first day swimming with Calder and the words he'd said: "It's not freakin' Ariel. Think *Silence of the Lambs*." But no matter how hard Calder had tried to impose a horror story on me, at the time, all I could see were possibilities.

There were three sharp knocks on Daniel's door. "Open

up, bro," said a deep voice on the other side. "I've got beer and cheese curds."

Danny just stared at the door, not making a move toward it.

"So . . . ," I hedged. "Do you want me to open it?"

"Maybe you can just wait in the other room for a second," Daniel suggested.

"Are you kidding me? Why did you make me come over here in the first place?"

Daniel shot me a nervous glance. "Just let me try to work it out on my own. If it sounds like I need help . . ."

"Whatever." I slipped out of the kitchen and into the bathroom on the opposite side of the kitchen wall. I leaned my back against the sink and picked the polish off my nails while Danny took some deep breaths. Then the security chain fell again.

"Dude, home sweet home!" exclaimed one of the brothers, bursting through the door and dropping something heavy on the kitchen counter. "Awesome summer party hou– What. Is. That?"

"What?" asked the other brother.

I heard the refrigerator door open. Danny was playing it ridiculously cool. "It's nothing," he said. The sound of his voice was followed by a *crack* and a fizz. "Want a Coke?" he asked.

"Like hell it's nothing," said the deeper voice.

Footsteps fell across the kitchen floor. "Is that a baby?"

"Of course it's a baby," Daniel said. "What did you think, I just decided to decorate the place in infant chic?"

Awesome, Danny, I thought. *Sarcasm should help a ton.*

"I don't understand," said the second brother. "You living with some chick?"

"No, I–" Danny floundered. "I–" The last strains of "Under the Sea" petered to a halt. I heard feet traveling across the floor, then Adrian cry out as he was lifted from the crib.

"Oh, no," said the first brother. "You didn't. Oh, God, please tell me you didn't."

Danny walked back into the kitchen. Adrian's wail almost drowned out Daniel's voice as he continued with his perfectly eloquent explanation: "I . . . I . . ."

"Is that thing hers?"

According to the bathroom clock, it had taken Danny's brothers all of sixty-five seconds to connect the baby to Pavati. Not a huge surprise since they'd spent a year rehabilitating Danny after Pavati had dumped him for Jack Pettit.

"After all that time deprogramming you?" the second brother asked. "I wasted the best year of my life."

Someone snorted and muttered, "Best year."

"You don't know," the voice continued. "What if that was supposed to be my best year? Maybe I could have been doing something great, and instead I spent it trying to get you over that bitch mermaid, listening to you bawling into your pillow every night, and now you've . . . Agh!"

Something big and heavy hit the shared wall between the kitchen and the bathroom.

The voice growled, "Tell me you aren't this stupid, Danny."

"Dude . . . ," said the other voice.

"Get your hands off me," Danny warned. "Can't you see I'm holding a baby?"

That was my cue to leave the bathroom. Danny was on his own, but I drew the line when it came to Adrian's safety. I had almost as much riding on his safe return as Danny did. If that meant diffusing his brothers' assumption about Pavati (correct though it was), I'd bite the bullet.

A second later I was in the kitchen. Danny's shirt had three sweat circles going down his spine, and he was holding the back of his head with one hand and cradling Adrian with the other.

"The baby's mine," I said. "Not Pavati's. Danny's letting me stay here with him, off and on."

"I remember you," said Christian, the one with the deeper voice.

"Likewise," I said. He'd believed I was a mermaid when we last met, although at the time, I wasn't. I'd used the brothers' misapprehension to my advantage then, the confirmation of their fears should only serve me better now.

"Get out," said Bernard.

"Hey, watch it!" Danny said, "This is my house. She's with me. I'll tell her when to leave."

"So you ditched one for another?" Bernard asked.

Danny said, "She's not *with me* with me, she's—"

Click.

Danny and I turned toward Christian, who was holding his phone up to take a picture of Adrian.

"Delete that," Danny said.

"I think Dad would be interested to see what you've been up to."

"Give it," Danny said, holding out his hand.

"What will you give me?" Christian asked.

I swallowed hard. If Christian and Bernard started talking, and Adrian's picture got passed around, someone might call social services, or the cops, or . . . *worse*. I couldn't let my mind go to that place.

These boys didn't know I was only a Half. They didn't know I had no electrical charge or hypnotic power. They didn't know I had no way to hurt them—on land, anyway. I'd have to compensate for my mermaid shortcomings with my acting prowess.

Doing my best Pavati, I pressed my palms flat against each other and began to circle them slowly. I kept my eyes downcast, until I'd taken a few seconds to build up the illusion of an electrical charge, then I slowly raised my gaze, looking through my lashes as Pavati did, focusing on Christian's eyes. His pupils dilated to the point I could see my reflection in them. For a second, I scared myself.

"Give me the camera, *boy*," I said. "Unless you want to make me angry."

"Give it to her," Danny said. "I don't want any trouble."

"You're already in trouble," Bernard said.

"Only if you make it so," I said, my voice a perfect Pavati purr. "I have no intention of hurting your little brother. He's only doing me a favor."

"In exchange for what?" Christian asked.

"His life," I said, and it gave me inexplicable gratification to see the hair on Christian's arms stand on end. "Now give me the camera." I took a step closer, and I could hear the tremor of his heart, wild and irregular. "You don't want to be on my bad side."

"Careful," said Bernard. "Back off."

I didn't acknowledge him, only held out my hand to Christian, who stared at my fingers with a healthy respect.

"What if I don't?" he asked.

"Do you want to find out?" I asked, switching over to Maris's threatening tone. I drew my eyebrows together.

"Just give it to her," Bernard said.

Christian dropped his phone into my palm, avoiding touching me. It took only a second for me to delete the photo and offer the phone back. When Christian tried to grab it, I snapped it away, then laughed like Maris, slowly sliding it into his front pants pocket.

He held himself rigid while I leaned in and, letting my lips graze his earlobe, whispered, "Smart boy."

Bernard slapped Christian on the shoulder and pulled him toward the door by his elbow.

"Not a word to Mom and Dad," Danny said.

"You're on your own," Bernard said. "We did our best." He pushed Christian toward the stairs and slammed the door behind them, leaving me and Danny standing in the kitchen. It was eerily quiet. Even Adrian looked stunned.

After a second, Danny turned and stared at me incredulously. "You can be really scary, you know."

I shrugged to play it off, but I was kind of proud of my performance. "You needed help, and now I need yours."

"What kind of help?" he asked. "I'm forever in your debt." He took a swig of Coke from his can.

"I think I need to break things off with Calder."

Danny choked and blew pop out his nose. "Damn, that burns!" Adrian began to cry again, and Danny grabbed a towel to wipe Coke off the baby's T-shirt.

"What's with you mermaids? Why can't you just be happy with the way things are?" He made a bottle with an already expert hand, then pushed it into Adrian's mouth. The baby fell instantly quiet, except for sucking sounds. "Although," Danny said, "I suppose Calder might understand it better than most, him being one of you and all."

"I *am* happy with the way things are. I don't want to do it. I *have* to do it."

"Holy hell, Lily." He rolled his eyes and turned to leave the kitchen.

"What?"

Danny stopped halfway across the floor. "Why would you want to ruin what you've got?"

"I don't want to ruin anything."

"Well"—he laughed once—"you're gonna."

I sighed and placed my hand over the pendant. "See this necklace?"

"All the time. Do you ever take it off?"

"It's telling me that Calder needs to go and find his parents. I can't go with him because there's something I need to do here. He'll never go without me if he thinks we're still together. That's why I need to break it off."

Danny tested out my words in his own voice, articulating

each word with a heavy dose of skepticism. "Your necklace is telling you that Calder needs to find his parents."

I nodded.

"Have you been huffing paint?"

"Thanks a lot. I thought you'd at least listen to me. Calder won't."

I followed Danny into the living room. The couch was pulled out into a bed that was covered in green and yellow zebra-striped sheets. Balled-up used diapers overflowed the small garbage can in the corner.

Danny sat down on the lumpy mattress. "If Calder thinks the necklace is handing you a load of crap, don't you think you should listen to him?"

I sat on the floor with the back of my fingers held under my nose. "Maris says he doesn't want me to believe what the pendant is showing me."

Danny nodded, and for a second I thought he was seeing things my way. "And, in the past, you've found Maris to be a reliable source?"

"No, but—"

"Lily, I think it's nice and all—Calder finding his real parents—but I don't think you need to break up for him to do that."

"I'm all ears. Give me a plan B." I pulled an afghan off the arm of the sofa bed and wrapped it around me. There must have been a draft, because a chill was running up and down my arms.

Danny laughed warmly, and his blue eyes sparkled against his tan skin. I was glad to see his mood change. He was really very cute. Sometimes I wondered what his life might have been like if he'd never met Pavati. I bet there were a lot of girls who wondered why he never noticed them.

"It's not rocket science, Lily. Ever heard of the Internet?" he asked. "Why can't Calder research birth records at your house?"

"Yeah, I thought of that, but at some point he'll need to start knocking on doors. We think they're in Canada. He's already said that he'd never go there without me." I chewed on my lip, thinking. "Maybe we don't have to break up. Technically. We could take a break for a–"

Danny tipped his head to the side and gave me a patronizing look. His dark hair hung across one eye. Clearly he thought I was being an idiot. I hoped he was wrong.

"And there's more," I said with a sigh.

"There better be."

"Maris and Pavati are fighting, and they each want me and my dad to join them. On a more . . . permanent basis."

"And . . . ," Danny prodded, his voice brightening at the sound of Pavati's name.

"Calder would rather poke needles in his eyes."

"I see. And you?"

I pulled my knees up to my chin and hugged my legs. "I would never join them without Calder, but my dad's considering it. I want to stay close to that situation. It would hurt Calder too much if my dad accepted their offer."

"Lily, you are the craziest girl I've ever met. You're telling me you won't do anything without Calder, but you're going to break up and send him away? Do you hear yourself? How does that make any sense? What are you going to do, just sit in your room until your *love-ah* gets back?"

I blushed. "Looks like it's working for you."

"Hurtful."

I got up, dropped the afghan on the floor, and walked to a bookcase where Danny displayed all his baseball memorabilia. Despite my quick comeback, his question had unsettled me, and I didn't want to give him the satisfaction of knowing that. He had a point. I didn't know how long it would take Calder to find his parents. And once he had, I wasn't one hundred percent certain that he'd come back. I knew how desperately he wanted a family—maybe even more than he knew himself. I saw how seamlessly he'd made himself a part of mine. The real thing would be irresistible.

For a second I thought maybe I *would* go with him, but I quickly dismissed the idea. I didn't trust my dad to know how to stand up to Pavati's and Maris's ploys, and then—in a year—there'd be the matter of Adrian. And what would become of Danny after that? I was more needed here than Calder would need me in Canada. And he would come back for me like he had once before. Wouldn't he?

Adrian made soft snuffling sounds as he drained the last drops from the bottle. Danny pulled the bottle from his lips and tossed it on the bed.

"Do what you have to do, Lily, but be ready for the consequences."

I turned to face him. "Good ones, I hope."

Danny raised Adrian to his shoulder and gently thumped him on the back. "Maybe."

13

CALDER

Two days passed since Jason suggested Carolyn be changed and during that time, I couldn't help but feel that something was seriously wrong between me and Lily. She avoided my eyes. She left the room if I entered it. When I caught up with her unexpectedly and tried to give her a hug, she only smiled wanly and pulled away, making some excuse.

Worst of all, when I asked what was bothering her, she'd just say, "Nothing. Maybe I'm not the only one with an overactive imagination." I wished I'd never mocked her for thinking Nadia was communicating with her. She was more offended than I'd realized.

I wanted to make things right between us. I wanted to tell her that I was sorry. If that meant letting her wear that blasted pendant every day and night, if that meant listening with rapt attention as she recounted all her Nadia dreams, so be it. Hell, I'd even take notes.

But really, more than anything, I wanted to tell her that I loved her, that I wanted us to be together forever, and that nothing should come between us. I wanted to prove that to her. I wanted her to understand.

So the next day, after putting the groceries away for Mrs. H, I pulled Lily aside and—against her protests—snuck her out the front door.

I'd spent all morning planning a romantic getaway in the woods. It was a scene right out of a John Hughes movie. I hoped she'd like the copper promise ring I'd made and hidden in a small velvet box. It felt ridiculously obvious in the pocket of my cargo shorts, but so far she hadn't noticed.

"Where are we going?" she asked as I pulled her toward the path that cut through the woods.

"You'll see."

She held her hand to her head so her floppy hat wouldn't fall off. "Stop, I can't run in sandals. Slow down or let me get different shoes."

"You're not going to need shoes," I said. "We're not going very far. Are you okay? You still look a little pale."

"The joys of being a redhead."

"I don't mean normal pale. I mean, you look kinda . . ."

"Don't say 'sick.'"

"Okay, you're not sick, but are you sure you're warm enough? We could go back and get you a sweatshirt."

She put on the brakes and pulled on my arm. "Tell me where we're going."

"We're already here," I said, leading her into a clearing, then pulling her into my arms and off her feet. Her hat fell off and her long, thick curls tumbled down her back. I inhaled the orange-blossom scent of her, burying my nose in her hair. This was perfect. Life was perfect.

My anxiety over the past few days evaporated, and I saw our lives with pristine clarity. I'd picked the perfect spot. The trees towered in a canopy above us. The ground was carpeted in moss and tiny white flowers—honeysuckle sweet. The early-evening sun streamed down through the pines, casting pollen-laden stripes across the private clearing and the patchwork quilt I'd laid out a few hours earlier.

"What's this?" Lily asked nervously. She looked down at the quilt and bit her lip.

Oh! Oh. I hoped I hadn't given her the wrong idea. The curve of her shoulders emitted a purple glow that burned up her neck and colored her lips. If she thought that I meant to suggest anything inappropriate . . . "What are you thinking?" I asked. "You're turning purple."

"I guess I am a little chilly after all," she said.

I took off my sweatshirt and gestured at her with my chin. She lifted her arms, and I gently, slowly drew the sweatshirt over her arms and head.

"Calder," she said.

It was now or never. Well, realistically it was now or later, but I couldn't wait for later. I took her hands in mine and pre-pared to give her the ring. The potential for rejection was the only thing holding me back. Maybe Jason was right. Maybe this wasn't something to surprise her with.

"You're not purple because you're cold," I said. "Purple is planning. I don't know what you're up to, but two can play at that game."

"Great," she said, drawing the word out. "Do I want to know what you've been planning?"

I pulled the ring box out of my pocket. Her eyebrows shot up. "Our future. I want to ask you . . ."

14

LILY

Oh my gosh. Oh, this is so not happening. Why did he have to make this harder than it already was?

I put my finger to Calder's lips, feeling the pulse in my fingertip beat against them. If I was going to send him away, we couldn't talk about a future. Not yet. Not now.

But knowing what I was about to do fed my desperation to keep him close. I could hear the ticking of my heart's clock, counting out each second before I said the words I had to say.

I was doing the right thing, but it was a leap of faith. No

matter what Calder thought he felt for me, how easy would it be for him to find that same happiness with someone else? Someone less pushy, less compulsive, less prone to visions of dead matriarchs?

Purple may be planning, but he didn't know what I was planning to say. He couldn't see the words that pushed against the back of my teeth. But he could see the anxious light fizzling around the corners of my mouth, radiating in my eyes. And I knew he wondered.

I also knew that I wanted something from him before I told him goodbye. He stood before me, dark swirls of hair falling into his green eyes, the sunlight glistening on his tanned face. I pulled his T-shirt up and off, taking in every line, scar, muscle, vein. I tried to memorize every inch of him as if he were a map and I was learning my way home, as if it were my last chance because I knew in my heart it might be just that.

"Um, Lily?" he asked, eyebrows raised.

Slowly, I sat down on the blanket and pulled him over me.

"Lily," he said. "Hold up."

I put my hand behind his neck and pulled his face to mine, kissing him once.

He put the box back in his pocket and laughed, saying, "Slow down. Can we talk?"

My fingers clenched at his hair. "We don't have a lot of time," I said. I hoped he didn't hear my voice shaking.

"Time for what?"

Stomach muscles tight, I rose off the ground to meet him. I knew I was confusing him, but he kissed me back anyway. His lips burned against mine. I moved my hands to his chest, and he took them in his own.

He leaned into me, kissing my forehead, then my cheek. I kissed his mouth, lips smooth, parting, slipping his tongue past my teeth. I wished for his fingers to explore my body, but he held my hands fast, now arms stretched wide, securing me to the blanket like a butterfly pinned to corkboard. *Lepidoptera,* I thought.

CALDER

I let go of Lily's hands and they were quick to find the small of my back. She pressed me into herself. The ferocity of it made it feel more like an attack than an embrace, but I rocked my hips against hers, watching the silver light in her eyes, the rose-colored glimmer at the corners of her mouth and the tips of her shoulders. I waited for her aura to tell me what she wouldn't say: to stop. Or to keep going. Or to explain what the heck was going on, because this was nothing like what I had been expecting. After barely a word from Lily in two days, this person was a stranger. A beautiful, exciting stranger.

She rolled me off her, following the rotation with her own body until she was on top. She hitched her skirt above her thighs. Her long hair tumbled onto my face. I held it back and kissed her throat, the hollow of her collarbone. . . .

My stomach muscles relaxed, then tensed with each breath, as she sank lower onto me, bending her body to meet the contours of mine.

"You're sure?" I asked.

"I'll tell you tomorrow," she said, her voice barely above a whisper.

I pulled away, ever so slightly. "Whoa. Wait. This was not my idea. We don't have to do this."

She shook her head and her long hair tickled my face. "That's not what I meant. I only meant that I wish I knew what I was doing."

"Well, I'd be very surprised if you did."

"I'm glad one of us does," she said, blood flooding into her cheeks.

"Actually," I said, "you're scaring me to death."

Slowly—so slowly I almost didn't notice—she slipped the metal button on my cargo shorts from its buttonhole. I held still, hoping she wouldn't, hoping she would. I was caught in a net, seeing the way out but not smart enough to take it.

"Lily, I love you. Please know I've never said that to anyone else, and that will never change."

She paused. A pale vibration of relief shone from her skin. "Good to know," she said, shutting off my protests with a kiss.

LILY

I took Calder's hands and moved them higher up my rib cage, all the while muzzling my inner chaperone. *Oh my God, you're about to have sex.* This went against everything I

126

believed in and all the advice I'd ever given my best friend, Jules. Why was I doing this? Maybe I wanted to give Calder a reason to come back. Maybe it was because, in my heart, I knew he wouldn't. Maybe it was because this would be my only chance to love him like this.

I silently counted to ten, the very core of me molten. Calder slipped my T-shirt over my head, breath catching in his throat.

CALDER

I'll count to ten, I thought. *If she hasn't stopped me by then . . .* But at seven Lily flash-burned with a pink fire I'd never seen before. I let out a low groan and gripped her waist, opening my mouth to hers.

And then her colors flashed to fear.

15

LILY

Calder jerked away from me, his breath running ragged, and my heart pounding against my sternum.

"What's wrong?" I asked.

"Not now," he replied. He grabbed my T-shirt out of the yellow bush and handed it back to me inside out.

"But–"

"Not until you're ready. Really ready."

My face burned with embarrassment as I clutched my T-shirt to my chest. "Seriously?"

"Get dressed," he said, not looking at me.

"But–"

Calder frowned at the ground, stifling my argument. I flushed scarlet as I awkwardly pulled myself together. I was such a colossal idiot. I wanted to crawl under a rock and die.

Calder sat silently by my side, not watching me dress, picking at the blades of grass that grew at the edge of the blanket. He rolled and spun them between his fingers creating the tiny sound of displaced air, but it wasn't enough to fill the silence between us.

I tried to stand up, but he said, "Don't leave. Just sit here with me."

So I did, but the silence continued, and it was excruciating. The muscles in his jaw bounced, making me wonder what he was really thinking.

Eventually, his forehead furrowed and the corners of his mouth turned down as he said, "Pavati told me about the letter she wrote you."

I eyed him suspiciously. It wasn't what I'd expected him to say. Was that all that was bothering him? "You know what she asked me?"

"Yes," he said, finally turning to me. He searched my face. "How long have you known?"

He closed his eyes to the apparently distasteful change in my colors and sighed. "A few days now. But, Lily, the last thing I want to do is fight."

"Who's fighting?" I asked, but I couldn't *not* feel irritated with him. Why hadn't he told me when he first found out?

Calder took a deep breath. He ran one of his fingers over the topography of my knuckles. "I'm not willing to give them what they want. And you should be more suspicious of their motives."

A strange rush of anger flared up in my chest, derailing me from my course. "You mean, they couldn't possibly like me for me? They couldn't possibly want me to be part of their family? Well, news flash, they do. And I think Nadia does, too."

Calder nearly did a double take, the change in my voice surprising him as much as me. "Of course they could like you for you, who wouldn't? I'm only saying . . . Lily, I–I'm sorry I've been so upset with you when you talk about Mother. Maybe if you tell me what you think you're hearing–"

"I told you. I don't *think* I'm hearing anything," I said. "Nadia is talking to me."

"Then, tell me what you *are* hearing, and I'll let you know if it really sounds like something she'd say."

"She shows me things. About the past. And what she wants for the future. I know how my grandfather came to have this necklace in the first place."

"That's easily explainable. Your subconscious probably just filed away something your dad told you."

"I've seen your birth mother. I've seen you as a little boy."

Slight trembling ran the length of his arms, and I could tell he was wondering how much detail about his past life I was privy to.

"Nadia wants you to find your birth family." There. I'd said it. There was no turning back now. The sudden anger I'd felt was quickly replaced by sadness because it was time to send him on his path.

"You're wrong," he said, his tone scoffing.

I closed my eyes and held the pendant in my fist. It took some concentration, but I did my best to mimic Nadia's voice, liquefying my words into a vaguely recognizable cadence:

"'Calder, when it is time,'" I quoted, "'when you know it's time, you need to go home. You need to find your mother.'"

"That's impossible," he whispered.

"Is it? A mermaid has no choice but to fulfill her promises. What if Nadia died with a promise unfulfilled? What if the compulsion to fulfill it was so strong, it followed her even after death?"

"That's impossible," he muttered again, pressing his knuckles to his forehead.

"I don't think Nadia is resting in peace," I said.

"Lily, I've told you, my biological parents aren't even a thought in my head."

It was when he lied like this that I understood him best. It wasn't that I didn't believe he'd let go of his human memories as soon as he was changed, but I also knew how much he wanted to belong to a family. He bent over backward to make my mom happy, and when I watched him helping her in the kitchen, or making his bed when she asked, I often thought *A momma's boy without a momma*, though I'd never call him that to his face.

"But that's just it," I said, putting my hand on his shoulder. "They should be a thought in your head. They should be much, much more."

"Why? Who says so? Has it occurred to you that this is more important to you than it is to me?"

"You started to search for them last summer. You said you thought they were from Thunder Bay. If it wasn't important to you—"

"It was only a fleeting thought. And it wouldn't have been even that much if you hadn't made me think of them. Truth is, maybe I was a little curious, but I don't *need* them anymore. I've already found everything I ever wanted. I've found a family that I want to be part of." His voice dropped to a whisper. "I thought I kind of already was."

I looked away and that small gesture stopped him short.

He leaned to one side and reached into his pocket. "Listen," he said, "I didn't mean to freak you out with this, and you don't have to read too much into it." He pulled out the small velvet box again. "If you don't want it you can say no."

He held it out to me, waiting for me to take it. "So are you going to open it? I didn't steal it if that's what you're thinking. But I want . . . I want to ask . . ."

"Do you know what I want?" I covered the box with a shaking hand—the soft velvet prickled against my palm— and gently pushed it back toward his pocket. "I want you to find your parents. That's what I want for you. And it's something you need to do on your own. Before you do anything . . . else."

The hurt in his eyes slashed at my heart. I wanted to kiss it away, but I couldn't move. All of my muscles had clamped down.

"I don't need my past," he said. "I want you. You are my future. It's you who makes me happy."

"But that's just it," I said. "Don't you see? Your happiness should not be completely dependent on me. *You're not whole.* Not yet."

"Who fed you that line? Pavati?" He grabbed my wrists, hard, and I twisted them to get free. "Don't trust them, Lily. She just thinks she'll have better luck with you if I'm out of the picture. They're queens of manipulation."

"Maybe you're right, but it doesn't make it less true. You need to find your parents."

"And what if I find them?" he demanded.

"What do you mean?"

"If I find them, then what? Do you think they'd just let me walk out of their lives again?"

"Well . . ." Admittedly, I hadn't thought about that. I assumed it would be hard for Calder to leave his family once he found them. I'd never considered that his parents would be the problem—that they would be the ones to not let him go again.

"That's it, isn't it!" Calder exclaimed. "You know I wouldn't be able to do that. Is this just some elaborate plan for getting me out of the way forever?"

"Calder—" I knew he'd react badly, but he was starting to scare me.

"Well, excuse my confusion, *Lily,* but what the hell was *this* all about?" He gestured angrily at the blanket and the imprint of our bodies still lingering in its fibers.

"I don't want you out of the way." I didn't. But I needed him to go. For him. For me. For Nadia. And for his birth mother, too.

"You're lying. I can see the lie all over you. Tell me the truth. You owe me at least that much."

"Nadia wants me to–"

"Damn it, Lily, she doesn't want you to do anything. She's dead!"

I looked up as heavy tears rolled onto my cheeks. "She doesn't feel so dead to me."

"She was my mother! You never even knew her! Believe it or not, the world is not yours to save, Lily. *I'm* not yours to save. Your dad, Sophie, Jack . . . If you'd let others take care of their own business instead of always–"

"Stop."

"Too much truth?"

I didn't need a mirror to know my face was red. My eyes glossed over and my lower lids flooded with the next set of tears. I stood up and my skirt fell to its full length. I had to get away. But Calder got up, too, and grabbed my hand, pulling me back to him. I pushed my palms against his chest.

"Lily, don't do this," he said. "I'll fall apart without you."

I winced. "Just go, Calder. Go to Canada. Find your parents."

"No!" he yelled.

In that moment, he reminded me of Maris, the way she once rose out of the water, staring down at me, her face radiant with fury. Calder's resemblance to his sister had never struck me as it did now. I took a step back. He grabbed my shoulders.

"Why are you doing this to me? What did I do?" he demanded.

"Nothing! Nothing. I'm not doing this *to* you. I'm doing this *for* you."

"Just when I . . ." He didn't finish that thought and I was desperate to know what it was. Instead he said, "I thought you loved me."

"I do," I said. "I'm doing this because I love you."

"That's bullshit and you know it." He laughed one hard laugh. "I always thought you were so much better than me. All this time I've been trying to improve myself. I kept thinking, if I could just be more like you. Kind and good and giving. But you're just like my sisters."

I ignored his attempt to hurt me. "Just promise me, Calder. Promise me you'll find your parents."

"Forget it."

"I need you to promise me."

He stared right through me for a long moment. I wished we were in the lake, and I could have heard the workings of his mind. It would have made it so much easier to prepare for his argument. Right then, if our hearts were timepieces, mine was a stopwatch, racing toward the finish line. His was an hourglass with the last grains of sand trickling out.

"Fine," he said. "I promise I'll go to Thunder Bay and search for my birth parents, whom I care nothing about."

I blinked, startled. "That's it? Just like that? You promise?"

The corners of his mouth twitched downward, and I watched as a green light simmered behind his eyes, then slowly darkened like a candle going out in an empty room. "Yes. Are you happy?"

I wanted to say, *Of course not. How could I be happy?* Why couldn't he understand this was never about me? I wished I could undo the harm I'd caused, to say, *Just kidding, I didn't mean it,* but instead I said, "Yes."

He bowed his head, and his hands dropped from my shoulders to his sides.

I took a deep breath and went to kiss him, but he turned his head and I missed his mouth. Still, I lingered on his cheek a second longer than I should have.

Then I walked toward the water.

His gaze bored holes into my body, but I never looked back. I hesitated only a second in the waves that pulsed at the shore. My skirt floated at my ankles, then my knees and thighs. I think I heard him say, "Don't," as I pulled my skirt up and over my head, along with my T-shirt, and dropped them both, leaving them to float in the shallows.

PART TWO

How fares it with the happy dead?
For here the man is more and more;
But he forgets the days before
God shut the doorways of his head.
   —Alfred, Lord Tennyson, *In Memoriam*, XLIV

16

CALDER

I didn't watch Lily leave. I slammed my palm against a tree. If she was going to walk away from me and swim right into Pavati's arms, I couldn't watch. If Lily didn't want me around anymore, that was fine. I didn't care. Not about her. Not about anybody.

Without conscious thought, I walked toward the water, but definitely *not* following her. Lake Superior was plenty big without Lily having to worry about running into me. Or me into her. I reached up with both arms, crossed them over my head, and pulled off my T-shirt. I dropped it on the ground.

It didn't matter where. I wasn't coming back for it. There was no reason for me to be on land anymore.

I stripped off the rest of my clothes, leaving the ring in my pocket, and took three long strides toward the water. *Goodbye, ground,* I thought. Goodbye to fooling myself into ever thinking I could be a permanent part of Lily's family . . . part of Lily's life. It had been a nice run. But it was over.

A cloud passed over the sun, and my mind matched the darkening light. The wind whipped my hair around my face. I stormed across the beach and made a shallow dive. I couldn't hear Lily. Not that I was listening for her. But did I really expect I would? She'd already proved herself capable of hiding from me in the water and, come to think of it, on land.

She could justify her reasons for sending me away anyway she wanted, but none of it made sense. After all we'd been through! Didn't she remember any of it? Didn't any of it matter to her anymore?

I'd been rejected. I had no one to blame but myself. I had nothing to offer. If only Lily had never made me hope for more. Never made me think we belonged together. Never brought me so far. Never taught me to love. I'd been right to fear losing her. I'd lost everyone else, hadn't I? But out of all the people I'd lost, she was the only one who'd chosen to leave.

I swam fast and far, bending the water behind me. The more I thought about it, the more I couldn't stop thinking about it. I shook my head, trying to clear the pain, but it was no use. The threads of depression thickened into ropes, which knotted themselves deep into the crevices of my brain. My heart seized. Without Lily, despair quickly crept in.

I hadn't been paying close enough attention. Like noxious vines once pruned back, they reclaimed the house as soon as the gardener left his post. For me, those vines were the urge to hunt, which I'd kept at bay for so long. Too long apparently. Eighteen months of abstinence were shrieking at me like an old woman trapped in a well.

A call for help cut through both the water and my self-pity, and I surfaced hungrily to find a stranded kayaker caught on the rocks. She was shrouded in the ashy gray of desperation, though when she turned and saw me watching, she showed no fear. Rather, a faint tinge of embarrassment, followed by gratitude—then the most delicious color of relief washed over her, flashing bright with an explosion of salvation. Oh, God.

"Wow, I didn't expect to see anyone else out here," she called. "I've caught a line on these rocks. I thought I was going to be trapped here forever. Give me a hand?"

She smiled, releasing a flurry of emotions that made my every synapse quiver with expectation. The water trembled and rippled away from me. Without thinking, I closed the space between us so quickly she had no time to react. Her sense of relief continued to flood my mind, my veins, surging for my heart.

It didn't take more than a second to flip the kayak.

My mind went blank, the world black. I ground my teeth together. The whole maneuver was instinctual. I didn't fight myself. I didn't think at all. It was like I'd never been out of practice.

Within seconds, I'd sunk my teeth into her life jacket and torn it into pieces, which floated toward the surface like neon orange petals in memoriam. Relieved of the vest, the girl's body touched mine. I clenched her to my chest, spiraling into deeper water that pushed the life out of her. Supple arms chilled and hardened as I wrung the last bit of happiness from her heart.

When there was little left but bone and skin, I released my grasp and let her sink.

Slowly.

Watching

her graceful

descent.

Her arms floated in front of her, rounded, a ballerina pose. Her long blond hair circled her head like a halo. But instead of rising, this angel was sinking.

Only then did the wretched horror of what I'd done wrench the fleeting jubilation from my mind, replacing it with a shame I had never known. She deserved better than this. What a disgusting creature I was.

Damn it.

I raced after her body, buoyed it up, carried it from the depths back to the beach. I stayed in the shallows. There was no time to transform.

I cradled the body in my arms and blew air into its empty lungs.

"Wake up. Please, wake up. Wake up. I'm so sorry. I'm so

sorry." Spit sizzled through my teeth. There was no excuse, no justification—not even a thin stretch of one that I could make myself believe. All that was left was this cold corpse lying in my arms, head tipped back, blue lips agape over too-white teeth.

"Please." I filled her lungs again. I shook her. Hard. "Wake up!"

I placed my palms flat against her temples and said a prayer—though I'd never learned exactly how. If I could have traded places with her, I would have. Maybe that was as good a prayer as any.

I inflated her lungs a third time, then pressed my face into her wet hair, saying, "I'm so, so sorry." Then, from some kind of nowhere place, she sucked in air like a vacuum.

The noise startled me, and I dropped her onto the sand. Her chest expanded. Her eyes bulged open. A feral growl of air raced through her. Before she was fully conscious, I pulled away into deeper water and watched from a distance as she rolled over in the sand, peeling back the hair plastered to her face, her chest heaving. She looked at her pebble-peppered hands, then collapsed back onto the beach.

She was exhausted. But she was alive.

That's it. Never again. But I could never go back to Lily now.

She was right; I was not whole and clearly I never would be. How could I ask Lily to waste her life with someone like me? The truth trickled icily through the veins in my arms, down to the tips of my fingers, tingling there. There was no escaping the past.

I snorted a short, humorless laugh. But that's what Lily wanted for me, wasn't it? For me to reclaim my past? Well, she'd got what she wanted. I hoped she was happy.

I swam to Red Cliff and found a safe spot to transform. Clouds were rolling in, and before I was done, a sharp wind brought the first pelting drops of rain, which pockmarked the lake.

The promising snap of laundry flapping on a clothesline drew me from the beach and up the bank. At the top, three small clapboard houses lined a narrow dirt road. One of them had pillowcases, socks, and several pairs of pants hanging out to dry—forgotten in the rain. I kept low, creeping in my nakedness along the tree line. When I was sure no one was around, I stepped into the yard and pulled some white gym socks and jeans off the line. The socks went on easily, but it was a struggle to get the wet denim over my legs, and when I did, the jeans barely reached my ankles. But at least I wouldn't get arrested for indecent exposure.

After another glance around, I took three quick strides to the back screen door and opened it slowly on squeaky hinges. A pair of leather work boots were lined up on the mat. I laced them on tight. They were still warm inside.

Less than a minute later, I ran from the house and up the gravel drive to the blacktop county road. My legs were still unsteady, and my knees buckled twice. I didn't know where I was going, but it couldn't be long before *someone* came by. If I could just get myself out of Bayfield—far away from this miserable lake, far away from Lily, somewhere inland—if I could do that, I wouldn't hurt anyone else, ever again.

Maybe the Black Hills of South Dakota. I could be the first landlocked merman of all time. I'd be legendary. Innovative. A real maverick.

Or just another idiot.

When I got to the road, I walked backward, holding out my thumb. The rain came down harder now, pelting my bare chest and washing my hair into my eyes. I spit water from my lips. The first three cars raced by without braking; their passengers craned their necks to look at me. I guess I looked a little criminal. Soaking wet, half naked, in too-small jeans and clown-sized work boots. The driver of the fourth vehicle must have been nearsighted because he stopped.

"Good Lord, son, where you going?" The man was about sixty, round in the middle, with gray stubble on his windburned cheeks. A bulbous nose balanced dark-rimmed glasses. He kept his left hand on the wheel and leaned across the empty passenger seat. Rain fell through the open window and left wet splotches on the leather seat.

"Thunder Bay," I said without thinking. *Ugh. Stupid promise. Why did I ever make it?* I knew better than to think my determination not to go to Thunder Bay could overrule my compulsion to fulfill my promise to Lily.

"I can get you as far as Duluth," the man said. "That's where I stop."

I hesitated. Rain wouldn't kill me, and the man looked like a talker. I wasn't in the mood for conversation. "Never mind. I'm good."

He laughed. "Don't be a fool. You'll drown out there. Plus, you're likely to cause an accident walking around

145

half-naked. What happened to your shirt?" He pushed open the door, and warm air burst out of the cab and hit my chest. I groaned, only now realizing how cold I was.

Grateful for the heat, I slid in beside him and prayed for my first impression of him to be wrong. It wasn't.

"You couldn't wait for the rain to stop before you started walking?" the man asked, chuckling in a way that sounded like he was gargling gravel.

"It came on suddenly," I said.

"That's the way everything is around here. It's like that song about the *Edmund Fitzgerald*. You know, the one about the 'witch of November come early.'"

I held my tongue and hoped he wouldn't start singing, too.

"Reach back behind me," he said. "My son left a T-shirt and a sweatshirt in here somewhere last time he was up. See it? Unless maybe the wife brought it in."

I dug around behind the driver's seat and found what he'd described. The T-shirt was inside the sweatshirt as if they'd been pulled off together. I pulled them on the same way.

"Looks like a wild one out there," the man said. Through my window I could see the waves churning into whitecaps. "Best those boats get back to the marina and zipped up tight. I used to work the ferry line when I was younger. Now, *The Island Queen*, she could cut the waves pretty good, but still . . . I never had the stomach for a life on the water." He patted his stomach and added, "Seasick."

There was a lump in one of the pockets of the stolen jeans. I pushed my fingertips inside and pulled out two wet dollar bills. "I don't have much to offer you for gas," I said.

The man chuckled again and rubbed the stubble on his chin. "I'm not about to take a young man's last dollar. Besides, just filled up. I'm good to go. This truck here is one of those new—whatcha call it?—economy gas guzzlers. I could make it to Iowa on one tank."

The man glanced over at me, and I held his gaze for just a second, pushing my will onto his. If I was going to search for my parents, it would be good to have a dependable vehicle. He stuttered, surprisingly susceptible to the amount of hypnosis I was putting off, and said, "Best vehicle I've had in a while. . . . I should let you take a turn at the wheel."

But then he looked away, and I lost my grasp on his mind. Hypnosis would only work with sustained eye contact. Without that, I couldn't connect my mind to his; I couldn't plant the thoughts I wanted to harvest. The only way to achieve it now would be to crawl onto the hood of the truck and stare at him through the glass, like a gigantic bug splattered on the windshield.

I snorted.

"You say something, son?"

I shook my head.

The road to Washburn wound down the hill and through the trees. As the rain came down harder, the man didn't take his eyes off the yellow line.

He could tell there was something wrong with me. I could see his nervousness sizzling on the backs of his hands, and that he was purposefully refusing to look my way again.

"How 'bout those Packers?" I asked, trying to get him to look over.

He raised his eyebrows. "It's the off-season."

"The Brewers, then."

"I follow the Twins," he said. "Ever since Kirby in ninety-one. Game Six."

I had no idea what he was talking about. "Yeah?" I asked, hoping that was enough to keep him going.

"When he made that jumping catch against the left center wall . . ." He chuckled. "He's like the patron saint of us short, chubby guys. Now, a young fella who looks like yourself . . . Well, I suppose you don't have much need for heroes."

"I don't know," I said.

The man turned west on Highway 2 toward Duluth and an hour later we were crossing the High Bridge into Minnesota. Up and up. Cars seemed to be passing closer than before. I was too far above sea level and, unlike in an airplane, there was no aisle seat from which to avoid the view. Instead, I laced my hands behind my head and put my forehead on my knees.

At the peak of the bridge, my stomach rose into my chest, then settled back into place as we went down the other side. The man asked, "Did I just help a fugitive cross state lines? You're not in some sort of trouble, are you?" I sat up, and he made the mistake of glancing over.

I hit my mark.

A streetlight flooded the car with a pale amber light, and I watched as his eyes widened and his pupils dilated. *Stop,* I thought. *Your gas tank is low.*

"Y'know, I think I should stop for gas," he said.

"You pay, I'll pump," I said.

His wipers went *thump, thump, thump* across the windshield as we pulled north onto Interstate 35. The old man exited the highway, put on the left blinker, and turned in to a convenience store. "Coffee?" he asked.

"Awesome," I said. "Why don't you have a seat at one of the booths. Take your time. I'll be in to join you soon." The old man's eyes glassed over as he climbed out of the truck and strode up to the building, never looking back. I was gone before he hit the doors. My only regret was missing out on the coffee.

17

LILY

Imagine pain so searing you think you'll go blind. Imagine a pain so liquefying that, to escape it, you would run naked down a city street and never care who saw. I was a horrible, terrible, disgusting person. I was stupid, too. And pathetic. And cold. Very cold. The memory of Calder's angry words rang in my ears, diminished only by the hurt in his eyes. I did that to him.

My heart leapt into my throat like a champagne cork, but even though I had got what I wanted, there was nothing to celebrate. For a second I considered turning around and running after him, telling him I'd changed my mind and that he was perfect and beautiful and whole. Just the way he was! And that I wasn't the soulless tramp he now thought I was. Maybe I'd tell him that I'd go with him to Thunder Bay and help him search.

But I knew I couldn't. I knew I wouldn't. Someone had to stay behind to keep an eye on Dad. And Danny. I had to trust that just as Nadia made me send Calder away, she would surely lead him back to me. She owed me that much.

When I'd entered the water, I'd meant to give Calder the impression I wasn't coming back, but I never actually made the transformation. With every ounce of concentration I could muster, I held myself together, refusing to abandon my body, focusing on my legs: muscle, femur, knee, all the way down to my pinky toes. I kept myself intact until I was sure Calder was gone, then–miserably–I went back for my clothes and collected his as well.

I cringed when I felt the ring box still in his pocket, but I pushed down all my feelings of dread and turned toward home. I really needed my mom.

I was halfway there when the rain started. I cupped my hands around my face to keep it from pelting me in the eyes. There was one consolation. At least I wouldn't have to explain why I was all wet; this way, Mom and Dad wouldn't suspect me of being in the lake.

When I got to the front door, my hand trembled on the doorknob before I stepped into the house. Despite the rain, I swore I could still smell Calder on my skin. I'd done the right thing, so why did I feel so terrible?

"Hey, Lil. How you doing, sweetheart? Where's Calder? Did he come in with you?"

I stared at my mom for several long seconds, eyes wide, before the tidal wave of shame hit me again. I felt every inch of separation between myself and Calder, like a great chasm was opening, one that I didn't know how to close. Despairing, I crumpled to the floor as Mom yelled for help.

The vibration of feet rattled the floorboards beneath my cheek. When I opened my eyes, all I could see was the linty space beneath the couch and the gray rubber curve of a wheel.

"Lily, what's wrong?" Mom's voice called from high above me.

My eyes rolled back as I sank deeper into the floor.

There was a hard *thunk* as Sophie dropped to her knees by my head and threw a blanket over me. The wool was dry and prickly against my wet skin and smelled like a campfire.

"Lily?" Sophie shook me by the shoulders, and my body twitched as if hit with waves of high voltage electricity.

"Does she feel hot?" Mom asked.

Sophie's hand felt small against my forehead. Her skin left a burning mark when she pulled it away. "No. She's cold. Really cold."

"Get a heating pad."

Feet ran out of the room. There was a banging of drawers and cabinets, then water running in the kitchen and then a *beep, beep, beep*. When Sophie came back, something soft and hot wrapped around my neck.

"Can you get her to stand up?" Mom asked.

Sophie attempted to lift me off the floor. "She's too heavy."

"Leave me. I just want to stay here," I said. I was so exhausted. Whether it was from resisting the physical transformation, or the emotional strain of saying goodbye, I didn't know. All I wanted to do was sleep, and I didn't care where. The floor was fine. I felt small. And very young. And I didn't care at all.

Mom said, "Shhh," and Sophie ran her hand from my temple around the curve of my face—over and over—until I thought there was no good reason to ever wake up. I slipped effortlessly into a dream. Nadia's voice filled my mind: *"Someone who loves you. Someone who loves you. Someone who loves you will show you how."*

Sometime later (minutes? hours?), the sound of crunching gravel added a familiar texture to my dream, followed by the rush of air as the front door flew open. Things of various weights dropped to the floor: a *thud,* a *clunk, clunk* against the door, the soft fall of fabric. "What is it? Where is she?" demanded Dad, missing the fact that I was the crumbled ball of blankets on the floor.

"Right here," Sophie said, and I opened my eyes.

It must have been late. Sophie was already in her pink fuzzy pajamas. I was embarrassed by the way everyone was worrying over me. It was nothing. I just needed to sleep.

Dad scooped me up and carried me into the back room. His arms were sure, and his footsteps even. He laid me on the daybed, like a toddler who'd fallen asleep in the car. I felt that somehow, with those footsteps, he was going to make everything all right. And I didn't have to be afraid.

But the thin mattress hit my shoulder, and his hands slipped away. The heating pad was back around my neck, and Dad piled more blankets on me.

Then Mom's voice was by my ear. "She's still freezing." She slipped a thermometer between my lips and a moment later Dad said, "Ninety-three point seven."

I shook in my woolly cocoon, arms stiff at my sides.

Dad held my wrist between his thumb and two fingers. "If I didn't know any better, I'd swear she was hypothermic. How did this happen? Where's Calder?"

I pulled the blanket up and over my head.

"Lily?" Dad asked. I don't think any of them had realized I was conscious.

"We had a . . . fight," I moaned. "More than a fight. I . . . We . . . We're taking a break." My nose was running, snot following the line of my upper lip. I wiped my sleeve across my face. I felt someone's fingers pull at the edge of the blanket, and I drew it tighter around me.

"Will he still sleep here tonight?" Dad asked.

I shook my head. "No."

There was a long pause, and I wasn't sure if the conversation was over. But then Dad asked, "Do you know when he'll be back?"

I sniffed loudly and flipped the blanket back to look at them all through the distortion of tears. "N-n-n-o," I said, the word coming out in multiple, staggered syllables. "Not exactly."

Mom bowed her head. "I don't like to hear that, Lily. I don't like the idea of that boy alone out there. He's not cut out for that."

154

I swallowed hard. What had I done?

"Is he gone forever?" Sophie asked.

Another wave of tremors washed through me. "Can we talk about this later?"

Dad said, "But—"

"I said, can we talk about this later?"

Mourning doves woke me up. I opened one eye to find Dad sitting in Mom's painting chair.

"You gave us quite a scare," he said.

"I'm sorry," I said. My voice sounded like sandpaper, and my teeth felt like they were wearing sweaters. How long had I been sleeping?

"Are you feeling any better?" He felt my face and neck. "You feel a little warmer."

I took an inventory of my body. "I'm fine."

"You're sure?" Mom asked as Sophie pushed her wheelchair into the back room.

"Yes."

Sophie climbed onto the daybed with me. My parents hesitated and looked at each other with worried expressions I didn't completely understand. I'd said I was fine, hadn't I?

"Because there's something your dad and I want to discuss with you. But we can wait until later if you want to rest."

"I'm fine." I struggled to a sitting position just to prove my point. My head spun and white flashes of light filled my eyes. "What do you want to talk about?"

Dad's face was disapproving, but he said, "Your mother

would like to talk about our discussion in the kitchen the other day."

It took me only a second to remember what conversation he was referring to. I thought we'd come to a conclusion on the issue of changing Mom. "It was a bad idea," I said.

"It wasn't a bad idea," Mom said. "I don't have much time anyway."

I dug my fingers into the blanket, clenching it tight. "Don't say that," I said in a hushed tone. Sophie curled into my side.

"It's time you girls knew." Her right hand trembled as she swiveled her chair to face us. The wheels caught for a second on the edge of the area rug and Dad helped push her over the lump. "I've been hiding things so you don't notice."

"What do you mean, 'hiding'?" I asked.

Mom and Dad exchanged a look that told me I didn't want to hear what they had to say. Because they had me surrounded—and I couldn't get up and run out of the room—I twisted the blanket to wring out the impending sense of doom.

Mom said, "I keep my hands moving so you don't notice them shaking."

I tried to interrupt, but she shook her head and made me listen. "I don't have a drink with dinner because it's hard to hit my mouth on the first try. I don't sit by the fire with your dad because the heat feels like knives. I haven't used the walker in months. For most people with MS, these symptoms go on for a long time, decades even. But not me.

It's not going to go like that for me. There have been some complications."

Sophie turned her face into my arm and hid.

"I just thought . . . ," I said. "I don't know what I thought."

"Your dad can see exactly how I'm feeling–emotionally– just like I know you can, Sophie." Sophie nodded against my shoulder. "But I didn't know if you were seeing it, too, Lily."

"Not like that," I said. "I've never been able to see a person's colors. And"–I swallowed hard–"I didn't notice the rest." Why hadn't I noticed? How could I be so insensitive? My God, this was my mother.

Mom stared at her hands, turning them over and studying them as if seeing them for the first time.

"She needs to be transformed," Dad said. "We've talked about it. We understand the risk."

"You're afraid of her out-aging you," I said, accusing.

"Not in the slightest," he said.

"Well . . . ," Mom said. "I have to say that doesn't appeal to me too much. But I'm afraid that'll be a moot point in the end."

"Mom . . ." Fear walked its prickly, cold fingers up my spine and down my arms. Her voice sounded like it was coming through a long tunnel. I stared at her as if she were speaking a foreign language.

"Even if it's not a complete cure," Mom said, "it can't be worse than what I'm dealing with now."

"You don't know that. Mom, look at me. It could be way worse."

"Lily, please," Sophie cried. "Do something! You need to change her."

"I can't." I was crying all over again. "You all know I can't! I don't have any electrical charge. You heard Calder." My voice broke on his name. I wondered where he was. What was he doing? How badly had I hurt him?

Mom said, "We have other options. Two, I think."

I hiccupped, holding back a sob. "Maris and Pavati? They aren't in the business of doing favors. And you're missing one important part, Mom. You're not dying."

"I am."

"No, I mean, you're not dying right now. Even if they would agree to change you, they'd have to stop your heart first. Is that really a chance you want to take? With them?" I turned to Dad. "You can't be serious about any of this."

"Desperate times call for desperate measures," Dad said.

"Really? You're going to fall back on lame clichés? This is Mom we're talking about!"

Dad hung his head.

Mom reached for his hand, and he took her fingers lightly in his. "This isn't your dad's idea," she said. "He's doing this for me. Because I asked him to. Lily. Baby. You need to at least ask. For me. This is my only chance."

"Mom, don't say stuff like that. You're freaking me out."

"This is my only chance," she said.

I shook my head, scrambling for a way out. It was too dangerous. "Calder would never let me even discuss it with them."

Dad said, "Listen, Lily. You know how I feel about Calder. I love him like a son, and I sincerely hope he comes home soon. But this animosity toward his sisters . . . he's stubborn, and he's holding a grudge, but his personal vendetta should not prevent your mother from finding a cure."

"Dad, I think he's earned the right to be bitter. And don't forget what they planned to do with you."

"To err is human, to forgive—"

I rolled my eyes. "If you had any idea how ironic you're being."

"Honey," Mom said, "if it's not too selfish of me . . . If Calder's going to be gone for a while, now might be the perfect time to at least test the waters, so to speak. There's no harm in asking his sisters. And he doesn't have to know."

"Mom, this is so unfair. You're ganging up on me, and you're taking advantage of Calder's being gone. What are we going to tell him when"—if—"he comes back?"

She leaned toward me and I moved to the edge of the daybed. When she reached for me, I took her shaking hands in mine. "Lily," she said. "Sweetheart. This is my only chance."

I threw back the blanket, and Sophie scooted to her left as I jumped off the daybed. After so many hours of inertia, my sudden movement startled Mom. She protested, saying I should stay put, sleep on the daybed for a while longer.

"I'm going to my room," I said, and I staggered through the house and up the stairs.

I pulled *MY SCRIBBLINGS* from my underwear drawer. It had been a long time since I'd tried to write anything worth keeping. I had so many different emotions racing through me, I thought I was ripe for writing a life-changing manifesto, something as deep and grief-gripped as Tennyson's *In Memoriam*. But I couldn't make the pen and paper connect. My head was too noisy, my thoughts too tangled.

I bent over the page and growled at it. My fingers were still cold and I had a hard time gripping the pen. I wrote a title:

APOLOGY

Then I underlined it. Twice. But nothing else came, so I crossed it out and wrote:

PROMISE BOUND

I tapped my pen on the paper like a woodpecker at a tree, but when that failed to extract any nugget of profound, poetic genius, I flung my journal across the room. It opened and flapped its paper wings for a second, then thumped pathetically to the floor, the cover torn from its silver spine.

A breeze blew through the open window and ruffled the poet portraits on my wall. Somehow, they looked sad and unfamiliar hanging there—like a memorial to someone I couldn't remember. Me, I finally realized.

With a burst of angry energy, I got up from my bed and went to the wall. Emily Brontë hung precariously from one corner. I tore her down, pulling off a large flake of paint with her. Then, with a cold shudder, I tore down Robert Browning, reciting through my teeth like a curse: "'The rain set early in tonight / The sullen wind was soon awake.'"

Charlotte went next. Then Matthew Arnold. "'It tore the elm-tops down for spite.'"

Down came Rossetti and Keats. "'And did its worst to vex the lake.'"

Then Yeats and Tennyson, with an agonized groan. "'I listened with heart fit to break.'"

I shredded them all, reducing them to nothing more than a useless litter of words and faces on my bedroom floor.

18

CALDER

The old man's absence amplified every other innocuous sound: the tires clunking over each crack in the road, the windshield wipers scraping on the glass, and something vibrating in the center console. Oh! He had left his phone behind. That was an unexpected luxury.

I did some impressive contortions to pull off my boots and wet socks while still maintaining speed, and stuffed the socks into the vents so they'd dry. I reached over to turn on the radio just to feel less alone, but before I could, I heard the thoughts of something on the roadside–thin, reedy animal thoughts calling *"Danger!"* and then *"Stop!"*

I looked up just in time to see a speckled fawn step into the road; its panicked mother was barely visible in the trees. The beams of my headlights caught the fawn's eyes, two silver moons, and I swerved, jerking the wheel too hard to the left. My tires skidded on the wet road, and though I felt like my body should be going one way, the truck spun in the opposite direction.

And then I was rolling. Tumbling. Down the embankment. Boots and cell phone and quarters flew through the cab. The truck hit with a jolt that was followed by a grinding shudder, as if the truck were shaking off the mud.

When the whole thing was over, I hung upside down and dangling from my seat belt. A wet trickle ran down my temple into my hair. I touched the spot with my fingers. Blood. *Damn it. Now what?*

Lake Superior raged and crashed against the rocky Minnesota shoreline mere feet from my window. For a second, I thought about swimming the rest of the way to Thunder Bay. But there was the matter of my newly acquired clothes and phone. I was going to need to keep up the human charade, at least until I could find a safe place to stash my stuff and maybe find some new clothes. The socks I'd jammed in the vents had disappeared.

I unlocked my seat belt and gravity took over. I fell onto the steering wheel—*hard*—then dug through the debris strewn over the cab ceiling to find the boots, the phone, and its charger. After I'd managed to get the boots on, I kicked open the door and stepped out—wet. And pissed. Any other time, the rain might have calmed me down, but tonight it only made me feel cold and empty and far away from home.

Climbing the embankment, I twisted my ankle. The soft ground gave way beneath me, and the mud suctioned off my boot and I stepped barefoot into the muck. I staggered around—hopping on one foot—before I was able to shove my muddy foot back into the boot. Sludge squished between my toes and up my ankle.

This whole thing was stupid. I had no interest in finding my family. The fleeting curiosity of last summer had long since left. And that's all it had ever been—curiosity—never a need. But that was the word Lily kept using. *"You need to find your mother."*

The only thing I needed was to be with Lily. What happened with the kayak girl was testament to that.

I fished the old man's phone out of my pocket and punched in Lily's number to send her a text:

Do me a favor. Check the beach N of your house. There might be a girl there who needs some help. She's probably gone by now. Hopefully she is. But just check. K? Bye.

Another minute passed and I added:

Call the police if you need to. Here's your chance 2 keep me from coming back.

I shoved the phone in my pocket and kept walking. Two hours passed before Lily responded.

Calder? Whose number is this? And I never said
    I didn't want you to come back.
ME: You told me to leave.

164

LILY: Not the same thing.
ME: Sounds the same to me.

Another twenty minutes passed.

LILY: Dad called the cops but there was no one there. Is it my fault whatever happened to that girl?

I stared at that text for a while. But I was too angry to respond. All I could think was, *Great. Now Jason knows.*

The wet leather boots tightened their grip on my ankles. I grumbled silently as I walked. The waves teased me, saying, *"You could be there by now."*

"Shut up" was all I said.

The rain finally stopped sometime after midnight. But a blanket of clouds snuffed out the stars, and the moon was nothing more than a hint. I followed Highway 61 north along the shore, yelling at the waves, yelling at my feet that were burning with a strange new sensation. I slipped my finger into the back of a boot and felt the skin on my heel tear away. The salt from my finger burned the patch of raw flesh. I was pretty sure mermen were not supposed to get blisters. This had to be some kind of crime against nature.

I hopped around on one foot and then the other, pulling off the boots and continuing the forced march in bare feet. I tilted my head back and yelled at the sky, "Would a goddamn car be so difficult? Where is everybody?"

Yes, yes, I answered my own question (because God knew *He* wasn't going to), *it's two a.m. Any decent person is asleep right now. Only thing stirring out here are psychopaths and rejects.* "Could you send me a fellow reject?" I yelled up at the sky. "Preferably one with a car?"

Nearly two hours after I rolled the old man's truck, I made it to Bon Chance, Minnesota (Unincorporated)—a hamlet with nothing more than a one-pump gas station, a bar, and a sign that read POP. 223.

It was four a.m., but as luck would have it, some guy had pulled off to the side of the road and was asleep in his car. The front bumper was dented and pressed against a lamp-post like he'd run into it. The pale flood of light revealed a dozen crushed cans and a crumpled pack of cigarettes out-side the driver's-side door. I set my muddy boots on the roof of the car and rapped my knuckles on the window. Once. Twice. Third time, the kid jumped.

"What the—?"

I twirled my finger in the air to suggest he roll down his window. It was an old car. He had to turn a crank, and the window lowered unevenly. He pressed down on the edge of the glass to finish the job. The yeasty stench of stale beer washed over me.

"What do you want, pretty boy?" he growled. I bent over and rested my forearms on the window frame. I couldn't tell if it was going to be easy to push my thoughts onto this bleary-headed guy—or difficult, given that he could barely focus.

"I want your car," I said.

"Yeah?" The kid leaned away from me and narrowed his eyes. "You going to fight me for it?"

"That won't be necessary."

"What's someone like you want with this piece of crap?"

"You got gas?"

"Enough." He pulled his lips back over a haphazard arrangement of teeth.

I pretended to consider the negotiation while casing the contents of the car. "Hmm. Tell you what, I'm feeling strangely generous. How 'bout I trade you a six-pack for your car?"

He didn't make any note of the fact that my hands were empty. "You think I'd trade my car for beer?"

"No?" I asked, pushing my will onto his. "You want to just *give* me your car?" The kid's mind turned slowly. It was like wading in molasses.

"Ha!" he finally said, surprising me with his volume. "Make it a case, and you've got yourself a deal."

"Done," I said, opening the car door for him to exit.

The kid climbed out and belched, blowing it in my face. "Guess you picked the wrong guy to negotiate with."

"Apparently," I said, sliding into the driver's seat, my feet ankle-deep in old hamburger wrappers. I kicked some of them out, then reached into the backseat and handed the kid his own case of beer.

"Yesss!" he said. Then he reached on top of the car and grabbed my boots, passing them to me through the window. "Fool like you . . . almost drove off without these. My mother told me you can tell a man's worth by his shoes. By the looks of these"—he snorted—"you must be the biggest loser on the face of the earth."

"You might be right," I said, and threw the car in reverse, spinning the tires in the wet dirt.

19

LILY

I slept late the next morning. Actually, I slept late into the afternoon and woke in a tangle of sheets, with two wet circles on my pillowcase. My sleep had been laced with dreams—but not the Nadia kind. Instead, Maris and Pavati and Mom and Dad had loomed over me all night in gruesome silhouettes, jabbing me with sticks and shoving me down onto the clattering rocks that lined the shore.

Peer pressure and social norms had never had much effect on me. In fact, sometime after eighth grade, kids gave up on the idea of me ever fitting in. Some kids called me weird, or worse. Others—like Jules, who herself was a specimen of social perfection, and Robby and Zach—stood by me. But pressure from my own family? Well, I didn't have the same kind of resolve.

How was I supposed to deny my mom her chance at a long life? But I didn't want to do what she asked of me. Even with the tentative peace between my family and Nadia's, the old history was not that old.

The Maris option was a no-go. Calder—I winced at the thought of his name—would never forgive me for trusting my mother to her. I trusted *his* judgment on that.

That left me with Pavati by default, but just barely. I'd never answered her letter, so that made a good enough place to start. She wanted something from me. Mom wanted something from her. We were both reasonable people . . . and that's where my mind stopped, because the thing she wanted from me—my alliance—wasn't something I could give. At least, not until Calder came back. *If Calder comes back.* And even then there was the matter of convincing him we owed Pavati our allegiance. Fat chance.

I wondered if Pavati would take an IOU. Could that be up for debate?

Debate, I thought, and pulled my phone out of my pocket and called Jules. She'd gone to the U without me, baffled by my unwavering decision to stay at the lake—a place she called "the death trap." I couldn't blame her. Her one and only visit had been a disaster that culminated with one of our friends attacked and nearly drowned.

"To what do I owe this supreme honor?" she asked, and

I immediately started counting backward in my head. How long had it been since I'd called? Six weeks? Seven? More?

"Hey, Jules. Got a sec?"

"Sure. I guess." Knowing Jules as well as I did, I could picture her narrowing her eyes as she spoke. "I'd love to hear how life has been treating you since you fell off the face of the earth."

I sighed. So it was going to be like that. "Sorry." There was an awkwardness between us that had never been there before. "I've been really sick. And it's hard to get good service up here. North woods, y'know."

"Yeah, I remember. So why are you calling now?" she asked.

I straightened the sheets, then tucked them in tight around and under my legs, making—it occurred to me—a mermaid's tail. "I don't know. I missed you?"

That softened her. "Aw, hon."

"And I could really use you right now." I flexed my feet, then pointed my toes.

Now she laughed. "Make note of the date."

"No, seriously."

"Okay, I'll bite," Jules said.

"You were in debate in high school."

"I know."

I rolled my eyes even though she missed out on the effect. "I'm saying, can you give me some pointers? I need to win an argument."

"With Calder?" she asked.

I closed my eyes and inhaled slowly. "Not exactly."

There were some muffled noises as Jules told someone to go on without her, then she was back to me. I broke out of my encasement and rolled over to get a pen and a café receipt from my bedside table.

"Coach would say, first thing, dress the part. Which means none of your normal costumes."

I wrote *dress the part* on the back of the receipt, then stared at my closet doubtfully.

"Then come up with two or three arguments for why your side is right. You can't even be a little iffy. You don't want them to smell weakness. Oooh, Lily. What are you up to? I'm starved for gossip."

"Keep going. Then what?"

"Don't get crabby. I'm skipping out on ice cream for you."

I was one of the few people who knew what a sacrifice that must be for her. Jules was a foodie at heart, the kind who ate anything and everything and still fit into size 2 jeans. "Just tell me what else," I said.

"Know what their counterarguments are going to be and have evidence to support your side and disprove theirs."

"Anything else?"

"Note cards help. Lily, what's going on?"

Suddenly the image of me, underwater with note cards and a flip chart, burst into my mind. I took a sudden breath and choked on it. "I don't think that'll work where I'm going."

"Where you're going? Oh my gosh, are you trying to convince your parents of something? Are you and Calder eloping?"

A sharp barb of adrenaline poked at my stomach as I

pictured the small velvet box lying in Calder's palm, the earnest question in his eyes. I tried to laugh Jules off, but it only came out as: "Heh."

"You are! You can't do that to me. I've had dibs on maid of honor since we were six."

"I know. It's not that." *It's far from that.* "So, thanks, Jules. I gotta go."

"Wait! What do you mean you've got to go? You just called."

I crinkled the receipt between my fingers, right in the receiver. "The line's getting a little fuzzy."

"Sure, whatever, Lil. I taught you that trick. But you'll tell me if you run off and do something crazy?"

"You got a deal."

After a few hours of rummaging through my closet, I picked the most Pavati-perfect, dress-the-part outfit I could find: a long peasant skirt and an embroidered vintage camisole. I curled my hair and loaded up the bracelets. When I was done, I studied myself in the mirror and adjusted the skirt lower on my hips. *Hmm.* I looked more like a fortune-teller than a Bollywood superstar, but maybe it would have the psychological effect I was going for.

I took a few moments to work out my key points, then walked down to the dock, jingling with each step, and hung my feet into the water. If Pavati still wanted to talk to me as much as I thought she did, she'd notice my scent and show herself. Plus, I wanted the security of land. Sure enough, I waited only five minutes before she slowly emerged in front of me–the top of her dark head, then lavender eyes, cheekbones, perfect lips, neck encircled by a silver band, which glistened in the fading sunlight. Water dripped from the tip of her chin. The lake rippled away from her bared shoulders.

"You look very pretty tonight," Pavati said. "Going some-where special?" There was a beautiful serenity to her voice.

Dress the part. Check. "Nowhere special."

She swam back and forth around the end of the dock, ten feet out, surveying me from all angles. "I don't know why I never noticed before. You have potential."

"Potential?" Hmm. Maybe I'd dressed *too* much the part.

"We could make a good team. Bait and lure, if you know what I mean."

Danny had once called human beings mermaid Prozac. I knew exactly what Pavati meant by "bait and lure," but by the looks of her, she didn't need any help from me. Her face practically glimmered–backlit by some poor soul's last smile.

"You don't really mean that," I said, shuddering. "You al-ways considered me the annoying Hancock sister."

"Try not to be so sensitive," Pavati said. "Everyone knows I have a soft spot for the little ones." She glanced up at the house. "Have you seen Daniel Catron today? How's Adrian?"

"How could you do it?" I asked. "Who was it?"

"Who was what?"

I threw my arms up in the air. I realized it was a ges-ture I'd picked up from Calder. "Aren't you supposed to be rationing yourselves? Hunting on some kind of controlled schedule?" *What was I doing?* Negotiating with a murderer. This was insanity. Pavati was no better than Maris, no less a monster. I would have walked away, but Mom's plea kept me rooted to the spot.

"I'm not a bad person," Pavati said, her voice thick with stolen serenity. "I do what comes naturally. It's not my fault I'm at the top of the food chain."

I groaned. There was logic in that, but it didn't make her hunting habits any less horrible. Still, could I really fault a predator for preying? Was the lion evil for hunting? Or the crocodile? Evil, no, I decided. Scary, yes.

She tipped her head, studying my eyes. Then she turned slightly, inviting me to follow. "Swim with me?"

I smiled at her question. I wasn't going to give her the opportunity to read my thoughts before I was ready to share them out loud. "Not tonight, but tell me this. Do you have any idea what you're doing to Danny? How can you play with his emotions like this? Particularly after what happened with Jack."

It wasn't what I'd come to discuss, but the question had been bothering me for so long I couldn't hold it in any longer. If I thought she had an ounce of humanity, some smidgen of charity toward a human being, then maybe I could stomach making Mom's ultimate request.

Pavati drew closer and her mouth tightened. "I thought we might talk about something else today."

I stared at her. Silent.

She inhaled slowly through her nose, then exhaled fast. "Jack Pettit was an unfortunate mistake."

"He was a human being, and you toyed with his heart until there was no humanity left. Now you're going to do it all over again with Danny."

She looked away. "I don't hear Daniel complaining."

I groaned mentally, but it was not lost on her.

"Lily," she said, her voice a warm purr, "you are still so innocent, aren't you?"

My stomach tightened at her question, and she tipped her head to the side as if she were reading my memories. I was right to refuse a swim.

"Men," she said, "were put on this earth for one purpose, and one purpose only: to perpetuate the species. Daniel Catron, at his young age, has already achieved his ultimate purpose. What is wrong with that? He should be thrilled."

"And what about love?"

"Love?" Her eyebrows shot up like birds taking flight.

"Yes, love," I said, annoyed. "Don't act like you've never heard of it."

"And you think *I'm* dangerous," she said, laughing at the irony. "Love is the most dangerous thing of all. My mother loved, and look where it got her." She paused and her expression turned smug. "Yes. Even you know I'm right. I have no use for love."

"Then what about your son?"

"Ah. Well." She shrugged. "That is a different kind of love." Her gaze left my face and she glanced toward the house. "Is he inside? Could you bring him to me? I'd just like to look."

"Danny took him to his house."

She bowed her head. "Is Calder with him, then? He said he wanted to keep an eye on the situation."

"Actually, he's gone away."

Pavati chuckled low and throaty, like she thought she was finally getting the upper hand. "Let me guess. You've decided to join me, and Calder refused to stay and watch."

"No, it's not that. I've been having . . . dreams. About Nadia. About your mother."

Pavati's eyes widened and she leaned through the water toward me. She was so close now I could almost reach out and touch her. Her gaze dropped to the pendant and then went back up to my face.

"That pendant you've been wearing, it stores—" she said.

"I know. But the dreams . . . it's not like I'm reading a history book . . . Nadia's . . . communicating with me. It's personal."

Pavati looked at me hungrily. It wasn't a hunger for my life—actually, based on how low I was feeling emotionally and what Calder had explained to me about absorption, I doubted she wanted anything I had to offer—but more like she was jealous of my dreams. I suppose that was right. If I'd lost my mother, wouldn't I be hungry for one last conversation?

"What did Calder have to say about that?" she asked.

"He doesn't believe it."

The feathery ends of her delicate fluke flitted through the air behind her. "So what does Mother say? In your dreams?"

"Nadia wants Calder to find his biological mother. She was quite insistent."

"The Thin Woman," Pavati murmured.

I sucked in my breath. "You know her?" I asked, my voice rising an octave.

"I know a little," Pavati said, sensing the upper hand her information afforded.

I got down on all fours at the end of the dock. The boards felt hard and splintered under my bare knees. "Tell me," I said.

She smiled. "Join me."

I shook my head, and annoyance flashed across Pavati's face.

"So why did you call me? If it's not about Adrian, and it's not about my letter, and if you refuse to join me, what more can you possibly have to say?"

The time had come. I wished I'd followed Jules's advice and brought note cards. My well-developed arguments were slippery and elusive in my brain. "Would you change my mother?"

Pavati's eyes flew wide with scandalized disapproval. "Absolutely not."

"Hear me out. I have something to give in exchange."

She looked doubtful, but said, "I'm listening." Her hands moved back and forth through the water.

"Adrian. Danny already understands that he holds the trump card. He'll use Adrian to get to you. I can guide him any which way I choose. If I tell him you'll follow if he runs and takes the baby, he'll run. If I tell him his best chance to be with you is to return the baby on schedule, he'll meet you at the pier."

"You know what I'd do to him if he ran. You don't fool me."

"Yes. But you'd have to find him first."

She clicked her tongue. "I'm surprised at you, Lily Hancock. I didn't realize you could be so unfeeling. Such a gamble to take with his life."

"Why won't you negotiate with me?" I asked. "What is my mother to you in comparison with Adrian?"

"It's about your sister," she said.

"My sister? What does Sophie have to do with this?"

"She is young. She still needs her mother. I won't be the one to take that away from her."

"Mom's illness isn't going to get better. We're going to lose her anyway. Sooner than you think." I crossed my fingers behind my back. Saying the words out loud made them more true—truer than I wanted them to be.

"I don't know that changing her would cure her, and I'm not going to take the chance of accidentally killing Sophie's mother. Your mother." After a pause, she rolled her eyes. "I know what you think of me, but believe it or not, I'm not completely heartless. I've been there. I wouldn't wish that on my worst enemy. Not even a Hancock."

"Then would you change me, too?" asked Sophie, coming up silently behind me.

I spun, a flash of panic burning across my chest. "Sophie, get out of here! Go back to the house."

Sophie set her jaw and folded her arms over her chest. "You can't make me. It's not fair. I want a vote in what's going on around here. You sent Calder away. What if I wanted him to stay? No one ever asks what I want. I want to be like you. *Both of you.*"

"Let's just see what develops naturally," Pavati soothed, her voice taking on a noticeably maternal tone.

"No," Sophie said. "It's never going to happen for me. Not naturally, anyway."

"You don't know that," I said. "Now go back inside."

"I did the chart," Sophie said.

Pavati and I exchanged a look. "What chart?" I asked.

"We learned in science about dominant and recessive genes," Sophie said. "Mr. Callahan showed us the chart for the redhead gene. You got that one, too, Lily. It'll work out the same with everything else. Lily will be the only one, and it's not fair."

"I don't follow," said Pavati.

"Mom had two human parents," Sophie said matter-of-factly.

Suddenly it occurred to me that I had no business trying to engage in a mermaid debate. My skills were paltry when compared with my little sister's. As young as she was, Sophie could be very persuasive; she always had the data to back her up.

"So?" I asked nervously.

"Dad had one human and one mermaid parent. That means that no more than half of his kids will get the mermaid gene."

"I don't think it's that simple," I said. "It took me seventeen years before—"

"Mom can't wait for me to turn seventeen. That's six

more years!" Sophie exclaimed, practically screaming. Pavati and I both took a step—or in her case, a stroke—backward.

"Sweetheart," Pavati said. "I'm not going to change you. It's not going to happen like that."

Sophie bowed to get her face as close to Pavati's as possible. She set her teeth. "Then I'll. Find. Maris."

"No!" Pavati and I exclaimed together.

"Ugh," groaned Sophie. She picked up one of my sandals and chucked it into the lake.

"Hey!"

She growled at me, then turned on her heel and marched up to the house, only pausing to yell over her shoulder, "I hate you both!"

Pavati and I watched her go. I wasn't ready to give up on our negotiation. "I have something more to offer."

"Go on," she said.

"I promised Calder I would never join you without him."

"That was an unfortunate promise to have made."

"But I didn't make that promise on behalf of anyone else. If you changed my mom, I could convince my dad to join you. You'd gain two. Even without me and Calder, you'd have the numbers against Maris."

Pavati met my eyes. "I won't change your mother. But convince your father to join me, and I'll give you Daniel Catron, emotionally intact."

I raised my eyebrows in surprise—a reaction that was interrupted by Sophie slamming the front door behind her. Both Pavati and I flinched.

After its vibrations dissipated, I returned my attention to

Pavati's lesser offer. "You'd promise to love Danny?" I asked. It wasn't what I wanted, but it was a significant move on her part. I couldn't ignore it. If Pavati was promising to love Danny, then she was promising to stay close to him. And if she made herself a part of Danny's life, then he wouldn't fall apart like Jack had. He wouldn't get desperate. He wouldn't resort to reckless behavior.

Before Pavati could answer, the front door opened again. It was Dad. Pavati ducked below the surface.

"Lily, are you out there? Sophie says you're in the water. What are you doing? It's not Friday."

Little liar. "No, Dad. Dry as a bone."

"Well, Gabby's on the phone. She wants you to go to some film noir festival with her in Washburn. What should I tell her?"

Pavati surfaced on the far side of the dock.

"I'll be up in a second, Dad."

The door closed again, and I turned back toward Pavati. "So?" I asked. "If my dad sided with you, would you promise to love Danny?"

"I would promise to let him think that I love him. That's the best I can do."

But something in the way she averted her eyes made me think it was only half the truth.

20

CALDER

Back on the road in the hamburger-wrapper car.

I slipped my fingers above the visor, dug through the center console and then the glove compartment, looking for cash. I came up with seven dollars and fifty miserable cents. It wasn't going to get me too far in Thunder Bay.

I lifted my foot off the gas and coasted. There was still the chance to turn around. Obviously I couldn't avoid my promise to Lily, but I didn't have to go all the way to Thunder Bay. I could research my parents from any coffeehouse with Wi-Fi. But the thought didn't last long, and I stomped on the pedal, pushing my speed up to eighty.

When it came right down to it, eventually I'd have to start talking to real, live people. I cringed at the memory of one of my and Lily's first conversations. "Didn't they look for you?" she'd asked. At the time, the idea had been beyond my comprehension. I had given my human parents so little thought over the years that it was difficult to imagine my death having made a lasting impression on them. Now I was going to start asking the general populace of Thunder Bay if anyone remembered me? Lily believed a three-year-old couldn't fall off a sailboat and be completely forgotten—even after all these years. I guess I had to trust that—despite my years of study—Lily understood human nature better than I.

Trust was going to be tough going, though, because right now, Thunder Bay was alien to everything I knew; it seemed impossible that anyone there would have heard of me. And who was I anyway? Tallulah had chosen the name Calder, so what name would I even ask about?

When I crossed the Minnesota border at Pigeon River, the customs officer waved me through. "I can let you go to Canada," he said, "but you better find your passport if you want to get back in."

Yeah, right.

I pushed the driver's seat back a few notches, stretched out my legs, and succumbed to the rugged and rocky landscape. The shadow of the mountains shrouded me, and mesas pressed against the roadside before breaking into a valley of sprawling farms, their wheat fields plowed and recently planted. After an hour or so, the valley gave way to pine trees and Mount McKay, hotels, a roadhouse, and

scattered gas stations before leveling out to more flat highway and ugly factories.

The expressway had taken me too far inland to see Lake
Superior, but I could still smell it, faintly, beneath the acrid
factory smoke that wafted through my car's vents. I turned
onto Arthur Street and made my way straight for the water,
trolling along the shoreline. Somewhere out there, too far
away, the lighthouse at Isle Royale blinked in the early-
morning sky. It was mirrored by the red light on my newly
acquired phone, blinking on the seat beside me.

I didn't know if I hoped for or dreaded another text from
Lily . . . or possibly worse, from Jason. . . . What would he
say about the girl on the beach? I didn't check to see who
was calling. Their disappointment in me was palpable across
the miles.

The waves, too, seemed to scold me as they chopped
against the strand. The lake wanted to reclaim me, but I
steeled my nerves. *Later,* I told it, and a wave hit the pier so
hard it sent an answering spray into the air.

I drove back up Arthur and stopped a person on the sidewalk to ask directions to the closest library. He pointed me
toward Brodie Street.

The library wasn't hard to find. It was an impressive
building: red brick and stained glass. Pale, lighter stone made
pillar-like stripes up to the roof. I parked the car. My rain-
soaked clothes had dried stiff. I missed the smell of the Hancocks' laundry soap; I missed Mrs. H folding my clothes,
treating me like her own son. . . .

I stripped off the old sweatshirt and threw it on the

passenger seat. I would have ripped off the scratchy T-shirt, too, if I thought I wouldn't get turned away at the library door. I entered and followed the signs to the reference desk on the main floor.

"Can I help you?" asked the girl behind the desk. Her smile was more of a smirk, and her eyes sparked in a way that gave me pause. Something about her reminded me of Tallulah. It wasn't just her hair, which hung in loose ringlets, the color of pale apricots. It was—as I originally thought—the way she looked at me: like someone who would come in for a kiss but bite my nose instead.

She pulled her hair back into a ponytail, exposing a Chinese symbol tattooed on her neck. Red-and-tan-striped feathers blended effortlessly with the baby-fine strands of hair behind her ears.

"I need to do some research," I said.

She rolled her eyes, saying, "Mmm-hmm," as if I'd just said I was Neptune's nephew.

"No, really." I rested my forearms on the counter and leaned toward her.

Unexpectedly, she made a *pfff* sound and rolled her eyes again. She returned her attention to the papers she was shuffling on her desk. "Of course you do."

"What's that supposed to mean?"

She leaned back in her chair and crossed her arms over her chest. "What do you really want?"

"A computer. Just point me to—"

"I suppose this works for you all the time, eh?"

"You suppose what works?"

"Come swooping in. Smile. Flash those white teeth of yours. Ask the library girl for a little help? Guys like you never do your own work. Well, I've got stuff to do, and you're not half as cute as you think you are."

That was it. I was giving up on girls for good. "You've got a serious customer service problem. Just show me how to work the computers and I won't bother you anymore."

She jerked her head in the direction I should go. "There are log-on instructions posted by each terminal."

"Thanks"—I read her name tag—"Chelsea. Big help. I got it from here."

She gestured with a graceful, though ambiguous, wave of her hand.

In the next room, several computers with bright blue screens hummed. I sighed at them in resignation. Admittedly, the girl had pegged me correctly (electronics had never been my strong suit), so I sat at the one in the farthest corner, half-shrouded by an overgrown ficus plant, where no one would notice me fumbling around. The table was scattered with scratch paper and short, stubby pencils.

For a second I just stared at my fingers on the keyboard, poised on the edge of God knows what. What did I know already? One: the name of the boat started with a *K* or an *R*. What I didn't know was if that memory was real or fabricated. If I'd screwed up on that detail, I didn't stand a chance. Two: registered in Canada to a husband and wife. Probably. And three: it was a sailboat. I was ninety-nine percent sure of that point.

I followed the instructions on the sheet, typing slowly

with two fingers until I got on to the Canadian transit site I'd found last summer. The site logged every vessel, air, and freight carrier registered in Canada. If my parents' boat was still in service it would be here. I went to the maritime page and plugged in Thunder Bay, then narrowed my search to only those vessels whose names started with a *K* or an *R*. Four thousand names popped up, give or take. I further narrowed the list, excluding tugs, freighters, and other commercial vessels. What remained was a startlingly short list:

Kanton Knees
Race Me
Rhapsody in Blue

Three sailboats. Three. Could it be that easy? I swallowed hard. Was I looking at my last contact with my human life? I wrote each name down and wiped my palms on my pants.

I stared at the screen for one long second, then, hovering the cursor over *Rhapsody in Blue,* clicked the mouse. The registered owner's name and address appeared: McIntyre; Farmer Road. I wrote them down on scratch paper and moved on to the owners of the other two boats.

I scrubbed away a shiver that ran down my arms. This time tomorrow I could be face to face with my parents. That quick. What would Lily think about that? Didn't matter. She was probably hoping it would take me longer anyway. I couldn't shake the feeling that this was all a ruse because she couldn't find the heart to break it off with me. She was hoping a long absence would make me forget her.

Agh. It might be only three sailboats, but it wouldn't be quick. This time tomorrow, there'd still be three because, as close as I was, it was the final step that I dreaded most: researching myself in connection with any one of these three vessels.

I didn't know what would be worse: to sift through all the stories of long-dead children, or to stumble upon my own reported drowning. Or worst yet: to discover there was no story to read at all.

I took a deep breath and blew it out slowly. Then, picking out each letter with my index fingers, like two birds pecking at seeds, I typed my first query:

```
Lake Superior child drown
```

I don't know what I expected, but a picture of me didn't pop up. Neither did a Wikipedia article on *Little Boy Lost at Sea.* I scrolled through the search results until settling on a newspaper archive site. Two hundred stories of drowned children between the years 1980 and 2000. The first was about a ten-year-old girl. And I knew her.

It was 1988. In my memory, I looked about ten, although by then I'd been in the lake for two decades. It was Big Bay–the same beach on Madeline Island that I'd brought Lily to last spring. I'd forgotten it at the time, but I remembered now. The little girl. Nadia watching from up the shore where we'd beached.

It had taken twenty years for the natural mermaid

disposition to catch up with me. Until then, I hadn't been touched with even a drop of sorrow. But when it did find me, it hit with a vengeance. For several nights, Mother had been worrying over my crying bouts, trying to pacify my tantrums. Maris convinced her it was time for my first kill; she was sick of me keeping her awake.

"There," Mother said. "She looks like a good one," and we watched the little girl on the beach for almost half an hour before Mother pushed me forward. I ran south along the shore, on uncertain legs, following the wavy line that separated the wet sand from the dry.

When I finally reached the little girl, my skin was dry and my feet felt solid under me. She was on her hands and knees, crawling around a mound of sand.

"What are you doing?" I asked in my younger voice, a scowl on my face.

"Building a castle," she said without looking up. "Want to help?"

I sat down and scooped at the sand, watching her and what she did, pushing wet sand into a fortified wall and poking it with a stick. I glowered at the misshapen building. If you could even call it that. It didn't want to keep its form. I stomped on the wall.

"Hey!" she said. "Don't do that."

"It's stupid," I said.

"You just need more water." She got up and dug a moat around the castle with a plastic shovel, then ran toward the lake with a bucket, filling it in the surf. Wet sand fell in heavy clumps from the bathing-suit ruffle that ran around her belly like a shrunken skirt. Yellow pinwheels of light swirled from her shoulders and her elbows and her heels as she ran. It almost made me cry out with pain, but I bit down on my tongue instead.

When she returned, I pressed flat rocks into the side of the still-standing castle wall. "Where's your mom?" I asked.

The little girl didn't look away from her work. "She's reading. Up there. By my dad. Where's yours?"

"Out there," I said, looking out toward the water. She didn't notice.

"My name's Ashley Marie Abbott," she said. "Everyone calls me Lee-Lee. What's your name?"

"Calder."

"Don't you have a last name?" she asked.

"Sometimes."

She looked up then, for the first time.

"Do you need more water in your bucket?" I asked.

"Yeah. It keeps soaking into the sand. A moat needs to look like a river. Like a doughnut river." She drew a circle in the air above the castle mound.

"I'll help you," I said.

"I only have one bucket."

"That doesn't matter," I said, shrugging. "I can get more water for you."

She stood up and ran for the lake. I ran behind her. I said, "If you fill your bucket out deeper, it won't sink into the sand so fast. You've been getting the water too close to shore. That's why it sinks in. It's not the good kind. It's already lost all the magic."

"Magic?" she asked.

"The magic water is out deeper," I said. "I used to be like you, but now I only play in the deeper water."

"How deep? Can I still touch?"

"If you're scared, you can hold my hand. I won't let you go."

"Promise?" she asked.

"Yes," I said. "I promise."

That's where the memory ended. Or, almost ended. Even now I could recall the effervescence of her yellow light fizzing in the recesses of my heart, making the world look bright and clean and hopeful again. That was all I let myself remember. I couldn't do this. There were far too many stories to read through. I didn't want to face any more names.

My phone was still blinking. I finally picked it up to see Lily's response to my last text.

Dad checked with the hospital. There was a girl who got hurt on the beach but they say she's fine. Thought you'd want to know.

I stared at those words, until the salty sting became too much to bear. I balled up my notes and threw them at the table. They bounced once and landed on the floor. When I couldn't hold back the tears any longer, I dropped my head into my hands. Shaking. Grateful there was no one else around. My vision blackened, and my soul swirled through me like water down a drain. I hated my memories. I hated

Lily for making me remember. No, it wasn't Lily. I hated me. If I could, I would have just lain down on the carpet and waited to die.

The Chelsea girl came up behind me and placed one hand flat on the table. Her nails were bitten down to nubs and painted black. I snapped my phone shut. She leaned in. Her long hair fell over my shoulder. "Everything okay?"

"Fine," I said, my voice rough.

"Sorry if I was rude before."

I refused to look up at her. "S'all right."

She didn't leave. Why didn't she leave? She kept talking. "You just seemed like one of those guys who thinks the library is some kind of joke."

I hunched over the keyboard and nodded.

"Well, like I said, I'm sorry about before. If I was rude."

I wiped my eyes with the back of my hand. Then I pushed my chair back and stormed out of the library, leaving the computer screen blinking behind me.

21

LILY

I didn't know a lot about film noir. Actually, I had to look it up on Wikipedia after I hung up with Gabby, but a night of cynical high-crime movies? Well . . . that seemed like a perfect distraction from the fact I'd just completely bombed with Pavati. Her promise to let Danny think that she loved him rang a little hollow now that I'd stepped away from the dock. It wasn't anywhere near what I'd set out to get in exchange, and what would I tell Mom?

So yeah . . . the distraction of a night out with Gabby, a little escape from reality, seemed like a decent way to kill the evening. Plus there was the added benefit that we wouldn't have to actually talk to each other, which meant I could avoid another conversation about Jack. Double whew.

Gabby was standing outside the theater when I pulled up. By the looks of things, the building hadn't been remodeled in nearly a century. Gabby mentioned it had once been a vaudeville theater, which made sense because the interior was ornate; the high ceiling was decorated with hand-painted cherubs and roses, and a red velveteen curtain with gold fringe covered the movie screen. There were only twelve rows of seats—each broken-spring chair covered in the same velveteen and mounted on a wrought iron base.

The best spots were already taken by the time we arrived, so we had to sit close to the screen to get seats together.

"Jack and I liked to go to these Bogart and Bacall marathons together," Gabby said, leaning into my ear. "Besides parentage, it was about the only thing we had in common. 'Dangerous love,' he called it."

"Yeah?" So much for a Jack-free night.

"He appreciated film noir from an artistic point of view," she said, gesturing dramatically on the word *artistic*. "I just find it ironic. I'm going to get popcorn. Want some?"

"No, I'm good."

Gabby tossed her sweatshirt onto the seat and left for the lobby. I dug around in my pocket for a half stick of gum I thought I'd left there. Violin music enveloped me as the curtains separated, exposing a screen crowned by an intricately carved proscenium arch. Prominent at the top: a life-sized mermaid, with peeling paint and glass eyes. No wonder Jack loved this theater. It sent the creepy-crawlies up my spine. Or maybe it wasn't the wooden mermaid at all—something cool and shivery was trailing up my neck.

"Lily," a voice whispered from behind me.

I whipped around and found Maris withdrawing her long, cool fingers.

"What are you doing here?" I hissed through clenched teeth.

"I'm a sucker for Bacall," said Maris with a thin-lipped smile. Her long blond bangs slipped across her face, and she pushed them back so I could better see her eyes. If she was trying to push her thoughts onto mine, the dim lighting was interfering. I couldn't feel any invasion of my mind.

"Be serious," I said, turning around to face front. I hoped I sounded irritated but controlled, because my heart was anything but. It raced in an uneven pattern of fearful spasms. What was she really doing here?

Maris leaned farther forward, her chin nearly touching my shoulder. I shuddered. She squeezed my neck with icy fingertips. "Have you ever known me to joke? How do you think we learned to be so perfectly human? Mother brought us to the movies every week. We even practiced our reading at the foreign film festivals. Subtitles, you know."

I turned my head only halfway to the left, saying, "I think you need further study when it comes to imitating humans." But I had to admit, it explained a lot. "Now get out of here. *Please.*"

"I can't. I need to talk to you."

I turned around again—this time to the right—as a woman

claimed the seat on my left. "How did you know where to find me?"

"Pavati."

"She told you?" I asked incredulously. That didn't seem likely.

"More or less."

Great. Gabby returned and Maris leaned back in her seat. Gabby ripped open a bag of M&M's and dumped them on top of the popcorn. "This was the way Jack liked to eat it," she said. She raised the popcorn bucket like she was making a toast. "To Jack."

"To Jack," I said halfheartedly, feeling Maris's death stare on the back of my head.

"May he rest in peace," said Gabby quietly.

I had a sudden surge of panic as it occurred to me that Gabby might choose this moment to bring up the dagger again. Right here. Right now. With Maris just inches away. We were so screwed. Obviously I couldn't see Maris's reaction, but I could feel the electricity in my hair. I whispered, "Gabby, I told you–"

"It's all right. We don't need to talk about this now." The last light went out in the theater and the projector went *clickety clickety* as the first silver frames of *The Big Sleep* appeared on the screen. As the names Humphrey Bogart and Lauren Bacall materialized in stylized script, Gabby leaned against my shoulder again. "You probably didn't know Jack well enough, but he was a romantic at heart."

"You don't say."

"*The Big Sleep* was his favorite."

Überdramatic music swelled like a wave, and the audience fell silent, except for some coughing. I didn't get past the first scene before understanding what Maris had been talking about. With the exception of hair color, the character of Carmen Sternwood was amazingly Pavati-esque. Or the other way around, I guess. The father, General Sternwood, sat in a wheelchair, requesting a favor.

Fantastic. So much for an escape from reality.

There didn't seem to be much ventilation in the theater, and the seats suddenly felt small and cramped. I pulled at the collar on my shirt and—would you believe it—Bogart's Detective Marlowe did the same thing.

Just as the Pavati character was described as a "little child who likes to pull the wings off flies," Gabby stopped eating her popcorn, her fingers frozen midair between the bag and her lips. I looked over and noticed a shiny tear trail on her left cheek.

"You okay?" I whispered.

"I know it's stupid, but I just wish I'd listened to Jack last year. About the mermaids. I wasn't a good sister to him."

"Hush! We've already talked about this. Jack was . . . confused," I said. It was the most generous adjective I could find. I sank down low so my head was barely above my seat back. Gabby turned to me expectantly, light and shadow flickering in silver and gray across her face.

"All those people," Gabby said. "Dead." The man sitting to Gabby's right shushed her, and she waved him off.

"Let's not do this right now," I said. "People are trying to watch the movie."

"They do this marathon every year. Everyone here has seen it at least a dozen times."

"Well, I've never seen it," I said.

Gabby said, "Sorry. I'll be quiet," just as Maris whispered through the space between my and Gabby's chairs, "Your friend isn't going to be a nuisance, is she?"

Gabby shot Maris a dirty look and said, "Sor-*ry!*"

The woman sitting on my left turned to scowl at me, then at Maris. I raised my shoulders apologetically. The last thing I needed was Gabby getting Maris all riled up, or making Maris think Gabby was another threat. I'd been down that Pettit road already.

"Dad bought a sonar for our boat," Gabby whispered.

"Shhh," I said, elbowing her hard. Maris's breath was cold on my shoulder.

When the first movie was over, the projection slipped seamlessly, without an intermission, into *Dark Passage*. I wanted to go. The seat was lumpy and uncomfortable, but more than that, knowing Maris was right behind me had me sitting so rigidly that by the end, my back ached and my head pounded. But I couldn't go. Gabby had me under surveillance, looking for the slightest word or gesture that might give her more clues into Jack's disappearance. And Maris . . . well, if I walked out, I was afraid she'd follow. Or worse, that she'd say something to Gabby.

It was nearly midnight when the double feature was over, and I thought I was going to die. When the lights came on, I shielded my eyes and turned to find Maris's seat empty.

"What did you think?" Gabby asked.

I massaged my left shoulder, then stretched my back. "Great cars. Lots of cigarettes. Awesome hats."

Gabby cracked a smile. " 'Bout sums it up. There's more tomorrow. *Key Largo* and *To Have and Have Not.* You in?"

"Actually, that might be a little much for me," I said, following her out into the lobby. I kept my head down but still searched for Maris. She was gone. Apparently, Maris could slip in and out of a theater as easily, and as silently, as she moved underwater. I had to hand it to her. It was mighty impressive.

As we headed toward our cars, I noticed a strange high-pitched sound. "New shoes?" I asked.

Gabby stopped walking. "What?"

"Your shoes are squeaking."

She and I both looked down at her feet. Right behind her heels, two gray-brown rats scratched, their tails writhing. One raced around Gabby's feet and climbed over the toes of her shoes. She screamed. I think I screamed. Rats? I'd never seen a live rat before. Well, except in the science lab, but those were kind of . . . cute.

"What are they?" Gabby shrieked. She hopped backward, lifting her knees high, but the rats followed her and three more joined them, matching her progress. Chirping and hissing, they slowly swept their tails back and forth on the pavement. My stomach rose up in my throat.

"Lily!" Gabby screamed, tripping over an empty beer bottle. It spun like a dial and clanked off the brick wall, ricocheting toward me. "Do something!"

"Do what?"

"Anything!"

I picked up the bottle and threw it into the rats' midst, but they ignored me. They were focused on Gabby and herding her into an alley, like border collies with a sheep. I kicked one, but it only bounced off the wall and ran to catch up with the others. Horror-struck, I watched as another dozen flooded into the alley after Gabby. My hand raised shakily toward my mouth.

"We need to talk," Maris said behind me.

"Gah!" I exclaimed, spinning around. Calder had once told me that he and his sisters could communicate telepathically with animals, but I'd never actually seen it in action. This was just plain sick. Gabby was still yelling my name from deep within the alley.

"Call them off. Now!" I cried.

"I just need five minutes alone with you."

I turned from Maris to run after Gabby, but Maris grabbed my shoulder and spun me around, dragging me away from the mouth of the alley. "What are you going to do about your mother?" she asked.

"What?" My head whipped back and forth between Maris and the alleyway. I couldn't see Gabby anymore, but I could still hear her screaming and kicking over trash cans.

Maris rolled her eyes. "I know what you told Pavati, and it made me curious. You're always getting in the way of things taking their natural course."

"Yeah, well, it's MS. I can't stop MS. Maris, please!" Out of the corner of my eye I saw a man and a woman enter the alley to investigate, then hurry out and run toward the theater. "Let's get the manager," I heard the man say. Maris seemed oblivious to the scene around us.

"Hurry up and ask the question, Lily Hancock. I heard Pavati thinking about it earlier this evening, and I don't have all night."

"I don't want anything from you."

"Well, you know I want something from you."

"Nothing's changed there."

"No, something has changed. Pavati has changed. I know you've talked. What have you told her?"

"Call off the rats."

Maris chuckled. "Fine. You don't have to tell me. I'm sure I'll catch your thoughts, or Pavati's, soon enough. Care to swim with me tonight?"

"Maybe another time."

Maris laughed again. "Fair enough. But I will help your mother, if you help me."

Maris's words shocked me into silence. For a second I couldn't move. Gabby's screams disappeared. I felt like I was floating somewhere above the sidewalk and below the beam of the streetlight. I was afraid to ask, but somehow I found the words. "If you change my mom, will it cure her?"

"I believe it would. An electrical shock like that to the nervous system . . ."

A man in a white shirt and black tie came running out of the theater armed with a broom. Another man, carrying a fire extinguisher and yelling a string of colorful epithets, followed him into the alley. Several others followed just for the show.

"Don't think too long," Maris said. "I'll do this for you if you align yourself with me. Mother put me in charge when she left. She trusted me. I'm the only one who can make this family what it should be."

I turned to face her again and asked, "And what's that?" The beam from the streetlight bore down on us. It cast eerie shadows across Maris's face, but her silver eyes burned through them.

"Powerful. Beautiful. The thing of legends. Pavati can't do it. She's too preoccupied with her offspring to think of the family's greater good. Join me, and I'll make you great, too."

The image she painted was indeed beautiful, exactly the way I'd imagined mermaid life back when I thought Tennyson's poetry was an accurate portrayal: underwater castles, music, pearls, and flirtations. My breath caught in my throat. I wanted that utopian vision; my hand involuntarily rose as if to grab it.

Maris smiled and looked down demurely, ending the dream.

I cleared my throat. "I think it's time to release Gabby."

Maris glanced casually toward the alley. "Jack Pettit's sister."

"That's right. But she holds none of the blame for Tallulah."

"Of course not. What do you take me for?"

I was tempted to answer but bit down on my bottom lip instead.

"Think about what I said, Lily. We could be great together."

Maris left, slinking into the gray shadows like a film noir character, or maybe more like the Pied Piper, because what looked like the black train of her skirt was really three dozen rats. And they were following the biggest one of all.

22

CALDER

By noon the next day, it was still raining. I stashed the old man's cell phone under the driver's seat and stepped out of the car, right into a puddle. The air was perfumed with the stench of swollen earthworms. My shoulders were stiff from having slept in the car, and when I opened the library door, the memory-scent of yesterday hit my wet skin like a slap to the face.

"You're back," Chelsea said as I walked in. "I was wondering if I'd see you again."

"Wondering hoping, or wondering dreading?" I asked, my voice expressionless.

"A little of both." That made me smile on the inside and maybe it showed a little on the outside, too, because Chelsea came out from behind the desk. "You left your notes," she said, handing me the balled-up list of boats, boat owners, and addresses, now pressed flat. "You left your computer screen open, too. You're researching drowning victims?"

I didn't answer, and she followed me to the same computer station I'd worked at the day before.

I wasn't going to read any more stories about dead children, whether I was the cause or not. I'd narrow my list down some other way. I'd hunt down each boat if I had to. Knock on doors. I pulled my chair up to the computer and logged in, continuing to ignore Chelsea.

She stood there awkwardly for a minute, then sighed and walked off.

I pulled up a new site to search for local phone numbers in relation to the names and addresses I'd found. Of course, it was possible none of the names I'd come up with was the one I was looking for. Perhaps the name of the boat had been changed at some point so all my research was off course. But I was banking on that not being the case. Even merfolk knew it was bad luck to change the name of a boat.

Chelsea came back with a Sprite and a bagel. She set them on the table to my left.

"Sign says 'No Food or Drink,'" I said.

"You look like you haven't eaten in a while. Besides, my mom's the head librarian. She won't care."

"I would think she should care most of all," I said, but Chelsea just shrugged.

"So what's your name?" she asked.

"Calder. Calder White."

"So what is all this research for, Calder Calder White? I'm thinking it's not for school. Am I right? I'm a senior." She rolled her eyes. "In high school. But my ex-boyfriend plays hockey for Lakehead University, so I'm used to older guys."

"Used to?"

"I mean, don't think I'm too young or anything."

"Too young for what?"

She laughed easily. "I'm just saying that if you want to go get coffee or something. If you need a place to stay tonight . . ." She stopped talking and put one finger on my notes. "How come you're making notes on these people?"

I covered the paper with my hand. "Just the names of some people I'm trying to locate."

She had no ability to read subtleties, or maybe she didn't care. "So what do you want with them?"

"I'm just looking for some information about who might have owned a certain boat."

"A boat?"

I'm speaking English, right? "Yes. A boat."

She slipped the paper from beneath my hand. "I don't know this first person," she said, flicking the paper with her index finger, "but the second one goes to my church, and the third one just checked out some books on Middle Eastern cooking."

"Who?" I snatched my notes out of her hand and read the name. "John McIntyre? He's here? In the library?"

"Not anymore. He left a few minutes before you came in.

I almost said something, but I didn't know what you wanted with him."

I stared at the library entrance. Had we passed on the sidewalk? I couldn't remember anyone in particular.

"I can help you, if you'd like."

"I don't need any help." I studied the address on the paper. Farmer Road. It meant nothing to me. I didn't know if it was ten miles away or right around the corner.

Chelsea folded her arms across her chest. "Suit yourself, but between the two of us, which one has lived here her whole life and knows every dead end, alleyway, and cul-de-sac?"

"I'm guessing that would be you," I said, ignoring her and pulling up MapQuest.

She leaned over my shoulder and hit the power switch behind the terminal. The screen went black.

"Hey!"

"Why don't you just consider me your personal chauffeur?" she asked, but it wasn't really a question.

"Why would you want to do that? I thought you said you were too busy for someone like me."

"Because my shift is over, and my friends all road-tripped to Ottawa for the Great Big Sea concert." She stared at me for a while as I watched my reflection in the dark monitor.

"Oh, come on," she said. "I'm totally bored. If you turn me down I've got nothing else to do. Also, because yesterday I thought you might be an arrogant asshole, but today you look kind of pathetic. Seriously. Are you homeless or something? Do you need some different clothes?"

I sniffed my shoulder. "That bad?"

"I don't know," she said. "There's a fine line between homeless and hip. Underneath the grunge nightmare, you might not be a complete disaster. Maybe even a regular guy."

I turned, finally acknowledging her persistence.

She had her apricot hair pulled back in a ponytail high on her head. I wondered if she knew what the Chinese lettering on her neck even meant. My guess was "peace," or "courage," or "honor," or any innumerable other words that had long since lost their meaning. And even if they hadn't, what did this girl know about any of them?

"Hey," she said, shoving my shoulder, "I was only kidding."

"Okay. Yeah. Sure. You can help. You don't need to drive me, though. I've got a car."

She hesitated. "On second thought, maybe I shouldn't go with you. For all I know, you're some kind of pathetic but maniacal serial killer."

"Good instincts," I said grimly.

She smiled. "I'll get my raincoat."

When we reached my car, someone had broken the passenger-side window. Glass littered the soggy seat and the hamburger wrappers were soaked from the pouring rain.

"Oh, man, that sucks," Chelsea said. "Did they take anything?"

"Just the radio," I said, shrugging. "There wasn't much else to . . . wait a sec . . . ah, crap, they took my sweatshirt. What the hell is wrong with people?" I quickly remembered the phone, but miraculously it was still under the seat.

"Come on." Chelsea grabbed my elbow. "My car is parked around the corner. We can get some duct tape and a plastic bag on our way back and patch things up. Towels, too."

"Fine. Let's go."

She released my elbow and let her hand bump against mine as if she wanted me to take it. I pulled away. If this was how things were going to go, I'd be better off on my own. But despite my misgivings, I slid into Chelsea's beat-up Honda Civic.

"Buckle up," she said.

She navigated the city streets, then the country roads like the native she claimed to be. We sat in absolute silence. I wrote the letter *L* on my fogged-up window.

Fifteen minutes later, Chelsea pulled up to an apartment building and disappeared inside. I compared the address to my notes. This wasn't where I thought we were going. When she came out, she had a small duffel bag stuffed tight. She tossed it onto my lap and got back behind the wheel.

"What's all this?"

"A charitable donation from my ex. He never locks his door, and he won't miss it. You need some more clothes if you're going to be running around town for a few days . . . or longer." I dug through the bag and found a replacement sweatshirt, a rolled-up pair of gym socks, two T-shirts, and basketball shorts.

Chelsea turned west at the light, away from the lake. I looked back over my shoulder at it as we pulled farther away. Paved streets gave way to gravel. Landscaping gave way to fields and wildflowers. Anticipation gave way to a strange feeling of stage fright. Fifteen minutes later, we arrived at 25 Farmer Road.

Chelsea pulled onto the side of the road in front of a sagging structure that I assumed was the John McIntyre house. It looked like a stucco shoe box. Someone had covered the southeast corner of its tar-paper roof with a blue plastic tarp. Two crows perched on the shallow peak over the door, and a German shepherd lay beside the front step. There was no car in the driveway. John McIntyre didn't appear to be home.

As much as I wanted this to be over, I was even more relieved to think I wouldn't have to start. I wasn't ready. What do you say? Hello, missing any boys? Um, Dad? Or worse . . . Remember me? What proof could I offer that I was me? I didn't know my name. I didn't know my birthday. I certainly had no good explanation as to why I looked nineteen when I'd been lost more than forty years ago. Good thing this McIntyre wasn't home. I wanted to leave.

"Chelsea—"

A pea-green Ford pickup pulled into the driveway. Chelsea turned to me with an easy smile. "Ready to see a man about a boat?"

The German shepherd made eye contact with me and pricked her ears. A low growl rumbled through her chest. *Leave,* she thought.

No threat, I responded. *We're only visiting.*

A second shepherd trotted from around the corner of the house, the tan and black hair on its back bristled. It sat by the back tire of the pickup truck, which was now parked. *Intruder,* it said. *Stay back.*

The man was still in the truck. I could see his head silhouetted in the back window. After a few seconds, he swung open the driver's-side door and put two mud-coated boots on the ground. He was in his mid-thirties, unshaven, with long hair pulled back in a ponytail. Too young to be my father. He patted the second dog's head. "What's wrong, Killer?"

"That's the guy," Chelsea said. "Are you getting out?"

"I don't know," I said. "This doesn't feel right."

"Feel right for what? You're just looking for information."

I looked down at my lap and laced my fingers together. My knee bounced up and down involuntarily. "I don't think he's the one I'm looking for."

"Seriously? You're not afraid of the dogs, are you?" I didn't answer, and she kept talking. "I'm sure they're friendlier than they look. Besides, how will you know this isn't the right guy, unless you ask?"

I steadied my knee. Then my voice. "I just know."

"Listen, I didn't drive all the way out to the boonies for nothing. I at least want dinner out of this."

The girl was persistent, I'd give her that.

"Come on," she said. "What's the worst he can say?"

Oh, I don't know, I thought. *That I'm a freakin' lunatic?* The second dog moved over to stand sentry by the steps as the man jogged into the house, a package under his arm.

"I guess you're right," I said.

"Of course I am," said Chelsea.

When we opened the car doors, the first dog tilted her head to the side. *Friend,* I said, and she sniffed the air between us.

Strange, the dog thought. She whined and laid her head back down on her front legs.

Chelsea ran up the three concrete steps and knocked. A second later, the door opened. The man looked through the screen door at me and Chelsea before finally recognizing her face. "Oh, hey," he said, glancing at his dogs, who were sniffing my feet. "Did I forget something at the library? You could have just called."

"Actually," she said, and elbowed me hard in the ribs.

"Actually, I'm looking for some information about your boat," I said.

"My boat? Is it okay?" He opened the screen door and stepped out. I took a step back.

"I'm sure it is," I said. "It's *Rhapsody in Blue,* right?"

"Yeah . . . ?"

"Have you owned it for long?"

"Five years. What's this about, eh?"

"I'm trying to locate its former owners," I said. Only then did it occur to me that I should have come up with some kind of cover story, but I didn't even try. My heart wasn't in it. "The people who owned it back in 'sixty-seven."

"Oh, that would have been my uncles. Mike and Jimmy McIntyre. I bought it off Uncle Jimmy after Mike died."

I sighed mentally. My instincts were right. He wasn't the guy. Still, I asked, "Did either of them have kids in the sixties?"

"No. Why?"

"No reason, really. Just curious, I guess. Well, thanks for your time." I turned and jogged back toward the car. Chelsea hurried behind me. Her hand came down hard on my shoulder, and she spun me around. Behind her, John McIntyre shook his head and went back into his house. One of the dogs barked twice.

"That's it?" Chelsea asked.

I grabbed her by the elbow and dragged her the rest of the way to the car. She got in. I glowered at the dashboard as if it were to blame for the way I felt right now.

"What's wrong?" Chelsea asked.

"I told you it wasn't the guy. It's not the right boat."

"Okay, so fine. Cross one off your list. There's no reason to get pissy about it."

"Sorry," I said. "I'm just tired." I leaned my head against the window.

"That's what you get for sleeping in your car."

I glanced at her without turning my head. How did she know that?

"Which," she said, "you won't be doing tonight. You can sleep on our futon. My mom won't mind."

"That's really nice, but there's something I've got to do tonight." I couldn't remember a time when I needed to swim more. Every inch of me thirsted for the water.

"Have it your way. But you are going out to dinner with me. It's the least you can do. I'm hungry for Chinese."

I plugged my phone charger into Chelsea's car lighter and, with a buzzing noise, the phone lit up. Lily's number announced itself in the display, nearly stopping my heart.

I didn't answer, but I wasn't mad at her. Even if she didn't want me in her life anymore, I believed that she wanted what

213

was best for me. Still, she could stop calling. It wasn't like we had anything more to say.

Chelsea misinterpreted my silence. "It doesn't have to be Chinese. Hey, are you all right?"

"I don't have any money," I said. "And, yeah. Right as rain."

23

LILY

It had been three days since Calder left, and Nadia had fallen silent. It was like I didn't know what to do with myself when I was sleeping. It used to be she woke me up by dragging me around the lake, dropping in on the ghost of my younger grandfather, or moping along the shore. Now she woke me up by making me miss her.

I don't know what I expected. I guess, since Calder was on his way toward finding his parents, and I'd done all I could to help that along, there wasn't anything more for her to say to me. But it still seemed kind of rude. Actually, it pissed me off. I was her granddaughter, after all.

But then, maybe Calder had been right, and I had been imagining her from the start. If that was true, if Nadia's silence was really nothing more than my imagination going dormant, then I'd sent Calder away for nothing.

I couldn't think about it. It had been the right thing to do. Torturing myself wasn't going to do either of us any good now.

I prayed for the dreams to return.

It was Tuesday, too early in the week for my normally scheduled Friday transformation. But I couldn't deny myself the calming effect of the water and ran across the yard, down to the shore. Slipping off my sandals, I walked the length of the broken willow branch, from the sand to out over the shallow water, unable to see it as just a branch. Now it was a permanent reminder of a mermaid's fury. I could almost smell the char where the split branch met the remaining trunk. The burned spot looked ominous in the shadows.

At the end of the branch, I sat down, surreptitiously looked around, and lowered myself into the water, which broke around my waist and soaked through my clothes, permeating my skin.

I gasped. It was colder with Calder gone.

The icy water was crystal clear, and I watched as my toes wriggled in the fine layer of pebbles. Slowly, taking deep breaths, focusing to keep my body intact, I lowered myself, inch by inch, all the way in and sat on the lake floor. I raised one arm, placing my palm flat on the bottom of the willow branch to hold myself steady.

The lake was quiet except for the low rumble of a motor.

When it passed, I heard a hard *D-D-Daniel,* followed by a *tk tk tk,* then a guttural noise, followed by a hard *eee,* then my name:

"*Li . . . lee . . . Han . . . cock. What about her?*"

I stretched my hearing out, searching for the source, finding the voices just west of Basswood Island. It was Maris and Pavati of course, but I wondered at the sound. Their voices rang so differently than in the past: high-pitched and shrieking, like wet cats in a well.

I quieted my thoughts, just as Calder had taught me last summer, so they wouldn't know I was in the water, too. I thought of Mom's white canvas, devoid of color, and made my mind do the same thing. It was a skill I'd gotten quite good at. Calder told me as much. He also told me he didn't like it.

"*Just tell me what you want,*" Pavati demanded of Maris, "*then get out of my way.*" The underlying threat shot adrenaline through my veins, and I was glad she wasn't speaking to me.

I could hear the sharp shift of sand. They were close to the bottom. Very deep. Maris delayed her response and when she spoke it was as if she had changed tactics, taking a near-motherly tone. "*No need to fight. Isn't this cozy? Just the two of us together again?*"

"*Make it quick, Maris. Say what you need to say, then you go your way, I'll go mine.*"

So they hadn't even been sharing a campsite? It was *that* bad?

Maris was speaking. I could pick out a few clipped sounds.

She seemed to be goading Pavati, but I couldn't make out the words. Whatever they were, Pavati did not take the bait.

"What does that have to do with Lily Hancock?" Pavati asked.

Maris leveled her accusation. *"You've met with her."*

"Once."

"She would be wise not to put too much trust in you," Maris said, and her sudden clarity made me think that she knew I was listening. Maybe I wasn't as good at quieting my mind as I thought. Maybe I'd let something slip, because Maris quoted a line from *The Big Sleep*: *"Oh, Pavati, you're just a little child who likes to pull the wings off flies,"* which made me even more suspicious that she was really talking to me.

But then Maris said, *"Lily sought me out,"* which confused me more than ever. Why would she lie like that if she knew I'd catch her in it? There was only one thing I knew for sure: Pavati would be super pissed about me talking to Maris. Maybe she'd even feel betrayed. I almost lunged toward their voices to explain my side of the story.

"You're lying," growled Pavati, and Maris howled in pain. The sound was so intense I almost sucked in a lungful of water. Maris screamed again. I wished I could see what was happening as clearly as I heard them.

"You cut me!" Maris gasped—both angry and surprised.

I didn't know what to do. Part of me wanted to swim out to intervene. The other part was screaming, *Don't be an idiot, Lily!* My track record with interventions was abysmal, and besides, why would I want to get in the middle of that? I didn't. But then I couldn't just stand by and watch my mother's only chances for a cure destroy each other.

"Lily wouldn't trust her mother to you. She wouldn't do that to her sister!" cried Pavati, and they both let out shrieks of agony as they tore at each other's flesh.

"I'm losing patience with this whole situation," said Maris. *"You have no idea how to manage this family."*

"And clearly you do? I'm tired of living under your rule and I won't subject my son to it."

"Your son! Evidence of your lack of restraint! You don't have the proper disposition to lead."

That was more than Pavati could stand. I heard the violence in her mind. I felt the impact as they launched their bodies at each other. But I couldn't tell who was winning, or if they both were losing.

"Will you tell her? The truth?" The voice was so strained, I couldn't tell who was speaking anymore. I had to believe they were still talking about me, so what "truth"? I searched out farther, sensing the pain in their thoughts, but then the pain was mine.

Someone grabbed a fistful of my hair and pulled me up out of the lake. I gasped and spit water from my lips and wiped it from my eyes.

"What are you doing?" Gabby Pettit yelled.

I slapped my hands down on the surface of the water in frustration, and Gabby let go. I'd been on the brink of learning something important, and now I'd never know. "I should ask you the same question!" I said.

"I was watching you," Gabby said. "Do you have any idea

how long you were under?" She wasn't saying it like she was impressed. It was an interrogation. Like the cop who asks if you know how fast you were going, when he clocked you himself and already knows the answer.

"You tell me."

"Ten minutes!"

Wow. Color me impressed. Probably best not to mention that I could go another fifty—at least in my transformed state.

"It's not funny, Lily."

"What do you care? It's none of your business."

"Like hell it's not my business. What is wrong with you?"

I turned toward shore and slogged through the water. My clothes hung heavy and tight against my body. I intended to keep marching to the house and slam the door behind me, but Gabby ran the willow branch like a jungle cat, leaping and tackling me to the sand. Or maybe I'd tripped and she'd fallen accidentally.

"Get off me!" I cried.

"You're going to answer some questions first," Gabby said. It sounded like a threat.

She had me by the shoulders and slammed me against the ground. I could feel the steely line of what I assumed was Sheshebens's dagger, tucked deep into Gabby's front pocket. Was she planning to use it on me?

I flipped Gabby over, gaining the advantage, and shoved her head into the sand. Then, in an almost Nadia-dream moment, I felt like I was having one of those out-of-body experiences—like when you're watching yourself from above and not completely recognizing yourself. My God. What was wrong with me?

Instinctively (and stupidly) I released Gabby and crawled for the water. I wouldn't fight her, but if this was going to continue, I wanted to be in the water where I had better control. Even if it meant transforming in front of Gabby, I wouldn't let her live long enough to reveal my family's secret. *Wait, what?* Did that thought really cross my mind?

Gabby must have realized what I was doing. She didn't follow me toward the lake but pushed herself up to a sitting position in the sand. "You wouldn't," she said, panting.

"Wouldn't what?" I challenged, though Gabby's question shook me. She knew. I could see it in her eyes. "And since when do you attack me?"

"Since when don't you need oxygen?" Gabby asked.

"Are you insane?" I asked, standing up. The water broke in ripples across the backs of my heels.

"Ha! Like my brother? Yeah. Maybe."

"Jack never attacked me with a knife." Only his hands, his lips, an iron chain . . .

Gabby closed her eyes and drew her knees up to her chin. I looked down at her as she took one deep breath, forcibly calming herself. Then she opened her eyes and leaned to her right, slipping the dagger out of her left pocket and throwing it on the sand beside her. It was a surrender. "I didn't attack you with a knife, but I do think I cut myself," she said.

"Must be karma," I said.

Gabby smiled a little. "I had enough karma the other night, thank you very much. Those rats–" She shuddered. "Whatever that was, I deserved it for what I put Jack through last summer."

I took a seat beside her on the sand, and we both stared

out at the water. Quietly. Still. Moving only to swat the occasional fly that buzzed around our faces and landed on our bare feet. I dug my toes into the sand as if I could seek out the water table. I was grateful that neither of us had done anything too stupid, though still irritated that I didn't know what was going on with Maris and Pavati.

For all I knew, they'd killed each other. But then two dark spots emerged in the North Channel. They were too far away for me to make out any details, but I had no doubt whom it was. The dark spots hesitated just above the waterline, then abruptly turned in opposite directions from each other and disappeared again.

I thought I caught the blue sequined sparkle of Pavati's tail. But it could have just been sunlight on the water.

"I came here to ask you a question," Gabby said. "You don't have to admit anything. Just tell me if I'm completely off base."

I fidgeted. "Try me."

"How long have you been practicing holding your breath?"

That seemed like a safe enough question. Hadn't I been doing that long before I knew my mer-potential? "A while," I said. "Just for fun. I like a challenge."

Gabby nodded. "Do you want to be a mermaid?"

"Don't be stupid."

"Just answer the question," Gabby said with an exasperated sigh. Her dark hair was growing out again, and the wind pushed it up and around her face so I couldn't see her expression. I played it safe.

"If being a mermaid is like being in one of Tennyson's poems, then yeah. Maybe."

"Who?" Gabby asked, finally looking at me.

I changed references. "If it's like Disney, maybe. I always liked that singing crab."

"But it's not like Disney," Gabby said.

"Gabby," I said, like a warning. It was time for this conversation to end.

"Could Jack hold his breath as long as you?"

I didn't answer that, and Gabby picked up the dagger. She rolled it over and over between her hands as she considered her next question, ignoring the fact that I hadn't answered her last. Or maybe she took my silence as an affirmation. She handed the dagger to me, and my fingertips prickled at the contact. The thing practically hummed.

"Do you see that?" Gabby asked, pointing out some of the markings along the handle. "It's an ancient language, but one of my dad's friends can read it."

"Dr. Coyote?" I asked.

Gabby raised her eyebrows at me. "How did you know?"

I shrugged. "He's my dentist."

"Well, yeah. Dr. Coyote took a huge interest in it. Asked me where I found it. Told me what it says."

"Which is?"

"This first part here"—she indicated with her finger—"is a name. Sheshebens."

Small duck, I thought.

"This other part took him longer to figure out, but he decided it says *Safe passage home*."

"Hmm," I said. I was already familiar with the story. "What are you going to do with it?"

"Dr. Coyote asked me the same thing."

"If he thinks it has historical significance, you should give it to my dad. He could take it to the college and get it submitted to a museum." I really hoped Gabby would be open to the suggestion, so I played it as cool as I could, as if I didn't care.

"I think I'll keep it for now. Thanks."

"Yeah, sure."

"So I have a theory," Gabby said.

I scooped wet sand with my hands and buried my feet up to my ankles.

"The dagger clearly means something." For a second she was distracted by it, and said, "It feels weird in my hand. It hums. Can you hear it?"

"No," I lied. "I think that's your imagination."

Gabby groaned. "Well, I think Jack understood it was connected to the . . ." She hesitated on the word, old doubts persisting. "Mermaids. At first I thought he was dead–that they might have even killed him with it–but I've changed my mind. . . . I think he left this as a clue for me. I think it means that he found them, and that he used the dagger for safe passage. Like a peace offering."

"Ironic, don't you think?" I couldn't help myself. My mouth was quicker than my brain.

"How do you mean?"

"A dagger as a sign of peace?"

"I think he went to them," she said. "I think they changed

him. Listen, Lily, I know you're not going to admit it to me, but my guess is, with what you were just doing, holding your breath like that, that you're planning to go to them, too."

I started to protest, but she put up her hand, saying, "That's why I'm not going to give you the dagger. I can't let another family go through what mine has. No one else gets a 'safe passage.'"

I still wanted to get Sheshebens's dagger back, but I took comfort in the fact that Gabby had come up with an explanation for Jack's disappearance that (a) satisfied her, and (b) required no retribution on her part. The last thing any of us needed was another Pettit on a crazed mermaid hunt. In her mind, Jack was still alive. Happy, even. And there was no one to blame for his disappearance but his own bad choices. That much was spot on.

I looked Gabby in the eyes and spoke solemnly. "I don't know if what you're saying is true, but I won't argue against it. And I promise you this: with or without that dagger, I won't abandon my family for a fantasy—real or imagined."

"Promise?" she asked. She stood up and slipped Sheshebens's dagger back into her pocket.

"Pinky swear."

24

CALDER

A cactus garden grew around a crumbling concrete wishing well that stood by the front door of the Tijuana Grille. Scattered pennies lay below the few inches of stagnant water. My stomach constricted at the memory of Lily's and my hunt for Maighdean Mara; Lily sprinkling old copper pennies onto the lake, shiny and patinaed circles both chasing the stony mermaid to her resting place. Man, I missed Lily. I wondered what she was doing right now.

I closed my eyes and pushed all curiosity out of my head so I could focus on the task ahead. *Look forward,* I told myself. *Not back.*

The hostess led us to a tiny table in the center of the darkened room. The walls were painted a deep purple. At least I thought they were, it was too dark to really know. The only glimmer of light came from the votive candles on the tables and the tiny white Christmas lights that hung in looping lines around the perimeter of the ceiling. Our table was uneven and rocked when I leaned my elbows on it.

"So," Chelsea said.

"So," I said.

A waitress wearing a poncho, a sombrero, and a just-kill-me-now expression stopped at our table with two glasses of water. I guzzled mine without taking a breath.

"Thirsty much?" Chelsea asked.

"Do you know what you want?" the waitress asked. Chelsea raised her eyebrows to suggest I go first.

"Why don't you order for us," I said. "You're buying."

"Two pops," she said to the waitress. "Coke okay?" she asked me. I nodded and swiped my finger through the votive candle's flame. "We'll have one burrito special. Two forks."

The waitress flicked her pen against her order pad, then walked off.

"I hope you don't mind sharing," Chelsea said.

I shook my head. "Thanks."

"No problem. Now, I know you're not from around here, but the traditional exchange for the burrito special is one life story."

I grunted at her.

"Spill it. What's so special about McIntyre's uncles having children born in the sixties?" She picked up a chip and bit down hard with her front teeth. The chip snapped in half.

I stared at her, my mind buzzing as I tried to think up an explanation.

"What?" she asked, chomping down on two more chips. "You can't expect me not to ask. What's with all the weird questions, eh?"

I passed my finger through the candle flame a couple more times, trying to come up with a semi-reasonable answer.

She pressed on. "Do the sixties have something to do with the drowning stories you were researching the other day?"

I knew it was a mistake to accept her help.

"Come on. Tell me why you care if that guy's uncles had kids."

I searched the restaurant for some lie-composing material. It wasn't like I could explain that the kid I had asked about was *me*. She'd write me off as a nut job, and until I got my window fixed I needed a driver. My gaze landed on a Day of the Dead diorama mounted on the wall. A pair of male and female skeletons dressed in wedding clothes, the male complete with top hat, danced around a red crepe-paper fire. Inspiration hit.

"There's something wrong with me," I said.

She smiled a little. "I figured that out for myself, thank you very much."

"It's not a joke. I'm . . . I'm dying."

Chelsea's hand drifted to her mouth, and her eyebrows rose toward her hairline.

"It's okay," I said. "It's just that two months ago I was diagnosed with a rare blood disease. My best chance is a bone marrow transplant, and the doctors say I'll have the most luck at finding a match with a close relative. Trouble is, my biological parents died when I was young, and I was adopted."

"Oh my God," Chelsea said.

"I'm trying to find my biological grandparents," I said, my foot bouncing uncontrollably under the table. I hoped Chelsea didn't notice the vibration in her water glass.

"It was a closed adoption, so I don't even know their names. But I'm hoping, if I find them, that they'll be able to help me . . . even though they really don't know me from Adam. I know the chances of this going well are pretty slim," I said, and swallowed hard. Chelsea interpreted it as desperation and leaned across the table toward me. "I guess that's what made me hesitant to talk to that guy," I continued. "You asked me about that. I mean . . . what do you say? How do you make that kind of introduction?"

Chelsea sat back—hard—against the wooden chair. "I'm so sorry. I wouldn't have pushed you so hard if I'd known."

"Why should *you* be sorry?"

She gave me a funny look, then her mood swung like a pendulum from sadness to . . . anger? Confusion? Ridicule? I couldn't place it. She said, "You tell me you're sick. I'm sorry to hear that. So sue me."

The waitress placed a white oblong plate in front of us. Whatever was on it was unrecognizable. Large. Yellow. Gloppy. Why do humans hide their food under so much sludge? Chelsea dug in, and long strands of what appeared to be cheese led from the plate to her mouth. I picked at the shreds of lettuce around the edge of the plate.

Chelsea took another bite and pulled the fork slowly between her lips. "Are you going to have any?"

I poked at the lifeless mound with a fork. "What is it again?"

"Seriously? It's a burrito."

"I guess I'm not that hungry." I scowled at the plate and pushed it closer to her. "One of the side effects of my disease: poor appetite."

She leaned across the table again. "So what do you have to go on?"

"What do you mean?"

"Clues. Documents."

The trouble with lies was that the more complicated they got, the more likely they were to unravel. I knew this. So what happened next was inexcusable. I said, "The only clue I've got is an old photograph of my biological mom as a little girl on a sailboat. I'm not even positive her parents were from Thunder Bay, but the boat had a Canadian flag and the name of the boat started with a *K* or an *R*. The year nineteen sixty-seven is written on the back of the photo."

She nodded and swallowed another bite. "Let me see it."

"See what?"

"The photo," she said, wiping her hands on a napkin and reaching across the table.

"I don't have it."

Her hand froze in midair. "You're kidding, right?"

I kept my expression blank.

Chelsea withdrew her hand and clicked her tongue in disgust. She folded her arms over her chest. "You mean to tell me the only clue you have to finding your family—*and finding a cure*—isn't in your wallet?"

I shrugged. "That's what I'm saying."

"You are seriously the weirdest guy I've ever met." She tossed her hands up. "Shoot, most people would have posted it on Facebook, made an appeal for bone marrow on You-Tube. Instead, you're running around a strange town, digging around in a freakin' library, and you didn't bring the only clue you have *with you*? Doesn't that sound a little unprepared? Are you sure you really want to do this?"

I looked away. I didn't want her to know that she'd nailed it. I didn't want to do this, but I'd bound myself to a promise and now I had to see it through. I couldn't even begin to get Lily back if I didn't at least try.

I flinched—startled by that bit of hope left clinging to my heart. It distracted me from the job of making my lie more convincing.

"There was a fire," I said.

"A fire?"

"I mean a flood." *Damn it.* "My basement flooded and the photo got ruined with a bunch of other things in storage. It took weeks to get all the boxes out of there. The cardboard was all soggy, kept ripping open . . ." I swallowed hard. "I had to do it all because my—"

"Exactly where are you from?" Chelsea asked.

Her interrogation was getting tiresome. My skin felt tight across my cheekbones, and my muscles uncomfortably dry. My bottom lip was split with hairline fissures. I didn't have the time, the patience, or the interest in discussing my past with this girl.

I leaned across the table toward her, watching as her

brown eyes melted like chocolate—so dark the pupils nearly disappeared. I looked through those expanding dark windows and pushed guilt into her mind and a little bit of embarrassment, too. She'd asked enough questions for one night.

Chelsea's cheeks flashed pink and she said, "Hey, forget about all those homeless cracks earlier, eh?" She reached forward tentatively and her fingers rested gently on top of my hand. It was an unusual color that hummed between her fingers and sifted across the back of my hand. I'd never seen anything like it before: light blue that faded to gray, then surged blue again.

"I really am sorry," she said.

Ugh. Pity. That's what that strange blue color was. I'd seen humans' excitement, joy, optimism, adventure, worry, fear . . . but never, in all my years, pity. I didn't like how that made me feel: small and powerless.

I was not to be pitied.

Behind me, the door opened and a cool rush of air blew into the room. It pushed a shiver up my spine and over my shoulders. I hunched my back to the cold and, without meaning to, leaned farther across the table toward Chelsea.

Two pairs of feet hit the terra-cotta tile in the entryway. Chelsea's eyes opened wide. "Kiss me!" she whispered, blue giving way to a surprised shade of flashing orange.

"What?" I growled.

"Kiss me! Quick! My ex just walked in with his new girlfriend."

Before I could respond, she grabbed me behind the neck and yanked me close. The table edge cut into my ribs. She kissed me hard. The salt on her lips burned through a crack in mine.

The new arrivals approached our table. Chelsea pulled back and smiled while I sat in stunned silence.

"Hey, Chels." Her tall, thick-necked ex loomed over me. He was wearing a Lakehead Thunderwolves hockey jersey. I suddenly remembered I was wearing his clothes. He gestured to the girl with him that she should go find a seat.

"Marc Parnell," he said, introducing himself. "I used to hook up with Chelsea."

"Shut up, douche bag," Chelsea said, her cheeks coloring.

"Nice talk, babe."

"Why don't you get back to your puck bunny?"

"Just stopped over to say hey," he said. "Y'know, jealousy is not your best look."

I cleared my throat and stood up. The guy was tall, but I overtook him by a couple of inches. I said, "I suspect you're barely a memory these days."

Out of the corner of my eye, I saw Chelsea smile up at me.

"I've done my best to make sure of that," I said. "If you know what I mean." Then I winked like Judd Nelson in *The Breakfast Club*.

Marc set his jaw. "Doesn't matter. I wouldn't be interested in your sloppy sec–"

But he didn't have the chance to finish the repulsive sentence because, without thinking, I pulled my arm back and let my fist fly.

It connected solidly with his mouth. Blood spurted onto his shirt (the one I was wearing), then ran down his chin onto his clean white jersey. It was the first time I'd ever attacked anyone on land. It made me feel . . . strange and . . . off-balance.

"Oh my God, Marc!" shrieked the girl he came in with. "Seriously? Again?"

Marc lunged at me, but I stepped back quickly, and he fell forward, onto the floor. He grabbed me by the ankle. I lost my footing and staggered against another couple's table, spilling their margaritas into the woman's lap.

The man yelled, "Hey! Watch it!"

Chelsea jumped up and grabbed me by the elbow. She dragged me out of the restaurant while the sombrero-clad waitress ran out of the kitchen behind us, yelling about the bill.

"Run!" Chelsea said through tears of laughter. So we ran. Fast.

We jumped in her car, and she peeled out of the parking lot, racing through a couple of lights. She glanced in the rearview mirror and asked, "Is he following us?"

I looked over my shoulder, but I had no idea what the guy's car looked like. "Quick, make a left here," I said.

Chelsea cranked the wheel and several cars blasted their horns, but no one followed. At first.

By the time we got to the end of the block, a blue car made the corner. Chelsea pulled into an alleyway, and then we bounced–hard–over railroad tracks. She turned left at a warehouse and then back onto the main drag. She hadn't been modest when she'd said she knew the city well.

After several minutes, Chelsea pulled the car between

two buildings and threw the gear in park. Then, without a word to me, she clambered out of the car.

I followed as she took off up a steep hill behind the buildings and ran up over the crest. The streets were narrow here, and poorly lit. We ran several blocks and collapsed, laughing, under a grove of trees.

"Oh, hell yeah," she said, panting. "Now . . . even I don't . . . know where we are. You better hope Marc doesn't either, or you're toast."

"I doubt that."

She flashed a toothy grin. "What you did back there. That was . . . unexpected. Weird. But strangely chivalrous."

"That guy's a jerk," I said. "You're better off without him."

"I know," she said. She took a few seconds to catch her breath; then she pulled a tissue out of her pocket and tried to wipe Marc's blood off my shirt. She let her hand not-so-subtly glance against my thigh.

Her touch seared me with the pain of loss and emptiness. I didn't want to be here. As nice as she was.

"Why are you helping me?" I asked, suddenly suspicious. "What do you want?"

"Nothing," she said, her tone defensive.

"That's a lie. Everyone wants something."

She kept wiping at my shirt, and her silence confirmed my suspicion.

After a few seconds she said, "Let's just say I have a soft spot for the terminally ill."

"I'm sure there's a hospital you can volunteer at." I removed her hand from my chest and tossed it back in her lap. Deep within my chest, the empty pit of loneliness yawned, openmouthed and jowly.

"And you're not so hard on the eyes," she added, grinning.

Here we go. I rolled my eyes, but my heart was black.

"Oh, come on. I was only trying to make you smile."

The air between us hummed with Chelsea's warmth. The open space between her lips was lemon yellow, like an exit door cracking daylight into a dark movie theater. Her happiness was my way out of the pain. And I wanted it. So help me God, I wanted it.

I slipped my hand behind her neck, and she kissed me—softer than the surprise attack in the restaurant.

I didn't think of Lily. Or more like, I didn't *let* myself think of Lily. No one could ever replace the fullness that Lily had once given me. But I was going to have to swim soon, and given that I would never make another absorption—never again take someone completely—kissing Chelsea was the closest life raft I could find. Whatever tiny bit of happiness I could steal from her now . . . Well, she was as good a temporary fix as any.

Who could blame me for jumping at that chance?

25

LILY

Ever since Pavati had denied Sophie's request to be changed, Sophie had been giving me the stink-eye silent treatment. She was good at it. Unfaltering. Not even Mom could convince her that it had gone on long enough—though she had no idea what had set it in motion. Maybe if Mom had known how miserably I'd failed with Pavati, she'd be mad at me, too. *I'd deserve that,* I thought bleakly.

In an effort to stage a treaty in the war of silence, Mom had sent us both down to the Blue Moon Café to make peace over a "hot drink" and maybe a "cream-filled something or other." I couldn't deny something hot would be nice. In the three days since Calder had left, I'd been unnaturally cold. I shivered in my bedsheets at night, and while everyone else was breaking out their summer wardrobes, I was still in sweaters. Today I had a purple crocheted scarf wrapped three times around my neck, and I still felt chilled underneath all my layers. It was as if I were shrinking, constricting like ice, day by day becoming a smaller, harder version of myself.

As for how Sophie was feeling, well, I didn't have to be able to read emotions to know. She didn't like being with me any more than *I* liked being with me.

"Come on," I said, dragging her roughly through the café door.

She dropped noisily into one of the bright yellow chairs as I went to order.

When I came back with her hot chocolate, she frowned at it.

"Aren't you going to drink it?" I asked, maybe a little too loud.

She kept her eyes on the cup and folded her arms over her chest in a sign of defiance. But she was too dramatic in her movements and accidentally knocked the cup over.

I jumped up, but Sophie didn't move. She just stared at the table and let the hot chocolate run dark and creamy across the table and onto the checkerboard floor.

I glanced at the shaggy-haired barista for a little help, but he avoided eye contact. "Oh, come on!" I exclaimed.

Mrs. Boyd poked her head out of her office. "What spilled? Oh! Lily. You've made quite a mess of things."

If only she knew.

To Sophie, Mrs. Boyd said, "That's okay, love. Just a little spill. Your sister will take care of it." Then she closed her office door.

Sophie made a *hmph* sound, the meaning of which was not lost on me. I growled at her low under my breath.

If only I could take care of everything. Put Calder's past back together, bring him home, save Danny from Pavati, pacify Pavati's concerns for Adrian, cure Mom, unify the family . . . There was a lot on my plate. I might as well add "bring about world peace." It wouldn't have made my list any more impossible.

I found the table-washing bucket in its usual spot behind the counter and sank my hand into the soapy water. I breathed deeply, feeling the flash of calm the warm water delivered, then extracted the terry cloth rag.

The tall boy behind the counter barely acknowledged me and bent over nonexistent work. It irritated me to no end. It was his job to clean up this mess. Not mine.

"What the hell is your problem?" I demanded.

He looked up, eyebrows raised. "Me?" he asked.

"Yeah, you. Why am I the one cleaning up the mess?"

"Uh . . . because you made it?" he suggested. Oh my gosh. He was a supreme idiot.

"Lily," Sophie said, her patronizing tone telling me to settle down.

I spun on her, surprised by the sound of her voice. I'd nearly forgotten what it sounded like. "Oh, so now you've got something to say to me?"

Sophie's face flushed.

The kid behind the counter said, "You should just stay home when you're PMSing so hard."

My eyes flashed hot. He did *not* just go there. "What did you say to me?"

"Lily," Sophie said again. I hadn't heard her get up from our table, but now she was dragging me by the elbow back to my chair. "What's going on with you?" she asked.

"Me?" I exclaimed. "You're the one who's had nothing to say."

"Don't blame *me* for being mad," she said. "You're the one whose colors are going all crazy these days. How am I supposed to react?"

"Don't do that," I said.

"Do what?"

"Rub it in my face."

She pulled her eyebrows together. "Rub what in your face?"

I looked around to make sure the barista wasn't listening. "Oh, come on. Don't pretend you don't *enjoy* the fact that you can see emotions while I can't." The sarcastic tone in my voice surprised me a little. I didn't know how much my inability bothered me until I said it out loud.

"Okay . . . ," she said, drawing the word out. "See, this is what I'm talking about. You should see yourself right now. Pretty gross."

I ground my teeth, not doubting her in the slightest. I'd felt it coming on for days—some weird kind of funk I'd never felt before. I missed Calder. Sometimes it felt like I couldn't breathe, I missed him so much. Sometimes I was so angry he'd listened to me when I told him to leave, but then I had to remind myself that that was my fault. I hadn't given him much choice.

The barista came up to our table. "Here," he said. "Mrs. Boyd said to give you this," and he set a fresh hot chocolate in front of Sophie, who looked up with a faint smile. The kid didn't look at me at all.

"You don't know how good you've got it, Sophie," I said

"You think?" She popped the lid off her cup and blew away the steam. "What about you? You get to do everything you want, and I never get to do anything. You got Calder. You get to be a mermaid."

"Hush now."

Sophie scowled at me and continued. "Now Pavati has this stupid baby. I bet you that Danny Catron will get to be with Pavati before me. She was mine first."

"Pavati was Jack's first," I said. "And I'm betting a hundred more before him. And they're probably all dead."

"Pavati would never hurt me."

I toyed with telling her the truth about what had happened last May—that Pavati had hypnotized her, used her as bait for Maris and Tallulah's purposes. Calder had told me every detail. But even though a little fear might have been healthy for her, I couldn't bring myself to do it. Instead I said coolly, "Pavati is not a good friend for you."

Sophie looked at me with pained eyes.

I sighed and examined my hands. "She killed Jack," I said, sneering.

"She only did it to save you."

"I know." I owed Pavati for that. "I know," I said again.

"So I've been thinking," Sophie said. "I bet Pavati would save me. If I fell into the water. Like maybe from a boat or something."

"What are you talking about?"

"I don't think Pavati would let me drown. She'd change me like when Calder was changed. She might not want to, but she would if she had to."

I was shaking my head vehemently before she was done talking. "Why has my family gone completely insane?"

Sophie ignored me. "If I were changed already, she wouldn't have any reason to say no to Mom. It's a logical solution."

"You're eleven. You don't come up with logical solutions!"

"Why are you so mean?"

I didn't know how to answer that. What I did know was that I couldn't let my mother die. And I couldn't let my sister throw herself into the lake to make Pavati do what I couldn't force her to do. Pavati's refusal to cooperate was leaving me no choice but Maris, and I was going to put that off for as long as I possibly could.

26

CALDER

Something tickled my nose. I opened one eye and found the culprit. My face was pressed into a patch of spongy grass. I took a second to appreciate the fact that my clothes were soaked in dew. Any bit of moisture was a welcome relief. Stiff-necked and groggy, I tried to remember where I was.

There'd been a fight . . . some hockey player chasing us in his car . . . I remembered running. Laughing. And a most unfortunate lapse in judgment.

I'd ended the kiss just as quickly as it had started, and abruptly changed the course of the evening by blurting out that Marc had probably given up by now and we'd better go get Chelsea's car. But we'd lost track of where we'd parked it, and after wandering dark streets until way past midnight, eventually we'd sat down under a tree to talk and wait for daylight.

We'd talked long into the night about my fake terminal condition, Chelsea's parents' divorce, and her cat's fetish for men's feet.

After a while, Chelsea made it perfectly clear that she was interested in something more than just a kiss, but I rebuffed her, telling her that I had a girlfriend, which didn't sound convincing to either one of us. Sometime after that, our conversation slowed to an uncomfortable silence. One moment Chelsea's bitter voice was in my ear saying something about me not playing fair, and the next moment, sleep.

I stretched out my hand and felt a bony knee. Oh, man . . . Where were we? What was that smell? Rotting meat?

I covered my nose with the back of my hand and sat up. *Ugh.* Apparently we'd crashed behind a Dumpster. There was a certain poetic justice to that. I felt completely disposable. And dirty. I didn't want to look at Chelsea.

"Morning," she said, equally baffled by our surroundings. They'd seemed so different in the dark. "I see you're still here."

By the tone of her voice, she was still offended that the kiss had never evolved into anything more.

I sighed. "Chelsea, I said I was sorry. It was nothing personal."

"Whatever," she said, pushing herself up to her feet. She picked at a few blades of grass that had stuck to her pants.

"I told you. I have a girlfriend. I couldn't do that to her."

It was the same line I'd been repeating to myself all

night. Like a skip in a record. Of course, Lily was much more than a girl—much more than a girlfriend. The word seemed trite and somehow vulgar when used to describe her. But the commonplace word was the best shield I had to either push Chelsea back or keep me from committing the most inexcusable of betrayals.

Chelsea made a sarcastic grunt. "Why do you keep telling me that? Seriously. I get it. I can do better than you anyway."

"Trust me. I'm very sure you can. I just didn't want to give you the wrong idea."

"The wrong idea about what?" she asked. "The idea that Whoever She Is doesn't care enough about her sick boyfriend to help him find a cure? The idea that if she really cared about you she'd be here?"

I let my gaze drift skyward. "It's more complicated than that."

"Doesn't seem very complicated to me. If my boyfriend were sick, I'd be there for him."

For a second, she looked around like she'd forgotten where we were. She didn't comment on the less than idyllic spot we'd fallen asleep in. Instead she said, "I promised you a futon. Oops." She looked up at a sign high above our heads: TIM HORTONS. ALWAYS FRESH.

"Timmy Ho's," she said. "I'm sure coffee and a doughnut will improve my outlook on life."

I looked up at the red script-like lettering. I had to admit, coffee sounded good.

"And if I'm not mistaken . . ." She dug around in her jean pockets. "Yep, I've still got my money."

She took my hand and pulled me to my feet. We made

our way into the restaurant and inhaled the sugar-laced air. Glazed and frosted doughnuts gleamed from the too-bright showcase that practically hummed with the "Hallelujah Chorus." Chelsea took her time picking out the perfect one, then ordered a "double-double."

"I guess I'll have what she's having, plus a glass of water," I said. I stagger-followed her to a table and collapsed into the booth. "I'm dying," I said.

Chelsea raised her eyebrows at me.

"No. I don't mean that. I mean I hurt all over. I haven't slept on the ground in a while."

"I'll make good on the futon tonight."

I shook my head. "I've got something I need to do later."

The corner of Chelsea's mouth twitched in a "we'll see" expression. She pulled my crumpled list of names out of her pocket and held it up in front of my face. The first one– *McIntyre*–was crossed off.

"How did you get that?" I asked.

"You gave it to me in the car yesterday. Remember? Really, if your head wasn't attached . . ." She smoothed out the list on the table and tapped her finger on the paper. "The next closest one is second on your list: George and Lenore Lee. They're the ones I don't know."

It would have been easier to read the list if I moved to the side of the booth she was sitting on, but everything still felt too awkward to get that close again. I said, "The boat's called *Kanton Knees*. Do you think that means they're from Ohio?"

Chelsea stared at me blankly.

"You know. Like Canton, Ohio? Of course, that's Canton with a *C*."

Chelsea shrugged. "Maybe they're being cute with spelling."

"Entirely possible," I said as I surveyed the restaurant. Two men in workman uniforms—the words *Kelley Electric* embroidered on the backs—walked in and flirted with the girl behind the register.

"I guess I never thought my family would be from anywhere other than here. Finish your doughnut. We can take our coffee to go. It should be easier to find your car in the daylight."

"No need to rush," she said. "They're probably not even awake yet. It's only six-fifty-two."

The sooner this was over, the sooner I could get back to Bayfield, tell Lily I had tried my best but I couldn't find anyone.

"Plus, we should at least get you a shirt that's a tad less bloody. Too bad Marc's duffel bag is still in my car."

I stared out the window at the electricians' van. My guess was that they had a couple of extra work shirts in the cab. At least an extra T-shirt. "Give me a sec," I said. "I'll take care of the wardrobe."

LILY

I hitched my long skirt above my knees and ran up the steps to Danny's apartment. Danny opened the door when I was mid-knock. He was unshaven, and dark purple moons hung under his heavy-lidded eyes. He turned away instead of greeting me. A pale yellow stain of baby spew ran from his shoulder halfway down the back of his white T-shirt.

"Hello to you, too," I said.

There were packs of diapers on the kitchen table, still in grocery sacks. Danny didn't have a job. How was he paying for all this stuff? He came back into the kitchen with Adrian and caught me reading the receipt for his recent purchases.

"Who knew how expensive diapers were?" he said. "Or formula. Do you know I used ten dollars' worth of coupons and still paid seventy for all this stuff?"

"But how–"

"Your parents have been really good about this. They've saved me over and over. I don't even have to ask, they just send me checks every couple of weeks."

My parents? I wasn't completely surprised, but maybe a little miffed that they hadn't mentioned this to me. What did they think I'd do? Pitch a fit or something? And then I realized, *Yeah, that's probably exactly what they thought.*

"Why don't you just get a job?" I asked.

"Because then I'd have to pay for day care. Do you have any idea how expensive *that* is? And you already said I wasn't supposed to impose on you or your mom."

Oh, right. I did say that. I reached out, and Daniel handed me the baby. He really was cute.

"Meet your cousin, Adrian," Danny said.

I looked up from Adrian's round face to Danny's worried expression. Cousin? I guess that was right. I hadn't thought of Adrian as anything more than Pavati's baby and Danny's ward. But by the look on Danny's face, I had underestimated a lot of things. For one, Danny was no longer looking at Adrian like he was a temporary problem. He was looking at him with love. Pride, even. When did that happen? This was not good.

CALDER

It was amazing how much daylight helped in locating Chelsea's car. We found it just where we'd left it, between the warehouses, looking no worse for wear. I half expected to find the windshield bashed in, but I guess Marc either wasn't as smart or as vindictive as Chelsea had given him credit for.

Chelsea jumped in the driver's seat and backed out from between the buildings while I read her the address on the paper. She made a few wrong turns, and we got stuck waiting for a train to pass for what felt like hours, but eventually we found the impressive-looking home of George Lee, owner of the sailboat *Kanton Knees*.

"Looks nice," Chelsea said. "Maybe you come from money."

I hoped not, actually. It would be easier to convince my family that I wasn't a con if there was no money to con them out of.

As it happened, I didn't have to worry about selling my

story to Mr. Lee. When the door opened, I almost laughed. I didn't know a lot, but I was pretty sure my people weren't Chinese.

Kanton Knees, I thought. *Cantonese.* I should have known. Very cute.

"Sorry to wake you," I said. "My mistake."

Chelsea ran behind me to the car, and we hopped in.

Chelsea pulled out a pen. "Well, I guess we can cross them off the list."

"This isn't going to work," I said. "You don't have to keep helping me. I'm wasting your time."

"Don't be an idiot. The last name on your list is Donna Brandon. I told you, I know her from church. It's not a waste of my time, and this will be the easiest one. I know exactly where she'll be in an hour and a half."

"Because you're psychic?"

"Because she sings in the church choir with my mom, and they're practicing at our house at ten."

LILY

Danny lay Adrian on a quilted mat and stuck a pacifier in his mouth. Adrian made sucking noises for a while, until the rubber nipple fell out of his spit-slippery lips, which kept moving in a rhythmic manner, as if the pacifier were still in place.

"It's hard to picture, isn't it?" Danny said.

"What is?" I asked. Adrian looked ridiculous sucking away on air. Just like a fish. I picked up the pacifier and stuck it back in his mouth.

"That he'll be one of *them* next spring. He looks so helpless now, but in less than a year he'll be swimming the lake, under his own power. Hunting . . ." His voice trailed off.

"I don't think that part starts right away," I said. "It takes them longer to grow into their need to . . . medicate."

"But he will," Danny said. "Eventually." He shuddered.

"I suppose," I said. I didn't like to think of it either. I was still haunted occasionally by images of Connor's dead eyes, even though he hadn't been a true mermaid victim.

"I don't like the thought of that," Danny said. "It's not right."

"Well, you never know. He might not. I haven't."

"You don't count."

That clipped comment sent my mood spiraling downward. "Well, if I don't count," I snapped, "how 'bout my dad? He doesn't hunt. Is that good enough for you?"

Danny's expression, first surprised, turned scrutinizing.

"Don't look at me like that," I said. It was almost a growl.

"Sometimes," he said, "Sometimes, you really don't seem . . ."

"Don't seem what?"

"Never mind."

I took two, long calming breaths. In through the nose, out through the mouth. I'd learned that from an early-morning yoga show. My temper was getting shorter and harder to control. I'd scared Danny. I could see that. What worried me more was that I'd scared myself.

"Sorry about that. Maybe I can talk to Pavati about Adrian. Maybe, when he gets older, she'll let Dad teach him how to override the temptation, too. Before he caves."

"Would you do that?" Danny asked, as if I'd lifted a boulder off his shoulders.

"Sure," I said. "I'd be happy to."

"Can I come along? When you talk to Pavati, I mean."

"Wait, what? No. No, Danny. Absolutely not! What do you think would happen? You'd light up like a Christmas tree if you got anywhere near Pavati."

"So? She needs to know how I feel about her."

"Yeah, I don't think that's the problem. I'm pretty sure she knows exac–" My words were halted by an epiphany. That little liar! That little freakin' conniver!

Pavati *did* care about Danny. And she'd cared about Jack before him. She didn't stay away from these boys out of indifference. She stayed away to preserve them. She knew just as well as I did that she wouldn't be able to resist them if they got too close. She loved them, and she wanted them to live!

But if that was the case, her offer to let Danny merely *think* she loved him wasn't a fair exchange for my and Dad's allegiance.

Of course, I couldn't tell Danny any of this. He'd probably go tearing off after Pavati like in some corny romantic movie. I could just see him running across a field of daisies . . . or more likely flailing around in a rip current. Actually, by the look of him, he might do it without any encouragement from me at all.

My phone buzzed and I looked down at the screen.

DAD: Come home now. Your mom's taken a turn.

Danny said, "It's not fair, you know, that you get to see Pavati and I don't."

I nodded bitterly. "Life's not fair."

CALDER

Chelsea's house was like all the others on her street: one-story, with a front door centered in its brick facade, a picture window on either side. Presumably it had been her mother who had tried to express some individuality with a white flower box under each window, filled to capacity with red and yellow tulips. They were pretty from a distance, but as we approached the door, my nose twitched at the odor of Styrofoam and plastic flowers.

From inside the house, the sound of women's off-pitch harmonies faded, while a few male voices carried a bass note. The end of the song gave way to chattering and the dull thud of chairs being moved around the living room.

"Sounds like they're wrapping up," Chelsea said. "Let's go catch Mrs. Brandon."

Chelsea opened the front door. She kicked off her shoes in the entryway and pulled me through. The living room, to the right, was painted sky blue. A navy couch was pressed up against the wall, and several high-backed dining room chairs stood in front of it. I stepped to the side as an older gentleman carried one of the chairs back to the dining room.

"Mrs. Brandon," Chelsea said, as she crossed the room to greet a woman with dark hair, a streak of silver in the front. She wore a lot of dark makeup, I thought, especially for a Saturday morning. Lily used to do that. The first time I saw her, she'd been ringing her eyes with thick black lines. She never did that anymore. I couldn't remember when she'd stopped.

"Oh, hello there, Chelsea," said Mrs. Brandon. "And who's this? Your boyfriend?"

"What's this about a boyfriend?" a second woman asked, entering the room with a coffee cake.

"Nothing, Mom," Chelsea said.

Mrs. Brandon took the plate from Chelsea's mother and placed it on the table. "We sounded good this morning, Gretchen," Mrs. Brandon said.

Chelsea's mom cut the cake. "It'll be better when Norma gets over her head cold. Chelsea, you should introduce your friend."

"This is Calder, Mom. I met him at the library. I brought him by because he has some questions about Mrs. Brandon's boat."

"What's this about our boat, eh?" Mrs. Brandon asked. "You're asking about *Race Me*?"

254

Chelsea nodded, while I eyed Mrs. Brandon speculatively. We had the same hair color. Maybe something similar about the eyes. I wondered if Chelsea was also seeing the resemblance, because her voice became more animated.

"Did your family own it back in the sixties?" Chelsea asked.

"Chelsea?" asked her mom. "What's going on?"

Mrs. Brandon chuckled and poured herself a cup of coffee from the decanter on the table. I watched her hands. They were still too young to be my mother's, but maybe a younger aunt? Or an older cousin?

She said, "I can't help you there, dear. Mr. Brandon bought it at a sheriff's auction in Milwaukee about ten years ago." She dropped her voice to a whisper. "Drug raid. Mexican drug cartel. I still can't believe that kind of crime gets this far north. Just terrible. But that's all you see on the news these days."

"Excuse me?" I asked, and Chelsea and the two women looked at me.

"Law enforcement confiscated a lot of property in the raid," Mrs. Brandon said. "Cars, boats, jewelry. They auctioned it all off. Mr. Brandon got quite the deal. Why do you want to know about that?"

"No reason," I said. "Thank you for your time. Sorry to bother you." I turned for the door without another word to Chelsea, her mother, or Mrs. Brandon. I'd felt so close. Now I just felt lost.

Behind me, I heard Mrs. Brandon ask, "Did I say something to upset your friend? Is that all he wanted to know?"

"Not exactly," said Chelsea, "but . . . Calder, wait up!"

I retrieved my phone and charger from Chelsea's car and was almost to the potholed street when she grabbed my arm and tried to spin me around. I shook her off me and kept walking.

"So that's it?" she asked. "You're just going to go? Even drug dealers have bone marrow. You're not going to give up like that, are you?"

"It doesn't matter," I said, mentally calculating the distance to the lake. I was walking fast now, and Chelsea was struggling to keep up.

"Where are you going?" she asked. "And what do you mean it doesn't matter? Let's go search arrest records. Let's go visit the prisons. Criminals or not, if they're family, you've got a shot. How can you throw your life away like that?"

"No need," I said, trying not to smile. I'd done all I could to find my family, but it was a bust. Was I disappointed? A little. More so for Lily because I knew how important she thought it was for me to find them. But more than anything, I was relieved. I'd fulfilled my promise to Lily, and now I could go home to her. If she'd still have me.

"What are you talking about? Would you please just stop?" Chelsea grabbed my elbow, and I shook her off again.

"Just leave me alone," I said.

Chelsea ran a few steps ahead and turned to face me, obstructing my path. I took a step to the right, and she put both hands on my shoulders to block my dodge. "I'm not going to leave you alone. I want to help you find your relatives."

"Chelsea," I said guiltily. "I'm not really sick."

She jerked her hands from my shoulders, and they hung there—midair—like she didn't know if she should celebrate or pound me into a pulp. "Why would you lie about something like that?"

"I lie about lots of things," I said. It was a jerk thing to say, but it was also the truth, and wasn't that better than another lie?

Her fists came down hard on my chest. "Why do you have to be such a prick?"

"Born that way, I guess." I pushed past her and kept on walking. It was three miles to the lake. I could smell it. I swear, Chelsea's artful string of profanity followed me all the way to the water's edge.

27

LILY

Nothing Dad said about changing Mom would ever make me think it was a good idea. But after my epiphany that Pavati might have more heart than we originally thought, Dad asked that I give her one more chance before I turned to Maris. If I could trust a mermaid (and according to Jack you never could), the safer bet was Pavati (lying sack of physical perfection that she was).

I tried not to think about what Calder would say about all of this. It wasn't hard to do. I had to look at the photos on my phone to remember his face. If left to just my memories,

I could barely picture him. The curl of his hair could be any number of boys' and his green eyes were faded to gray in my mind. It terrified me that I was losing my connection to him.

Reluctantly, I sought Pavati the only way I knew how, swimming out from the end of our dock and calling her name halfheartedly, even at the risk of Maris responding.

The lake was not as clear as usual. The winds had pulled at the water the night before, stirring the bottom. A millennium of pulverized sandstone and iron ore clouded my perception of what was right and what was wrong. Once, these waters had been home to Maighdean Mara and her offspring. Her devotees had given gifts of tobacco and copper. But there was no sense of devotion in the water anymore—no sense of love. It was a cold and brutal place. I barely recognized it.

I called again, and a moment later Pavati emerged from the silt-clouded expanse—breathtakingly beautiful as always, and this time, when she invited me to swim with her, I agreed.

Maris's suggestion of a mermaid utopia was still firmly planted in my brain, and as I swam with Pavati I let my imagination go to that place, fantasizing about what life could be for me, for us as a family. I couldn't get over how right it felt. But rather than give me hope, it brought me into a funk because without Calder, how utopian could it really be?

As we swam, Pavati listened to my thoughts, sometimes smiling, sometimes touching my bare shoulder when my thoughts turned dark. I ignored her attempts to console me; I couldn't afford any distraction from my singular purpose. I was giving Pavati one more chance to help my mom.

The water gave me courage. I was just about to broach the subject when Pavati said, *"You look like Mother. Did Calder ever tell you that?"* She turned to look at me, then averted her eyes while she reached one arm forward and one arm back toward me. *"I can see you don't want to talk about him."*

"No, it's okay." I exerted an extra amount of energy to keep up with her. Why did she have to be so beautiful? And fast? *"He may have mentioned it."*

"Same hair. Same eyes. There's something about your nose. More turned up than hers I think, but the resemblance is striking. Maris doesn't like that, you know."

I looked questioningly at Pavati. *"Why would she care what I look like?"*

"She resents the position you're in with Mother, and your having her pendant."

I snorted. *"It's not that great. I haven't slept in months. But Pavati, I want to talk to you about—"*

Pavati smiled but refused to look my way. I knew I was in a bad mood, but it must have been worse than I thought by the way she avoided looking at me.

"I can tell you haven't been sleeping," Pavati said. *"You're beat. Do you want to take a break? There's a sunny little bay on the south side of Raspberry."*

"Too many sailboats," I said.

"Not today. Not enough wind."

I followed her up to a bright spot on the water, through

the glitter of sunlight, then through the glassy ceiling of the lake.

Pavati pulled herself up onto a large boulder and pushed her dark hair off her face with both hands. She combed her fingers through her tresses. "I haven't seen Maris in a while. Have you?" She looked down at me quickly with the tiniest flash of suspicion.

I shook my head, and it seemed to mollify her. "The thing with Maris is . . . What I want to—"

"Maris tries too hard," Pavati said, her lavender gaze straining to fix on my face. "She's worked her whole life to bend us all to her idea of how this family should run, and look where we are. Tallulah is dead. Calder has run off. Your father is acting like more of a Half than you are. None of you are hunting—not that I'm complaining about that part. It does make it easier for me."

That last comment threw me back to my visit with Daniel earlier this morning. It was the other reason I'd sought out Pavati.

"Danny is starting to worry about that," I said.

"Worry about what?" she asked, her eyes narrowing. She flipped her cobalt tail slowly, menacingly, against the rock, like a cat flicked its tail before pouncing.

"Adrian needing to hunt," I said.

Pavati closed her lids slowly, like a sated lizard, and leaned her head back to soak up the sun's rays.

"Does he need to worry?" I asked, swimming closer to her rock. The waves I created sloshed against the freckled granite.

Pavati made a dismissive sound.

"I'm serious," I said. I put one hand on the boulder and pulled myself halfway out of the water. "And I guess I'm curious. Why do you still feel the need to hunt?"

"I don't understand," Pavati said, looking down at me, her eyes flashing with lavender brilliance. I could see how Jack and Danny had both fallen for her.

"You're a mother," I said, dropping back down into the waves.

"Yes," she said. Suspicious.

"And happy about that."

"Very." Although I couldn't see colors like Sophie did, I couldn't help but notice the flash of heartache in her voice.

"So . . . ?" I hedged.

"So . . . ?" she asked, mimicking my inflection.

"I just thought if you found happiness in your son, you wouldn't need to absorb it from other sources. Neither would he."

"What on earth gave you that idea?" She laughed and the sound soured my mood.

"Calder," I said grimly.

"Calder," she scoffed, but then she saw how her tone hurt me. She closed her eyes to the muddy colors I must have been putting off, and softened her voice. "Calder is imaginative. I'm sure he was able to convince himself of that. I'll remind you that my mother was a mother four times over, five, really. And she was the most insatiable hunter of all of us."

"Do you think Calder's hunting now?" I asked, bracing my heart.

"Away from you? I think we can be fairly certain he

is." Pavati said it in a way that was both matter-of-fact and sympathetic.

I couldn't imagine it. I couldn't let myself believe it.

"That's hard for you to picture," she said, slipping back into the water and treading closer to me. Her hair was half-dry, and it curled and looped around her face. "I can see that. His methods aren't like Maris's, but he used to be an effective hunter. Until he met you. But now . . ." She left her thought to hover in the air between us.

"What are his methods?" I asked, not really wanting to know but at the same time not being able to resist asking, as if knowing any detail about his life—no matter how disturbing—might keep him from drifting further away from me.

"I don't want to upset you anymore." She scrunched up her nose. "Your emotions are really quite repellant today. Perhaps we should talk about other matters. You still have a decision to make. You and your father's allegiance for Danny's sanity? Do we have a deal?"

"What methods, Pavati?"

She sighed. "Calder is fairly good-looking, wouldn't you say?"

My heart quickened as I realized where she was going. I had a flashback to a girl sitting on a bench outside the Blue Moon Café, dangling a flip-flop from her foot, licking her fingers.

"He's not so much for the snap-and-grab. That's Maris's method. Just like me, Calder is the follow-me sort."

I knew how that went. I'd felt Calder's hypnotic pull many times. The second time we met, I followed him into the woods and let my sister go off with strangers. How easily

I had given up on all rational thought. How easily I would have followed him into the water. For a second I was jealous of whoever was with him now, no matter what her fate.

"Does he always hunt girls?" I asked, looking downward.

"They are attracted, not threatened. Most men, on the other hand, see him as a threat, so they sour. They're not worth the kill. With some exceptions, of course. But girls have always proved the most satisfying for him. They tend to fill—"

"You know what? Never mind. I don't need to hear any more." She was speaking of his past, I told myself. This was not the Calder I knew. And besides, I needed to get this conversation back to Mom.

"If you joined me, Calder would follow you," Pavati said. "You have that same effect on him as he has on others."

"I don't think so."

"You don't think he'll come back?"

I didn't answer Pavati right away. For now, it was just a fear. As soon as I spoke the words, they would be true. So instead of answering her directly, I said, "I haven't heard from him in a while."

Pavati raised her eyebrows and dove. I bleakly followed and listened as her memories traced backward to the point where song lyrics began to lace her thoughts. The words were sad, as was the mildly familiar melody. The first lines lifted with the lilt of a lullaby:

I can hear you well, though your thoughts are far away.
Do not be sad about the one who wanders on the waves.

I myself am thinking on the one I've loved and lost
Not in waves and water, but from love's sweet bitter cost.

"*What is that?*" I asked. "*I think I've heard it before.*"
"*A song Mother used to sing to Calder as he fell asleep at night.*
You made me think of it."

Pavati's memories of the young Calder painted a more comforting picture than her account of his hunting techniques. I yearned to replace one image for the other and begged Pavati for more. "*Is that it? Is that the whole thing?*"

"*Let's see . . .*" Pavati thought, then continued:

The child-starved heart; the hands wrung dry, o'er the
  waves Mick Elroy cries.
The woman walks a white trenched line of feet and peb-
  bled sand.
And would ransom all the dear sweet sons we've lost be-
  yond the strand
But I lie quiet waiting, Son, for the time we've not yet
  reached
When I will send you back to those who walk weeping on
  the beach.

"*Why?*" I asked, touching her arm. She looked at my hand before she looked at my face.

"*Why what?*"

"*Why did Nadia sing such a sad song to a little boy?*"

Pavati picked up her pace, and flipped her blue fluke just

past my shoulder. *"I don't know. But toward the end, in the weeks before she died, it was nearly every night."*

"Who's Mick Elroy?" I asked.

"No idea," she said, turning abruptly to face me. I could feel the warm buzzing heat of her thoughts in mine. I tried to push them away, to gain control of the conversation, but I was not as talented as her. Pavati continued, *"Some human, I suppose. Maybe a lover. The name of one of her prey?"*

That didn't sound right. *"Did she normally make up lullabies about her prey?"* I scoffed.

"Well, when you put it that way." Then she groaned, saying, *"Get a grip, Lily. You look disgusting."*

Pavati was fast. Very fast. I struggled even harder to keep up with her as she tore away, and I could tell our time together would soon be over. But I wasn't done with her yet! She'd distracted me from my initial purpose. Only now did I realize that had been intentional—how every time the thought of Mom's transformation entered my brain, Pavati had stripped it from me.

She was giving me no choice but to turn to Maris, and I hated her for it.

Hearing my thoughts, she said, *"I told you, I won't take Sophie's mother away from her. Quit trying to ask me."*

"Mom's taken a turn for the worse," I said. *"It's now or never."*

"It's never," she said, and there was a firm resolution in her face that I knew I could never shake.

With that, I turned my back on Pavati and sped through the water, arms pointed forward, like I was the figurehead on a ship. I powered my way to shore. Calder was gone. Mom was slowly leaving us. Everything was falling apart. I was going to have to go in the house and tell my family that I had failed. Tell them that we had no choice. That we were going to have to make a deal with the devil.

My despairing thoughts were unnaturally loud, and my cry pierced the lake—only a hair's width, but a long needle of sound that spiked north, never pinging back, never blocked, interrupted, or redirected.

"Calder!" I cried out, scaring myself. The sound shattered my heart like a bullet through glass.

28

CALDER

The midmorning air was May cold. I wished I'd stopped to get my car, broken window and all, because it would have been nice to run the heater for a while. But more than warmth, I needed the water to clear my thoughts and make a plan. I was just too relieved. Too happy, really, knowing I'd given this parent-search thing a valiant effort. So I'd come up empty. So what? I'd never promised Lily that I'd find them, only that I'd look. Promise fulfilled. Check.

If Lily was skeptical, I had at least five baffled witnesses—seven, if I counted Marc and the puck bunny—who could attest to the fact that I had been here. I thought Chelsea would back me up on at least that much. The only question was: would Lily still have me?

I tightened my fists and watched the skin split in razor-thin slits across each white knuckle. Would it have been nice to find my parents? Maybe. But I told myself I didn't care. Not enough to matter, anyway.

Standing with my knees pressed against the guardrail that separated the road from the lake, I watched the waves chop into silver wedges of home. With happy anticipation, I pulled off the electrician's T-shirt and tied it in a knot around a sapling that clung to the sandy soil. I was just about to do the same with my jeans when Chelsea pulled up alongside me in her car and let it idle. She rolled down the passenger-side window.

"You can't get naked on the side of the highway without getting arrested," she said. "Trust me, I've tried."

I glanced back quickly to find her frowning at me.

"Are you going to stay and watch?" I asked. Honestly, at this point I didn't care.

She got out and stood on the far side of her car, her arms resting on the roof. "Maybe," she said. "What do you think you're doing? Where are you going?"

"I need to clear my head," I said, yanking down my jeans.

"Jeez, Calder, what the hell? I didn't think you were serious. Put your clothes back on. You must be certifiable."

"You think I'm crazy? Well, you might be right," I said, smiling. I checked to make sure my cell phone and car keys were still in the pocket, then I folded up my jeans and anchored them under a rock beneath a scrub bush. I climbed over the guardrail and ran down the hill toward the lake.

"Calder! Stop it! Are you trying to kill yourself?" Chelsea cried.

I heard her feet run around the front of her car, and the swish of tall grass as she climbed over the guardrail. "Come on! There are a lot easier ways than drowning. Calder, come back. You're scaring me."

I glanced over my shoulder, and she was right. Her aura was a gravy of colors all blending to a mustard brown.

"Sorry," I said.

"Quit grinning at me. What is wrong with you?"

I crawled over the large boulders at the shoreline and down to the debris-strewn sand. I waded in. "Don't wait around. I'm not coming back."

"I'm calling the police!" she cried.

"You do that."

Chelsea slid on the steep slope and let out a yelp as her feet slipped out from under her. She fell, sending down a tumble of gravel that raced me down the hill to the bottom. "I hate you, Calder White!" was the last thing I heard before I dove.

I closed my eyes and reached forward through the cold, dark water. My blood fizzed like snow on a power line, then slowly burned through my muscles. The explosion in my ears raced toward my feet, and I was momentarily blinded by the bright bursts of pinwheeling light before I cracked open like an empty shell. My God, how long had it been?

The breathtaking relief of it made me scream out loud. Fish scattered as my silver tail released and propelled me away from the wretched city.

"I hate you!" Chelsea screamed again, making sure, wherever I was, that I would hear.

I prayed she was the only one and that Lily wasn't out there, somewhere, thinking the very same thing. At the thought of Lily, my imagination took over. I could swear I heard her voice in the waves, distorted but piercing the spindrift: *"Calder!"*

But she was too many miles away for that to be true.

The strength of my stroke was now tenfold. I reveled in the speed. My mind filled with the new sounds and unidentifiable vibrations of this part of the lake: the buzzing, whirring sound from manufacturing plants, the low groan of ore boats loaded with taconite.

Time passed quickly.

Above me, ferries and shipping vessels pockmarked the surface, but I whipped my tail, obliterating them all in the blur of my wake and sending me deeper into the increasingly darker depths. I swam in the direction of Isle Royale, the largest of all the islands, while three sturgeon followed close behind.

As the hours passed, the sun became too weak to reach me, and my body temperature dropped uncomfortably. I climbed toward the light and followed the contours of Washington Harbor and the archipelago's shore. I circled the craggy satellite islands, the black rocks scattered across the water like beads from a broken necklace.

Five times I circled the big island, sometimes stopping to harass disinterested wood ducks that bobbed along the reefs in Siskiwit Bay.

My head hadn't felt this clear in days. I could suddenly see my mistakes, the miscues, the misunderstandings. Lily did want me, or at least she had still wanted me when she sent me away. She did it out of love, and I slapped her in the face for it. I recoiled at the memory of my angry words, how they'd pushed her away.

I saw the blond girl on the beach, wrung nearly empty but still gasping for air. I prayed she had recovered. I prayed she'd forgive me, though I'd never deserve it. I hoped Jason would let me back into his home, his family. . . .

But most of all, I hoped—despite everything—that Lily would forgive me for not believing her when she told me about Nadia. Lily had been confused and hurting, and I had told her I didn't want to hear about it.

As soon as I got back to land, I'd call. I'd beg her forgiveness. I'd tell her I was coming home. I'd tell her that I didn't belong in Thunder Bay. I didn't belong to scruffy ponytail man, or the early-rising Chinese, or drug lords, or church ladies. I didn't belong to anyone here. I'd tell her that, if she'd still have me, I wanted her forever. That would never change. But *I* would.

I would be a better man. I would be the man she deserved.

The sun set, then rose again. It crawled across the sky until it hovered, pink, swollen, and sated, over the western horizon once more.

On the third day, I surfaced alongside the rocky shoreline

and came face to face with a moose, who watched me from the conifers that lined the shore. It laid its ears flat and licked its muscled upper lip.

You don't belong here, it said, stomping to assert its territory. So now I was getting it from a moose. It had to be true.

29

LILY

My body trembled in response to the morbid silence that filled our house. We'd spent all night together as a family. Dad built a fire. He made Mom's favorite meal: beef Stroganoff and Caesar salad. Her "last meal," I couldn't help but think. And it wasn't a stretch. She'd been imprisoned by her disease, and now she was heading off to die. Even if things went the way we all hoped, she'd have to die first. That part was unavoidable.

We had forced conversation through dinner, with meaningless talk about weather and Girl Scouts and groceries.

After the dishes were cleared, we played the world's most somber game of Monopoly. Mom was the horseman. It was the easiest piece to grab, but even then Dad had to move it around the board for her. She didn't seem to mind.

To look at her complacent expression, you wouldn't know what was coming. I didn't know if that was because Mom didn't truly appreciate the danger, or if she simply was not afraid to die.

We made eye contact across the game board. She smiled that Mom smile—content and proud and full of love—and I realized it was none of those things. She was keeping up a good front just for us, because she didn't want us to be afraid. She was protecting us even now. I wished I hadn't seen that in her eyes. It made it worse.

Sometime after midnight, we all fell asleep downstairs: Mom and Dad on the couches, Sophie and me on the floor. None of us wanted to break away from the family group. We would stay together to the end, and hope that we'd have more time after that.

When morning came, Dad and I were the first ones up. We busied ourselves in the kitchen, quietly making coffee and pulling together the essentials Dad thought we would need at water's edge: a warm blanket, a thermos for the coffee, a wool hat—things that, should Mom transform, we would be able to warm her with afterward. Dad worried aloud about shock. If he was also thinking about a bigger threat, he never let on.

"I don't like this," I whispered, my voice breaking.

"None of us do," Dad replied as he screwed the cover on

the thermos. He held his hand over the top for a few seconds before packing the thermos in the bag.

"Maybe Maris won't come," I said.

There was a beat of silence before Dad said, "She'll come."

I rolled the blanket tighter and made a second attempt at getting it to fit in the bag. It didn't seem to want to go either.

"You're sure about your promise to Maris?" I asked. "You know you can't go back on it."

"I know that," he said woodenly. "I can already feel it."

I got the blanket in the bag and pulled the straining zipper closed. "I'm glad Calder's not here to see this."

Dad turned from the counter and stared at the floor. "Because he'd stop it?"

I shook my head miserably. "Because he'd feel so betrayed. Maris . . ." *Jeez,* I still couldn't believe it. "How did we get to this?"

"Jason," Mom called from the couch.

"Coming, sweetheart." Dad left me and went to help Mom. I followed him into the living room. He picked Mom up and set her gently in her chair.

Mom's pale yellow fleece reminded me of a dandelion held under the chin—sweet cream butter. I leaned down to hug her, inhaling the familiar scent of her lotion and the warm smell of sleep.

"Mom," I whispered.

She tapped my back in a light rhythm. "It's going to be okay, baby."

Sophie took longer to wake. I wondered if she was faking sleep so as to prolong the sounds of Mom moving around the house. Was it possible the seriousness of what we were attempting was finally sinking in? If only there were enough time to turn back. But now that the plan was set in motion, it felt like an enormous stone rolling down a hill.

"Are we ready?" Dad asked. He stood at the door, duffel bag in hand, the hint of tears in the corners of his eyes. He swallowed hard, and I watched his Adam's apple drop, then rise like a fishing bobber in water.

"Ready as I'll ever be," Mom said in an eerily cheerful voice.

Sophie slipped her hand in mine and squeezed hard.

We moved slowly, as a group, down to the water's edge. Dad pushed Mom's chair over the uneven ground. It felt like a clumsy funeral march. It was a funeral march.

When we got to the water, Dad lifted Mom from her chair and laid her in the shallows where she could sit. The water broke gently over the tops of her legs.

She cringed. "It's so cold."

"Go ahead," Dad said, nodding at me. "Call Maris."

Trembling, I walked to the end of the dock and stared out at the lake for a long, hard time. I glanced back at Mom, and she nodded encouragingly. When I could feel Dad just about to say something, I sat down on the dock's edge and lowered myself in. I hoped Pavati was too far away to hear. Then I closed my eyes.

"Maris," I thought. *"It's time."*

I didn't hear any reply. Neither did I feel any rush of movement within a mile's radius from the dock. Maybe I'd get lucky and she wouldn't hear me. I could buy another day.

"Maris," I called again, this time stronger, but with a desperate sob in my voice.

There was a rush of current, and when I opened my eyes, Maris was mere inches in front of my face. Our noses nearly touched.

"Oh my," she said, her voice like honey. I almost heard her say the word. *Honey. Lily, honey. "You are a mess, now, aren't you?"* It wasn't a question. She tsk-tsked me mentally, like a scolding mother hen.

I stared right through her without a response.

"I can see how much you're suffering, Lily. You are more fully mer than you know, than perhaps I've even realized. The pain . . . I can help with that. I can show you how." Then she cocked her head to one side. *"Are you tempted? Let me help you."*

My heart twinged at her words, which confirmed everything I knew but had been trying so hard to ignore. *"My mother,"* I said.

"I saw her," she said. *"Jason, too. He knows I can make no guarantee?"*

I swallowed. *"He does."*

"And he will side with me against Pavati? No matter what?"

"He will."

"I need to hear it from him."

I surfaced and pushed my wet hair back from my face. Maris surfaced as well, but she had swum away from the dock and was facing the shore, where my parents sat with the waves breaking over their legs. I tried to ignore the panic that was clearly evident on Mom's face. She moved out deeper, still sitting, but now the water broke around her chest.

"She needs to hear you promise, Dad."

Dad stood up and looked directly into his sister's eyes. "I promise to give my allegiance to you," he said, "as head of the family."

I watched a flicker of memory flash across Maris's face. Did she wonder if he was good for his promise? Did she wonder if he was more like his father than their mother? Was Maris *also* afraid?

Maris dove, and a second later we all watched in horror as two pale hands grabbed Mom by the ankles and slowly pulled her deeper.

I put one hand on the dock to steady myself. This was wrong. Dad needed to stop this now. It wasn't going to work.

Her arms drifting out to her sides, my mother formed a cross as she floated on her back. I could feel the vibration in the water of my mother's heart thudding inside her chest, racing to a point where I hoped it might stop of its own accord.

Mom closed her eyes as Maris continued to pull her out deeper. Then Mom's ankles dipped below the surface, followed by her knees, her body arcing slowing downward until . . . she was gone.

Only now did Dad react. He took two quick steps into the water.

I pulled myself up onto the dock and scanned the water in a panic. There was no struggle. Was Mom so willing to die that she could override the instinct to fight drowning? Or was she simply that weak?

I couldn't see her. I couldn't see Maris. I could hear nothing. The absence of sound was more frightening to me than anything that had come before. How could they have both just disappeared? I looked back at Dad in terror. Sophie stood beside him, clinging to his arm.

Before any of us could speak, a sizzling sound broke the silence, followed by a bright flash of light. A second later, Mom's body floated to the surface, facedown in the surf.

Maris came up and pushed my mother's lifeless body away from her as if it were nothing more than passing driftwood. "Now you are free," she said to Dad. "Come with me."

Dad ran into the waves and pulled Mom's body to shore. "What have you done?" he howled.

"She was holding you back," Maris said.

"You were supposed to reinvigorate her!" Dad cried.

"It's too late for that. I told you it might not work."

"You bitch!" I cried, dispatching birds from the willow tree with my scream. "You didn't even try!" The dock shook like an earthquake under my feet.

Dad dragged Mom up on shore. He flipped her over and blew air into her lungs. "Come on, honey," he whispered, filling her lungs again. "Carolyn, come on, baby. Breathe."

Sophie stood–paralyzed–looking at me in horror, her eyes huge with fright. Her mouth hung open in disbelief.

I drew my fingers to my forehead. The light hurt my eyes; there was a grinding sound, like metal on metal, in my ears. I couldn't think straight. I needed to get away. My mind fell dark with grief and rage and shame, like a black velvet curtain drawn over a window. I crumpled to my knees, then fell forward. My head struck the iron boat cleat on the dock.

And Nadia was back.

30

NADIA

MAY 8, 1945

I stop outside a record store on Ashland's main street. A taxidermist's eagle is featured prominently in the window below a banner that reads VICTORY in red, white, and blue letters.

Not for the eagle, I think, but nonetheless, a celebratory flag waves from every doorway. Men in hats talk animatedly on the street corner, and women with rolled hair hurry arm in arm to buy their newspaper. A few cry. But not prettily like they do in the movies. Theirs is an ugly, soul-wrenching sound that sickens me. Victory came too late for some.

My reflection in a storefront window catches me off guard. I cradle my pregnant belly and try to make my way up the crowded sidewalk, before stopping again, three doors down. The humans around me are loud. Their emotions are a whirl of high excitement and jubilation. Their war is over. My head spins. I stagger down the sidewalk, toward a pay phone.

I had no intention of doing this today. I had planned a private spot, not here, so far from the lake. But I can never get anything to go according to plan. I stop at a boarding-house and knock. It takes the woman in the faded housecoat a long time to answer. She is putting on lipstick. I can hear a radio blaring "God Bless America" from the kitchen.

She takes one look at me and leads me to a back room with a cot, around the corner from a kitchen stove that radiates heat throughout the room. Now free of the crowds, my head stops pounding. The woman gets a cold towel and lays it on my chest. It's wet, and my body instantly relaxes.

She calls a doctor, but it's too late. I am already delivering a baby girl.

Maris.

Later that evening, while the woman sleeps off her martinis, I wrap the child in the clean sheets from my cot, slip out the back door, and catch a cab to the college. The driver happily leaves without his fare, and I find an open window on the ground floor of the science building.

I climb three flights and at the top I inhale. Following the father's scent, I trail the wall to the third door. PROFESSOR JOHN BISHOP is stenciled on the door.

I leave the baby with a note.

SEPTEMBER 3, 1966

I would never say what I was really thinking, but humans always strike me as a little odd with their many limbs, all gangly and hanging. Even when I don their strange vestiges, I avoid my reflection. So why Tom Hancock has accentuated his legs with black-and-red-striped pants, I cannot begin to comprehend. Worse, he has taken to wearing a pair of shoes he calls winklepickers, which sit neatly beside him now. His bare feet dig into the sand, which is cold with the changing seasons. I like his T-shirt, though: Jefferson Airplane. The waves thrum against the sand as he strums a guitar he calls Gibson.

Tom turns the knob on his transistor radio and picks up the Mamas and the Papas. They're dreamin' on such a winter's day. . . .

His long hair hangs in his eyes. He has grown out his sideburns. He says, "Tell me I'm not like the others," while he clumsily picks out some chords.

It is probably not a good idea, but I tell him the truth. "You are not like the others. You know that." I hear the veracity of my words in the tumbling cadence of my voice and hope he does, too.

"Do I?" he asks. He taps a pack of cigarettes absentmindedly against his thigh.

"I will be back in the spring. I promise."

He grins broadly. He knows a mermaid can never break her promise. "That's what I needed to hear. I knew it all along," he says, though I know that is not true. I have shared too much of my life with him. He knows too much. I am not made for love.

"You will take care of him," I say, touching our three-month-old son, Jason, who lies on a pile of blankets beside me. He is the most beautiful of all my children, and that is saying something. Never before have I stayed with a father this long, stayed with my baby this long. "And when I return, you and Jason will both join me."

Tom pulls back with a questioning look and blows a long stream of gray smoke from between his lips. "We haven't talked about that before."

"Come to the water," I say. "I will change you. Then we can be a family—as complete a family as this lake has ever known. That is something I've never offered the others, Tom. Now do you see how much I care?"

"Change can be good," he says, fidgeting with the radio, looking for a new station. The signal screeches like dolphins in the Gulf. "Maybe someday . . ."

"Someday has come early," I say, teasing him with a finger drawn down his spine.

He chuckles. "Yes, I've always suspected you were the real November witch." He rolls over on top of me, brushing the tumble of hair from my face. "Just a beautiful storm, coming when some innocent man least expects it."

"Do not joke," I say.

"Okay, but it's still not time."

"It is," I say. "It's time for my family to be together."

MAY 2, 1967

Tom Hancock has left the front door unlocked. From the hallway, I can hear his bedsprings groan as he turns over. A woman's sigh. I feel the urge to wring her sleeping neck, but can do nothing here on land. Instead, I climb the narrow staircase, touching the pictures on the wall. At the top, I trail the dark corridor to the nursery and step inside, inhaling the sweet baby smell. Vanilla and lavender.

"What are you doing, Nadia?" Tom asks from behind me, his voice dangerous but calm. He is beautiful. Even more beautiful than I remembered. I want to protest the woman sleeping in his bed. He should be with me. But I am afraid and so I feign control and say, "Jason is a year old. He's walking."

"I won't let you take him."

"Watch me," I say too loud, while he glares down at me.

"Quiet. Diana is sleeping."

Tom closes the nursery door and turns on a small lamp, flooding the blue room with light. His warm hand covers my shoulder. "Find someone else, Nadia. Start another family. Leave Jason with me."

"He belongs with me," I say.

"Over my dead body."

My heart sinks with his betrayal as he slams me against the wall. I grit my teeth as the chain around my neck snaps and snakes its way over my shoulder and hits the floor.

"This isn't over, Tom. You made me a promise."

"Some promises were meant to be broken," he says.

I straighten my shoulders and say, "I want my family to be together."

Tom's face transforms into an expression I cannot read: Grief? Worry? Hope? If it's hope, it leaves an unmistakable glow. Tom reaches down and takes Namid's pendant from the floor.

JUNE 28, 1967

Almost two months later and the seeds of my hope have been scorched by Tom's silence. I scramble every suicidal thought I have, but as young as Maris is, she's amazingly intuitive. She swims far behind me, lurking behind the rocks, watching me with worried eyes.

She follows me into deeper water, watches my dark descent. The waves above us rage into whitecaps. A sailboat passes, hurrying back to port. The wind changes tack, and the shadow of a boom swings overhead. There is a scream and a splash.

I see my son, Jason, plummeting through the water. He is as graceful as a poem. But he does not transform.

His pale arms and legs pull at the water. He makes no progress. Air bubbles rush out of him like a rabble of silver butterflies. He is sinking. His eyes close. The vibration of his heart trembles in the water. The cold slows it steadily, until there are too-long gaps between each beat.

It is not Jason. It is someone else's son. And it is almost too late.

Maris calls to me in the water. *"No,"* she says. *"We don't need him."* Her cries capture Pavati's and Tallulah's interest, and they are quick to come see.

Maris is too young to hide her thoughts from me. She thinks I save the boy because I am dissatisfied with her. Nothing could be further from the truth, but I am too preoccupied with saving the little life to correct her.

Tallulah, I see, loves him already. With a burst of light, the boy is silver-tailed. Just like her.

JUNE 28, 1973

Pavati and Maris have gone off to hunt. I am watching Calder and Tallulah chasing each other, darting through the wake of a Boston Whaler, careful not to catch the attention of the man and woman who sit somberly at the wheel, neither of whom look left or right, least of all behind. As far as I can tell they do not speak to each other.

Suddenly, the man cuts the engine and the boat stops as if it's hit a stone. The water lunges and tosses the boat before settling to a calm.

I call Calder and Tallulah back to me, and Tallulah hides behind my arm. A seagull lands on the waves, and we look up to see an arm reaching over the side of the boat. It lays a strange object on the water. There are a few beats of silence before the boat pulls away.

Calder swims up after the strange floating thing. He returns with a circle of flowers, woven together on a wire frame. It is all roses and ivy with a satin banner that says OUR BOY.

Calder is careless and the banner floats away. He bows to Tallulah and places the floral wreath on her head like a crown.

She laughs, saying, *"Now I am the queen and you are my king, and someday you and I will lead this family."*

"And we'll make Maris eat wormroot for breakfast," Calder says.

"You two be nice to your sister," I say.

Laughing, Calder chases Tallulah to the bottom, and my heart aches for the one this wreath was meant for. And for my poor boy, as well.

APRIL 1, 1978

Five years later, Tom Hancock returns to the lakeshore. If I had passed him on a street, I might not have recognized him, but his scent is immediately recognizable in the water.

I hesitate, searching to see if the mousy woman is with him. But Tom is alone. I consider ignoring him. Then I consider killing him. Then I sense him leave the water, and I am lured closer by the fear of losing him again.

The lights are on in the old homestead. I wonder how I hadn't noticed. He sits at the end of the dock, and I peer at him from the dark shadows of the willow tree. Gone are the striped pants of the 1960s. His hair is cut short.

He drops his legs in the lake, then pulls them back. He is fishing, I realize. Fishing for me. I do not reward him that first night.

For two more nights I watch him. He sighs and searches the stars. When he looks back at the water, he is startled to find me within inches, staring up at him from the waves that slosh against the dock. I put one hand on the splintered boards and pull myself up, water dripping from my hair, my nose, my chin. He scrambles backward like a crab.

I don't say anything, but stare at him through burning eyes.

When he offers me no apology, I flip and dart away.

Two days pass. I watch as Tom continues his vigil on the dock. Now and then he calls to me, "Nadia!" and his voice tugs at my heart.

When I emerge the second time, his face washes over with sky-blue relief.

"Why are you here?" I ask.

He exhales. "I needed to reassure myself that I hadn't imagined you. I needed to know that you were real. The other night . . . was that you? I convinced myself it was a dream."

I have no answer for this. Isn't our son proof enough that I am real? And why should he be the one reassured? Where is Jason?

"You are alone?" I ask, my eyes glancing to the nursery's dormer window.

"Jason is dead," he tells me. "I thought you should know. You deserved to know."

"Liar!" I cry, though the possibility that Tom is telling me the truth churns through my body, erupting in a white light that blinds me.

The burst of energy shoots from my body across the water. It slices through the willow tree, severing a branch and continuing through the trunk and down to the ground. The tree groans, then splinters. The long willow branch crashes onto the water and a shower of small green leaves fills the air.

Tom jumps to his feet and watches the trunk heave, its pulp burned black. When he looks back at me, his eyes are sad, but his aura doesn't quite match his expression. They are close, but his emotions are more confusing than convincing. A part of me, the very core of me, says that Jason is still alive. But I don't trust myself anymore. I cannot ignore the fact that Jason has never come home to me. I can't believe there is anything so strong that it could keep him away this long.

AUGUST 20, 1983

Another five years, and I still cannot be consoled. Grief and doubt have overtaken me, and I refuse to seek their cure. Maris implores me to hunt with her. The water is warmer than usual and it has drawn more swimmers from the sand.

I curl up in a sea cave, lay my head against its smooth sides, and refuse to come out.

Maris has swum with me for thirty-four summers, her small body matured only to a human prepubescent. She begs me to come out of the cave. She hears Tom Hancock in my memories. She tells me he lies. She tells me she can see the lie on his face. That Jason is still alive. But I cannot trust Maris. Or I am too far gone to care.

"Please!" Maris pulls at my arm, her hands sliding down its length before reaching my fingers and letting go. "I'm begging you. I don't want to be in charge. Don't go. Don't leave me."

"It is your family now. Do what is right. Keep them together. Take care of Calder. You know how much he looks up to you, and I know how much you care about him."

A wave of horror washes over her. "You wouldn't tell him."

"Don't tell him the thing he most needs to hear?" I ask, managing a weak smile.

"He won't pay attention to me if he thinks I'm weak."

I lift my head, though it is as heavy as a stone. "Love doesn't make you weak, darling. You're stronger than you think. I'm counting on that. I know you won't let me down."

"I don't know how to do this."

"Listen to me. This is important. If your brother is alive–as you believe–he may still choose to come home. Something has held him from us. Be vigilant. Watch for him. If something keeps him from us, free him from the problem."

Maris squirms and scowls at the water. "What is he to me?" Her black tail glints in the sunlight that streams through the mouth of the cave. "This is all his fault."

"No. This is my fault." I'm tired now. I manage to find just a little more voice. "Jason is your family, and family is the most important thing. Do what you need to do. Promise me you will."

Maris fights the words, but ultimately we close our eyes together, and I hear her say, "I promise."

31

CALDER

Just after daybreak, I returned to where I'd stashed my clothes, under the scrub bush. From there I hitched a ride to the library, where my car had gathered several parking tickets. I assumed it was Chelsea who'd been kind enough to write *F.U.* in the grime and dirt on the driver's-side door.

I got in, plugged in my phone. It lit up with a text from Lily.

> I'm sure u don't want to hear from me. If
> you've moved on I can't blame you. Idk maybe

u don't even have this phone anymore. But
if u do . . . does Mick Elroy mean anything
to you? I think it's important

No, I thought. This search is over. I'm done. I did everything I could. Besides, no Mick Elroys had showed up as
registered owners of *R* or *K* boats.

If it weren't Sunday morning maybe I could have gone
back to the library and checked, but it was closed until
tomorrow and I wasn't going to stick around that long. Except that—

Damn it. My compulsion to fulfill the promise clamped
around my heart like a vice. It froze my feet at their spot. Apparently the search wasn't as over as I'd hoped.

Chelsea had programmed her number into my phone
and, unwillingly, I dialed it.

"Screw you," she said.

"Good morning, Chelsea. Is that the way you greet
everyone who calls so early?"

"Why aren't you dead?" she asked, and I could tell this
time it was honest curiosity and not a sarcastic retort.

"Not my time, I guess. Listen, what do you know about
the name Mick Elroy? Does that mean anything?"

"I'm not talking to you."

I sighed and rolled my eyes. "Just knock your phone on
the wall then. Once for yes. Twice for no."

There was an overly dramatic pause and then a dull thud
on the other end.

"What does it mean?" I asked.

"There aren't enough ways of knocking that."

"Okay, so how 'bout in relation to the people we talked to yesterday?"

Silence.

"Chelsea, come on. Please. I need to look something up. The library's closed."

More silence.

"You still there?" I asked.

"Yeah, I'm still here. Fine. Come on over. You can use my laptop."

It took me a while to find Chelsea's house again. They all looked the same on her street. Ultimately, I recognized the white window boxes and the chemical smell of plastic flowers. I pulled to the curb. Chelsea met me at the door in her pajamas and led me inside without any greeting or questions about what I'd been doing for the past three days, or even about our parting scene. She looked seriously pissed, though. This was going to have to be quick.

"I might have some new information," I said.

"Yeah, so you said." She opened her computer without looking at me and said, "What do you want to search?"

"Plug in 'Thunder Bay' and 'Mick Elroy.'" Then, on a hunch, I suggested adding the name of ponytail man's boat, *Rhapsody in Blue.*

Chelsea typed in the name, but she did it like a surname–McElroy–and my heart gave a weird kind of lurch. Three articles popped up. Chelsea clicked on the first one:

FATHER, SON LOST IN LAKE SUPERIOR
Thurs. June 29, 1967

By RICHARD OLIVER, Staff Writer–Ontario dive teams joined the efforts of Wisconsin Fire & Rescue, as well as the U.S. Coast Guard yesterday to locate the body of Liam McElroy (Thunder Bay) and his three-year-old son, Patrick. McElroy and his wife, Margaret, were returning from a two-week excursion of the Apostle Islands on Mrs. McElroy's brothers' boat, *Rhapsody in Blue,* when their son fell overboard. McElroy was also lost when he dove in the lake after his son.

"It ends there," Chelsea said. "Is this what you were looking for?"

I couldn't find my voice. My head was a whirl of fragmented images: a red box of raisins, the sensation of falling, the sounds of a splash and screams. A boat. A maple leaf flag. A dark-haired woman. I was stunned and panicked to the point of speechlessness.

Chelsea rolled her eyes and exited out of the article, clicking on the second article, which was about a charitable fund being set up for the sole survivor of the McElroy family.

She exited and clicked on the third. It was a section of a newspaper announcing engagements and weddings. The post referred to "Margaret (Molly) McElroy, formerly of Thunder Bay." Seemed she had remarried. The name of the groom seared the synapses of my brain.

"Chelsea?" I said, finally finding the air to speak.

"What?"

"Thanks."

She eyed me doubtfully, then said, "Whatever," slapping her computer shut.

I ran for my car.

My eyes were wide in the rearview mirror. Patrick? Did I look like a Patrick? A rush of heat flashed through my face and then the tears came, wild and furious.

How is it that every life I touched lay in ruins? My father was dead because of me. Nadia was dead because I had not been enough to fulfill her need for a son. And what about the Hancocks? Could they have avoided their true nature if they had never met me? And now what about my biological mother? Was there at least one life that I could salvage?

As the image of my mother flashed across my mind, a guttural cry built up in my chest and broke past my lips. Salt-laced tears stung my eyes, and I could barely keep them open to see the road. I bit down on my hand to restrain the sound that was tearing at my throat.

Grief. Or joy. Or loss. No label fit. So much time lost. That was what bothered me most. She'd been so close for so long. Why hadn't I ever recognized her touch? The curve of her cheek? Was I so far gone?

No. It couldn't be true. There must be some mistake. Even if I had lost all memory, what mother wouldn't recognize her own son? What kind of mother was she that she wouldn't have known me? I'd been so close. How could she have let me slip away? Not once, but over and over and over again. I hated her. I loved her. I didn't care anything about her. I wanted her. I wanted my mother. I felt small and alone.

Then, just when I thought I might pull myself together, the faded image of my father sinking in the lake brought a new sound of agony to my lips. I wiped my face with the back of my arm. How many people had died because of me? My father had only been the first. Maybe I wasn't being fair to myself when it came to him, but how could I deny it? He was dead because of me.

A truck blared its horn as I veered across the center line, the sound swelling, then fading away as I swerved to the right and skidded in the loose gravel on the shoulder. I put the car in park and threw my head back, howling and bashing my skull against the headrest, over and over and over. My face contorted, unrecognizable in the rearview mirror. I'd never felt so hopeful or so low. So ashamed and in such a hurry to make things right. But I couldn't turn back time. I couldn't change the past. I could only run pell-mell into the future.

I abandoned the car and sprinted for the lake, just beyond the tree line. I couldn't wait any longer for this road to carry me home.

32

LILY

Waking was like coming out of the grave. My room was dark,
the curtains drawn, alarm clock unplugged. There were no
sounds in the house to confess the time. No coffee gurgling,
no Queen on the stereo, no smell of onions frying in a pan.

My Nadia dreams still lingered on the fringes of my
mind, but, slowly, I shed the cloak of death and found my way
back to reality. My head pounded and my shaking fingers
found the very real goose egg on my forehead. It throbbed,
and I remembered the sickeningly dull thud of my head hit-
ting the boat cleat.

"How are you feeling?" asked a low voice.

It startled me and, not yet certain of my surroundings, I nearly rolled out of bed. "Who? Dad?"

"Are you okay?" he asked.

"Yes," I lied, not wanting to confess what I had known for quite some time. Ever since Calder had left, the mermaid's black cloud of despair had been slowly descending until I was deep within the well. Too deep. And I didn't see any way of climbing out of this hole I'd dug for myself.

Even Dad's voice tunneled away from me, getting smaller and smaller like the circle of light at the top of the well. I could barely see him sitting there in a wooden chair in the corner of my room. I was conscious of only one sense. It was as if the world I'd known had been sucked into a black hole, and all that was left was a high-pitched keening in my brain. Mom was dead.

"Mom?" I asked, my voice trembling, my heart a heavy anchor in my chest.

"She's fine," he said. "Well, not fine. But alive."

I didn't believe him. I'd seen it all firsthand. He was lying to pacify me. But I wasn't a child. He couldn't treat me like a child. "Maris killed her," I said.

"Almost."

Yes, he was a very good liar. "I failed!"

"It wasn't your fault," Dad said.

I shook my head, trying to clear the wailing in my brain. It drowned out the sound of my own voice. "It is. It is. Mom's gone, and now you're bound to your promise. You'll have to leave and join up with Maris."

"I told you. She's alive. But you are right about that last part. We only asked Maris to try, and there were no loopholes when it came to me."

"I'll kill her!" I screamed, tearing at my blankets. I didn't care if Maris thought she had been *freeing* Dad from the so-called problem. *I* would be her problem from now on.

Dad looked at me with a puzzled expression, which only made me angrier.

"Maris," I explained, as if my threat required further explanation. "I'll kill her."

"Lie down, Lily," Dad said. "You hit your head pretty hard. You've been sleeping for two days. You must be starving. I'll go make you some tea and toast, then I'll explain everything."

As soon as he was gone, I whipped back the covers and went to the window. My feet were unsteady from lack of use. Staggering across the floor on pins and needles, I bumped my hip against the dresser. The screen on my cell phone lit up. It was ten a.m. and there was a text from Calder:

Lily? You still there?

Unfortunately, his message did nothing to pull me out of the hole. It was too little, too late. I scrolled back and found my original message to him:

Does Mick Elroy mean anything to you? I think it's important.

I couldn't remember what my message meant, or why I'd wanted to send it. I dropped my phone on the floor with a clatter and pulled back the thick curtains that covered my window. The bright sunlight was an assault on my eyes and a personal insult. *Stupid sun. Stupid ball of gas making me go blind.*

I slung both legs over the windowsill and slunk across the porch roof. Dropping to the ground, I crouched beneath the downstairs windows and looked toward the lake, which lapped at the shore like a thirsty dog, all tongue and slobber. The very smell of it—an icy coldness, if cold has a smell—attached itself to the center of my brain like a lead sinker that, when released, plummeted down my central cortex, through my nasal passages and my throat, burning past my heart, to the cold empty pit of my stomach.

I was gone before Dad came back with the toast.

A black web of misery spun out from the center of my body. When it felt like the last bit of life had been pulled through my final fiber, I found myself standing in the lake with no memory of having crossed the yard.

A face appeared no less than twenty feet in front of me. A rippling circle broke around her square shoulders. Would Maris really make it this easy for me to kill her?

"Lily," she said, without any hint of apology for what she had done. Her voice threw gasoline on the fire raging inside me. I charged into the water, my hands drawn like claws.

She didn't retreat. Her tone was soft. Soothing even, like balm to my splintered mind. It was a well-practiced sound, as if she had been confronted by someone like me a million times before. There was no concern on her face at all, which only made me angrier.

I snarled, swiping at her cheek. She dodged the blow, saying, "I see how low you've fallen."

"That's ironic!" I screamed, aiming for her eyes, my fingers like talons. Within seconds, Maris was directly behind me, one arm wrapped around my waist, the other around my throat. The image was that of an orderly subduing a mental patient with a straitjacket. I was still in human form, but she was not. The disparity of our physical states made her infinitely stronger. I couldn't break away.

"I can help you," she said, her voice like butter.

"I'll take a pass on any help you're offering," I said, straining against her arms.

"You're not feeling well," Maris said.

"You think?"

Maris's coal-black tail undulated beneath us, slowly pulling me out deeper. "I know how to help with that," she said. "Do you think you're the first of our family to fall so low? I know you're angry. Maybe rightfully so. But there's no need to suffer. Let me do at least one good thing here. One good thing for you."

"I'll feel better once Calder gets back," I growled, remembering his text. I knew it was a stretch.

Maris clicked her tongue behind my ear. "You can't be serious. He turned his back on his human family. Then he turned his back on us. You're just the next in a long line of abandoned people in Calder's wake. We're creatures of habit, and *leaving* . . . that is his."

By this time I'd been in the lake for more than a minute. The change was rippling through my body in uncontrollable waves of energy. Maris released me and backed away as my body exploded and my clothes tore away, floating to the surface.

I wheeled around. We were now evenly matched. Or so I thought.

"Calder hasn't turned his back on his family. He's looking for them," I countered.

"You're sure?" she asked, still annoyingly calm.

Of course I wasn't sure. Not at all. He could be anywhere, doing anything. This was all my fault. Just like always–I wanted to make things better, but I made them worse.

I lunged at Maris, but she flipped under my arms and came up behind me.

"Lily, I know what you need. It doesn't have to be this way."

I shivered in response. I never felt cold when Calder was here.

"Seriously," Maris scoffed, breaking her calm exterior for the first time. "I will never understand anyone's aversion to survival. There's nothing wrong with acknowledging your nature."

Once more Maris's eyes dropped to my neck. Although we weren't submerged, I could tell what she was thinking–that I wasn't worthy to wear her mother's pendant.

Maris said, "I can see this isn't coming as easily as I thought it would. I blame myself for not taking you under my wing sooner. I was hoping you'd reach this moment on your own."

"Hoping?" I sneered.

Maris clucked her tongue again. "Expecting. I expected you to reach this moment much earlier."

This moment? So that was the help she was offering? She was going to teach me to hunt? "Calder can resist the urge," I challenged. "And so can I."

"Sure, he *has*," she said, shrugging. "Calder has always experimented in self-control, but there hasn't been just *one* experiment. There have been many over the years. Too many to count, really. He always falls off the wagon for a few years before trying again. No one can deny themselves forever, and that includes you, Lily Hancock.

"We all wear the mask–play pretend, put on a good show for human eyes. But in the end, you are who you are."

"And who are you, Maris?" I asked.

"Me? I am the best choice to lead this family. Mother believed I could keep this family together."

"But you didn't."

For the first time I saw her falter, but she composed herself. "I was young. I didn't know how to play the mother role. Obviously I made mistakes."

"Tallulah," I said, hoping the sound of the name would cause her pain.

"And Calder, too," said Maris, unflinching. "I don't want to make the same mistakes with you."

Oh, she was good. Too good. The black cloud of my heart churned stormily inside me. Without wanting to, I heard myself say, "You'd help me?"

"Back then, I was too young for the responsibility. I was

too young to shoulder my siblings' grief. Revenge was the only thing I understood, so it was the only thing I had to offer. I can see now the damage that caused. And yes, Lily Hancock. I can help you."

"I feel so empty."

"I can fix that. Trust me. No need to feel ashamed."

PART THREE

Thy voice is on the rolling air;
I hear thee where the waters run;
Thou standest in the rising sun,
And in the setting thou art fair.

—Alfred, Lord Tennyson, *In Memoriam*, CXXX

33

DANIEL CATRON

I lifted the bottom of my T-shirt and scrubbed the yellow pollen from the Hancocks' kitchen window so I could peer in. No one had answered the door when I'd knocked. No one seemed to be inside. Not even Mrs. Hancock, whom I'd never seen leave the house. All the lights were off.

Huh. Maybe it was a good thing.

I'd reached the end of my rope when it came to Pavati blowing me off. I'd spent the past three nights lying awake, trying to figure out the best way to find her. I hadn't gotten any sleep, and that had nothing to do with Adrian. It was basically now or never. Or at least now or succumb to insanity.

Knowing Lily, she'd probably try to talk me out of what I was planning. So it was a good thing she wasn't around. Maybe my stars were finally aligning, if stars ever aligned for me. Yeah. Funny.

But I couldn't help thinking that maybe the Hancocks' absence was, like, fate or something. Maybe Pavati wanted to see me just as much as I wanted to see her, and maybe she'd been waiting for an opportunity like this where we wouldn't be interrupted or judged or yelled at. Maybe she'd done something to make them leave for a while, just in the hopes that I'd stop by. *Maybe freakin' maybe, baby.* It was about time I found out. I mean, it wasn't like I could be *re*-rejected, right?

Adrian lifted his head off my shoulder and sniffed at the cool air. "Yeah, buddy. You and I need to get out more, don't we?" Seriously, that apartment was getting majorly depressing. There were only so many episodes of *Cops* one guy could stand, and I'd run out of variations on macaroni and cheese: mac 'n' cheese with mushrooms and onions, with spaghetti sauce, with tuna, with Cajun spices; in a pinch I'd invented leftover macaroni soup.

I pulled Adrian's bottle out of the diaper bag and stuck it in his mouth, carrying him like a football in the crook of my arm. He'd already lost one sock somewhere in the trip from my apartment to Lily's front door. I pulled off the other and dropped it on the hood of my car as I made my way toward the water.

Do I call her name? Do I go underwater and call? In the past, Pavati had always just showed up, without any effort on my part. I used to think we had some deep emotional connection because she always showed up right when I was thinking about her, but then I realized I was always thinking about her, so it wasn't so cosmic after all.

When I reached the end of the dock, I sat down cross-legged and propped Adrian up between my legs. I took off my shoes and socks and dropped one foot in the water. Nothing said come hither like sweaty feet, right?

I pulled my foot out, laid Adrian's head on one of my shoes so he was comfortable, then dangled my hand in the water. *Come on, Pavati. Don't be shy.*

The lake looked dead. I couldn't find a single pinprick of an air bubble, a rippling circle . . . nada.

"Pavati," I called out. I glanced over my shoulder at the house just in case someone had been home all along. For a second I thought I saw an upstairs curtain move, but there was still no one.

"Pavati!" I called, louder this time.

Adrian cried. His bottle had rolled away. I popped it back in his mouth and balanced my other shoe on his stomach to hold the bottle in place. I pushed myself farther over the edge of the dock and dropped my whole head underwater.

I called again, this time into the water, *"Pavati!"* Bubbles fluttered past the sides of my face.

I listened, but didn't hear anything other than a boat motor. I pulled myself out, flipping my wet hair back and drenching the rest of me. Adrian startled when the cold water sprinkled his face, and he cried out. The bottle clunked onto the deck boards.

"Sorry, dude," I said as I popped it back in his mouth.

The boat I'd just heard appeared around the bend and came surprisingly close to the Hancocks' dock. When it was just twenty feet out, I saw a girl was driving it. She had chin-length, thick black hair and piercing eyes that told me she wasn't one to take any crap. Binoculars hung around her neck. Gabby Pettit. Damn it. What did *she* want?

She cut the engine.

"Is that you, Catron?" she asked.

"What?" I put my hand to my ear as if I couldn't hear her.

She smirked, so I guess I wasn't going to win any Oscars for this performance. "What are you doing here?"

"I came to see Lily," I said, "but she's not home." It was a lie, of course, but I hoped Gabby couldn't tell.

"I didn't know you two were friends."

I shrugged. "Sometimes. When the mood suits her." I didn't want to play nice with Gabby. (She'd shaved my eyebrows off at Jimmy Watts's party sophomore year.) But I had to be careful with what I said. Lily had told me Gabby had suspicions about mermaids and her brother's death.

"Yeah, I know how that goes," she said.

"Where are you headed?" I asked, an idea suddenly occurring to me. If Pavati wasn't going to show herself close to land, maybe I could get her attention farther out. It would be worth spending time with Gabby if that was the payoff.

"Nowhere in particular," she said. "Just cruising. Is that . . . is that a baby?"

Adrian was pulling the last drops out of the bottle with a dry sucking sound. "I'm babysitting for my cousin." It hurt to deny him as my son, but I knew lies were going to be a permanent part of our future. "Want to give us a ride?"

Gabby looked at Adrian hesitantly. "Is that okay with its mom?"

"I'm pretty sure. His mom is a . . . water enthusiast."

She paused.

Come on, please, I thought.

"Well, if you're sure it's okay. I could use an extra pair of eyes."

"What are you looking for?" I asked, dreading the answer and wishing I didn't have such a big mouth.

But most of all, I was hoping–hoping Pavati would forgive me for using our son as bait.

34

GABRIELLE PETTIT

Danny Catron had been kind of a putz in high school, but he seemed to have filled out quite a bit since I saw him last summer at that horrible camping trip to Manitou Island. And I was glad to see his eyebrows had grown back. In a way, now that he was older, he looked a little like Jack. Same coloring, anyway. Different eyes, though. Who had blue eyes like that?

In fact, now that I thought about it, Catron wasn't bad-looking at all. But there was something else—and not just his eyes or his mild resemblance to Jack—that kept my attention locked on him. Some distant memory of a fight. In the woods beyond the bent chain-link fence where kids went to light up in the morning before school.

Only about ten of us had gathered because the fight hadn't been well advertised. Besides, it was a family matter. Brother on brother. Danny was getting the shit beat out of him, which wasn't that interesting on its own, but the older brother said something that now, in retrospect, held possibilities.

"Mermaid," he'd said. "Effing mermaid."

Was it a coincidence Jack and Danny had both found their way to Lily Hancock? I doubted it. And what was with this baby?

"I'm babysitting for my cousin," Danny said. "Want to give us a ride?"

The baby wriggled on the dock, head nestled in Danny's well-worn Nike. His cousin must be a real piece of work to put him in charge of a kid that small. "Is that okay with its mom?"

"I'm pretty sure. His mom is a water enthusiast."

Smooth, Catron. Okay. I'll play along. We can see where this goes. "Well, if you're sure it's okay. I could use an extra pair of eyes."

"What are you looking for?"

"Did you hear about my brother Jack?"

Danny's face went slack, like he'd had a stroke or something, but his silence was all I needed. Obviously he knew all about Jack, and then some. I started up the boat and brought it up against the end of the dock. Danny handed me the swaddled baby, which felt surprisingly solid for something so small.

Danny picked up his shoes and threw them into the hull, stepping over the side rail. The bottom of his T-shirt was smeared with some yellow gunk. With my luck the baby was a puker.

Danny took the kid back from me right away. Maybe he wasn't such a bad guy after all. A dude with a baby. It was cute in a bizarre kind of way.

"So, you heard about Jack?" I asked again, since he didn't show any sign of answering.

He swallowed and looked down at his feet. "I heard he died. I'm sorry to hear that."

"Where did you hear that? From Lily?" I folded my arms over my chest.

He shook his head, eyes still downcast. "It was in the paper."

"The paper said he was missing. His body has never been found."

"Oh. Right." He nodded. "I guess I just assumed."

"What would you say if I said I thought a mermaid took him?" I paused to let that sink in.

Danny looked up. His eyes flashed and he dropped onto one of the seats, his face turning a little gray. "I don't know. That it sounds a little crazy?"

"Maybe." I studied the lake surface that lay between the Hancocks' dock and Madeline Island. "But where would two crazy people look for a mermaid?"

"I don't know what you mean."

I sighed for effect. "You're a terrible liar, Catron." Then I turned back to face him and smiled consolingly.

Danny fidgeted on his seat and wrapped the blanket tighter around his little cousin, who'd fallen asleep. "I suppose I wouldn't be looking along the shoreline," he said. "I suppose I'd try deeper water."

"Hey!" called a voice. Danny and I both jumped, and jerked our heads toward the darkened Hancock house. Lily's little sister was running across the yard for the dock. "You guys going for a boat ride? Can I come, too?"

35

CALDER

There are some moments in life you plan for. You've imagined it so many times you have to remind yourself it hasn't really happened. Not yet. Maybe not ever. And then all of a sudden, it's a day like any other, maybe a Tuesday, and you're standing in The Moment.

For me, it was like riding on top of a soap bubble. I barely breathed for fear it would burst, and I would fall to Earth, and my mother would see me for what I was: unworthy, floundering, and clumsy. Because for all my imaginings, I didn't know how to do this.

I watched my mother through the window, seeing my own reflection superimposed over my view of her as she moved around the room, touching this, straightening that. Her hands . . . My God, I remembered her hands, and a small red box of raisins in them. I followed the fingers to the wrist, up the arm. Was this the right face?

She must have felt the intensity of my stare because she looked up, then paused–surprised–before her face broke into a smile. I followed as she waved me toward the blue door and turned the dead bolt. She left the Closed sign in the window.

I stepped inside, inhaling the rich scent of ground coffee beans and the sweet slip of sugar glaze. "Mom."

Another pause, but this time accompanied by a jerk of her hand. My eyes followed her every movement.

"Excuse me?" Mrs. Boyd asked.

Without planning, I threw my arms around her neck. She staggered back from the force of my weight and caught herself against the table.

"Calder? What's wrong? What happened?"

The scent of her was a time machine. I was three years old again, sobbing on her shoulder with no ability to make voice and teeth and tongue work together and give meaning to the sounds coming from me. I clung to her too tightly, and she tried to break away.

"Mom," I said again.

"I don't know what's going on with you, Calder." She shoved me, and I let go. "But I don't appreciate it."

"It's me," I said.

"Yes, I see that." Her pinched lips told me she was both annoyed and embarrassed about how I was behaving.

"I'm Patrick."

A flash of pink joy turned to black as her hands shook like aspen leaves. "Get out."

"It's really me."

"Get out!" she demanded, louder.

"I'm Patrick," I repeated, suddenly comprehending how ridiculous I sounded.

"Patrick is dead."

"I'm alive. I can show you," I said, pulling her toward the door.

She yanked back her hand. "I'm not going anywhere with you. I don't know how you know about Patrick, or what you're trying to do, but I want you to leave."

A swirling array of color spun out of my former employer—*my mom*—like a box of melted crayons. She was crying. In my impulsiveness, I'd hurt her again. I didn't know if I should step back or put my hand on her arm. I didn't know if I should stay or run.

"It's me," I said again, as if the words should have been enough.

"I don't know why you're doing this," she said, "or what you think you have to gain, but you don't look anything like Patrick." She searched my face. Perhaps hoping to find something to make her believe? "Your eyes are all wrong."

"I can explain that," I said.

"And you're far too young to be my son."

"I see," I said, bowing my head. I gathered the bits of

information I had that might convince her and hoped against hope that they'd be sufficient. "It was the *Rhapsody in Blue*. It was my uncles' boat. I fell overboard, and Dad dove in after me."

"You could have read that somewhere. Calder, why are you doing this?"

"Raisins," I said.

"Excuse me?"

"You gave me a box of raisins. Right before I fell out of the boat."

"Impossible," she murmured.

"Please," I said. "Come with me down to the lake. I want to show you something."

Her eyes widened and her jaw fell; her aura changed from confusion and grief to hope and possibility. She moved her shaking hands to cover her mouth and spoke through her fingers. "The Star of the Sea? The redheaded woman who sat with me on the rocks?"

I didn't know what she was talking about, and I shook my head. "I don't remember much else," I said. "I don't have anything more to convince you with."

She laughed, startling me. "That's the most convincing thing you've said so far. If this were a con, you'd have done better research."

A smile pulled at the corners of my lips but quickly faded. "I want to take you to the lake. What I need to show you . . . I can only show you there."

Her serious expression returned. "Because it's her, right? She's back?"

"Who?"

"The Star of the Sea. Our Lady."

So all these years it was someone else she'd been hoping to see. I was going to be another disappointment.

"She appeared to me one day," Mrs. Boyd said. "Years and years ago. She told me she'd send Patrick home. I didn't believe her, of course, but still I prayed she'd keep her promise."

Ah. Nadia. Lily was right all along.

"She did send me home," I said slowly, hoping the weight of my words would convince her. "I'd like to explain. Please come with me, and I'll show you."

"But you're still too young," she said, doubt returning.

"I know, just please come." I took her hand, and she stared at my fingers, running her thumb over the back of my hand.

"Too young," she said, but she took a step toward the door.

I led my mom to the fishing pier by the playground and told her to wait, then I ran toward the trees.

"Where are you going?" she asked.

I turned and walked backward a few steps. "Just over there for a second. I'll be right back." But once I reached the trees, it took me longer to get up the courage than I had planned. What would she do? Would she scream? Would she run? I worried she'd get tired of waiting and head back to the café.

Deep breath. Deep breath. You have nothing to lose. Everything to gain. Nothing to lose. Deep breath. Don't be a coward. This is your mother. Your mother. Deep breath.

After what seemed like hours, I waded into the lake, out of view but close enough to hear my mom walk the length of the pier, the creak of dry splinters under sensible shoes. In the near distance, I could hear the dull rumble of an approaching boat. I'd have to make this quick.

I submerged and swam underwater, making the transformation a hundred yards out, then swimming back to the shore head-on. When I surfaced, cutting through the bands of light and the disk of sunlight, she had left the pier and was standing on the shore. "What on earth are you doing out there?" Then her hand went to her heart. "Is the Lady here, too?"

"No," I said. "Not anymore. Or . . . at least . . . not where we can see her."

She smiled. Embarrassed. "Then get out of there before you catch your death of cold."

I raised my hands from the water, palms facing her. "Not yet. I want to show you the reason why I don't look the same, why I look too young." I dove, flashing my silver tail in an obvious display, the kind of reckless thing I would normally never do so close to shore. When I came up again, she'd fainted dead away.

Gah! It was a completely stupid thing to do. What was I thinking? How could any mother accept a son like this?

"Mom?" I called, barely more than a whisper. I swam in and pulled her out to three feet of water. Maybe the cold would revive her.

When she came to, frantically blinking her eyes, I let her go and retreated a hundred feet so as not to scare her again.

But this time, there was no fear in her eyes. Her face glowed with unrestrained amazement, a bright white light streaming from every pore. She burned with light as if she were her own solar system. A million stars against the dark water.

It was the most beautiful thing I'd ever seen.

36

MARIS WHITE

Below the spot where Lily and I swam, a crayfish was caught in some lost fishing line, the other end of which was tangled in a leaf. He was dragging it like a ball and chain. Lily surprised me with an ironic laugh that cut off all thoughts in my head. It wasn't really funny, which told me how far Lily had fallen. Still, the human trill of her laugh reached my own hungry soul. There hadn't been any good hunting yet this season.

When we were little, Pavati and Tallulah would try to copy the effervescence of a human laugh. They could rouse up only a hollow imitation. Not so with Lily, even though, right now, her laugh sounded more maniacal than joyful.

It struck me how Lily didn't realize how powerful she could be. That was a good thing. I didn't need another competitor, but I could use a follower. I didn't know how everything got so out of hand. Wasn't it just last spring I could turn Pavati, Tallulah, and Calder in whatever direction I wanted them to go? That was how it should have stayed. I couldn't put my finger on the moment when I lost control.

Still, if I was losing Pavati, this Half was a good replacement. My dark colorations made me the better stalker, but just like Pavati's blue shimmer, Lily's color would make her the better lure. Beautiful. With that innocent expression that drew people to her. It would be a binge-worthy feast.

Pavati was proven and true in this regard. Given a choice, I'd prefer to stick with a tested hunting partner. If only that baby hadn't interfered with what I'd spent years cultivating. What I wouldn't do to subtract it from the equation.

When I refocused on Lily, I saw the cloud descend on her face. I could hear the cat-hissing static in her brain. She glowered at the crayfish now as if she wanted to destroy it.

"Why do you fight yourself?" I asked.

Lily covered her ears with her hands and shook her head. "I JUST WANT IT TO STOP!"

I drew closer. I meant it as a comfort. "You feel the worm inside your mind? Feel it twist? There is a cure for that, you know."

Lily looked at me with a pained expression.

"Follow me," I urged.

A low growl rumbled in Lily's chest.

"That's right. You were born for this life," I said, low and soothing. "Human beings, they were born to sustain you in this life. It's nature's plan, Lily. There's nothing wrong with being at the top of the food chain. You don't have to apologize for being what you are."

"I can't," Lily said, but it was a lie. She knew she could. In fact, she knew she would. "But I have to, don't I? If I don't, I will die right here. I can't let my parents find me dead. That would be cruel. I couldn't do that to them, so I will hunt for them. I owe them that much."

I nodded. It was as good a rationalization as any.

"Don't fight it," I said, my voice falling deep and low, soft as velveteen. It was good advice. I could watch the urge aligning itself within Lily, see it tumbling over her vertebrae like water over a rocky, shallow creek, branching over her shoulders and down her arms to her fingertips.

Lily's hands clenched and unclenched, seeking some invisible body. Her thoughts roiled like thunder, pounding out all other sound. Her legs gave way. The water came up to meet her face.

"Dive, Lily!"

It wasn't so much a dive as a collapse. Lily crumpled, falling inelegantly into the water. Her skin split and tore, finally exploding in a riot of pink sequins. But it didn't matter to me how she entered. What mattered was how she was going to leave.

I raced along beside Lily, pushing her forward. We listened to the sounds of the lake, but there was nothing human. No swimmers, and there was not enough wind for the slower-moving sailboats. Lily was already giving up. She was pathetic.

"Don't give up so easily," I coached. *"They'll come. There's always someone."*

"No one's in the water today," Lily said.

"Then lure one in."

"How?"

"Lily, you're a stunningly beautiful creature. Do what comes naturally, but you'll need to move fast. There can be no hesitation, or they'll sour. Strike. As soon as the impulse hits, you must strike and dive."

Lily groaned, imagining the feeling that would fill the empty recesses of her heart. To feel what she'd once felt so easily and taken for granted . . .

"Listen," I said. *"Someone is talking."*

"They're not in the water."

"No, but they're close to it. You need only ask. They will follow you."

The current pulled Lily's hair across her face, and she drew her arm over her eyes to clear her view. She smirked at me with red lips. Then suddenly—like some supreme gift—the body behind the voice entered the water.

Lily and I both gasped with exaltation as a white-hot explosion of unrestrained joy burst from the woman, more exquisite than anything in recent memory.

"Strike!" I cried

Lily's thoughts echoed back to me: *"Yes!"*

"Do not hesitate!" But then, from a different direction, a

familiar scent flooded my senses . . . though not firmly rooted in my memory . . . Pavati's child? Pavati's child was in the water? How could this happen? My luck was finally changing. If I could do away with Pavati's child, there'd be no more need for this silly standoff between us. Things could go back to normal. We could finally be a family again.

Pavati raced up from behind us, yelling, *"No! He's mine!"*

Lily Hancock was all but forgotten.

37

PAVATI WHITE

A boat motored overhead, then pulled away, cutting the engine and dropping anchor some fifty yards from the pier. I waited for the customary fishing line to drop, but nothing happened. Instead of the leaden plunk and the thin, spiraling fizz of the sinker, there was the faraway sound of Maris and Lily talking. I groaned. Same old, same old. As soon as my back was turned, Maris was always right there, setting her hooks, making her play.

I would have followed them, but a new scent shot through the water. It took me by surprise and sent flashes of memory across my mind—like a slide show of flickering light.

Me, huddled in a cave, pressing my palms against my pregnant belly, drumming my fingers against my taut flesh. Ripe with expectations.

My baby, nestled against me in a dark cave, as my skin tightened with dehydration, and I whispered my dreams in his ear, telling him that it would all be fine. That we would be reunited soon.

Me, crying. Begging Maris for more time. Would he forget me? Would he remember my face? Would he know the look in my eyes that said I loved him?

Maris, telling me to shut up. That I wasn't the first person to give up a child. A year was nothing. And *so what* if he forgot me? It would be easier if we weren't tied down by a child.

My baby's sweet smell in the water? What was he doing out here? My ears were full of sound, ringing. My mind fell numb. I squeezed my eyes tight and searched for Daniel Catron's scent, but he was absent. I didn't understand. A prickly flash of goose bumps ran the length of my arms.

Had Adrian fallen in? He was too young to transform. Had Daniel Catron lost his mind? Had he thrown our child overboard? Lily was right. This was my fault for having neglected him.

I tore off in the direction of Adrian's scent, only barely aware that it was the same path the boat had taken, and then just as quickly as it had appeared, it was gone.

What? Where? I jerked around, left, then right, searching

331

the water. Fear clutched at my mind and dragged me to a place I didn't want to go.

Maris hurled herself in my direction. Her thoughts told me she was focused on Adrian, her senses not as keen to him as mine were. She tracked the memory of his scent, not realizing he was gone.

"Mine!" I warned Maris. How dare she touch him?

Daniel's voice yelled from the boat, "I see her!" The words were followed by a splash—too big for Adrian.

Maris followed the sound—and so did I. Myself, out of fear. She, with a mind for destruction.

When I located the source, it wasn't Daniel or Adrian. It was Sophie Hancock in the water. Her golden hair trailed upward as her body sank a few inches below the surface, her arms extended as if waiting for something . . . or someone.

"Stay away!" I warned Maris.

Then Daniel's peppery scent flooded my senses. What was this insanity? His strong arm reached over the side of the boat and plunged deep. I watched with gratitude as he yanked Sophie out of the water.

Maris beat me to the boat, and she rose out of the waves, cracking her tail like a black bullwhip against the aluminum sides. An unfamiliar female voice screamed.

"Stop!" I cried. *"Maris, leave them alone!"*

Maris turned on me, whirling with a black swirl of her tail, blocking my line of vision. She pulled back like a cobra about to strike, her shoulders hunched, her thoughts snarled. She lashed out at me with one arm, fingers aimed at my eyes.

"Pavati!" Daniel cried from the boat before diving into the lake.

"*Idiot!*" I cried out to his deaf ears.

Maris turned her attention from me to Daniel, who was floundering ridiculously toward us. Maris wondered what to do with him—her third potential target in less than a minute's time. Still, she was not one to be too picky.

"*I'm doing us both a favor,*" she said to me before ensnaring Daniel in her arms, making an inescapable cage. She pulled him toward the bottom, her voice screeching in his ears.

I cut off her path, swiping at her face with my fingernails, beating her back with every muscle in my body. She twisted and headed north, a silver train of bubbles sweeping behind her.

I chased, and when I caught up to her, pulled her hair, snapping her neck back. Her body buckled, and Daniel broke free. He kicked for the surface, and I heard a boat motor start up. Seconds later, he was climbing back into the boat. His feet kicked at the hull, making a dull thudding sound in the water.

Maris seethed at me, her brow shadowing her eyes. She glared and pulled her lips back over her teeth. Then she came at me, biting down on my shoulder and tearing at my flesh.

I tasted my own blood in the water. We were mere feet below the surface. She wrapped her arm around my neck, her elbow just under my chin, and her tail churned the water until, from the surface, it must have looked like a feeding frenzy.

Maris tightened her choke hold. My vision faded to a

blank canvas. I lost touch with sound. It was as easy as falling asleep, but still my tail twitched. There was a scream from the boat: "Who are they? Do you see Jack with them?"

Another splash and I felt Daniel back in the water. He was a slow learner. What could he hope to achieve? But I had to applaud his courage.

Daniel swam directly at us, fighting hard against Maris's grasp on my body. He pulled at her arms, prying her hands from around my neck. There was a slashing motion, a flash of a copper-handled dagger, and I opened my eyes to see a line of red corkscrewing away from Maris's body before dissipating into a pale pink smear in the otherwise clear water.

Maris howled in outrage. She lunged, barely missing Daniel. Merely wounded, she charged and rammed his chest so hard I heard his heart skip, then stop.

"Daniel!" I cried. I didn't think twice.

I placed both palms flat on his chest and closed my eyes. An electric jolt shot from my hands, shocking his heart. Daniel's eyes flew wide, and his body contorted, writhing in pain as the seams of his swim trunks split and his body transformed—blue and gold, with flecks of black.

38

LILY

It was like an atomic bomb had been dropped on Bayfield. Joy exploded from the woman's heart and flooded the water. My own heart leapt from my chest, leading my body, seemingly meters ahead of the rest of me, screaming with both pain and ecstasy, pulling me forward.

Maris's voice cheered in my head: *"Strike!"*

My own thoughts raced forward: *"Yes!"*

"Do not hesitate!"

Someone yelled, *"Mine!"*

No, mine! I thought. After all this they were going to steal my prey for themselves? Were they really that cruel to toy with me like that?

Then another familiar yet somehow unplaceable voice: *"NO!"*

The woman was waist deep, deep enough for me to swim to her without getting caught on the sand. My mind was a vacuum; my body worked on instinct. I lunged for the light, my fingers grazing a sodden cotton dress, feeling the softness of her arms, the backward arch of her body as I yanked her off her feet.

Maris was right. It was all too easy. I clutched the bright light to my body, spiraling deeper, reveling in the joy that permeated my skin and filled my mind, hearing Pavati behind me, screaming, *"Stay away!"* as I tore the woman away from the dock and deeper, farther from shore.

Stay away? Stay away from what? Am I doing it wrong after all? Doubt trickled in, but happiness still seeped from the woman into my mind—like sugar dissolving, a slush, then a syrup, then a nectar—so I must have been doing okay.

But then I felt another body close to me. I was being chased. Pavati wanted to strip me of my catch? What was she doing?

Maris said, *"I'm doing us both a favor."*

I was so confused. I didn't understand the directions they were shouting at me. I dragged the faceless woman deeper into the lake and would have succeeded in finishing her, but I was rammed from the side with such tremendous force that my arms flung open.

The woman crawled for the surface, coming up under an

aluminum boat anchored fifty yards from the pier. The dull thumping sound of several panicked feet against the bottom of the boat vibrated through the water.

I lunged after the woman before she could be pulled out of the lake, but someone bit my arm and tore me away from her.

I swiped at my attacker's head, but whoever it was ducked and twisted, and came at me from the other side, shoving a hand under my jaw, pushing my head back. I snapped my teeth as a warning and curled into a ball, twisting under my attacker's arm and bolting after the woman, who had just cut the surface like a long, sharp knife.

39

CALDER

It was a nightmare. How could I have been so stupid as to lure my own mother into the lake? Had I lost every single brain cell? But I must have had a few still working because it took me less than a second to realize what was going on. It was as I'd always feared: that without me, Maris would get her hooks in Lily, that nature would take its course, that in the end Lily would be no better than me.

But Lily *was* better.

I could still stop this! I would not let my mother die. And I would not let Lily lose her humanity. I yelled through the water at her, *"NO!"*

I couldn't hear Maris, but I could see Lily's reaction to something she said. It gave her just a split second of hesitation, and in that bit of broken concentration, I made my move. I bit down on Lily's arm and jerked my head to the side, pulling her with me. With a gasp of surprise, her arms flew open. I watched to see if my mother would sink. Or was she still alive? She scrambled to the surface, a flurry of bubbles behind her. Thank God.

Now Lily took advantage of *my* distraction and swiped at my head. Her fingers grazed my skull as I turned at the last second and came at her from the other direction, pushing the heel of my hand under her jaw, pushing her head back so she could not attack. She struggled, twisting her neck back and forth, snapping her teeth at me as if possessed by a demon. Her eyes were wild, unseeing. She curled into a ball like an acrobat, twisting under my arm and bolting after my mother. It was too late for my mom to provide any more positive emotion—the water had fallen dark—but did Lily realize that?

Two silent figures cut the water: one black as coal, the other a blue jewel.

Maris tore after my mother. The realization that I couldn't fight all three of them dropped like a lead weight in my stomach.

"Mine!" Lily called after the other two.

"Lily, no!" I called to her. *"Look at me. Stop. Please stop. This isn't you."*

One of my mother's shoes had fallen off in the struggle, and her foot hung limp. She was cold. Too cold. Lily caught up to me and seemed to be taking instructions from her new family. She circled her fingers around my neck as if to strangle me, with no apparent recognition. She was strong, but I was stronger. I wrapped my arms around her, pressing her body to mine, and raced her away from the scene.

Behind me I heard one shoe-clad foot and one bare one kicking against the outside of an aluminum boat. Someone had pulled my mother to safety! Now if they only had the good sense to get her back to shore.

Lily squeezed my skull between her palms, pushing my face away from hers.

"Lily, look at me. Open your eyes," I begged.

A scream erupted from her, the likes of which I'd never heard before. Wild and primal and desperate and despairing. I covered her mouth with mine, letting her scream fill every recess of my body, absorbing her pain into my mind, my bones, my muscles. The dark descent of her heart was excruciating to bear. I hardly recognized her as Lily. Her lips were cold and steely against mine; her nails dug into my shoulders. Though she tried, I wouldn't let her wrench herself away from the kiss. If that was what this was. I would gladly absorb this misery from her because the thought of her killing my mother—anyone, really—was so much worse.

I felt Lily's despair seep in, slowly pooling through me with inky darkness, as if she were writing on my heart with a leaky pen. I didn't fight it even when my stomach constricted with nausea and my fluke convulsed beneath me.

Seconds into the exchange, I felt the change in her: the softening of her lips, the faint smell of citrus in the water, the weight of her hands turning from a push to a pull as she held me closer.

340

She gasped, first with exhaustion and then with surprise. I didn't know if the surprise came from her coming back into herself or from the wretched sight of me. I had never felt such anguish as that which I had just taken from her. From the way the world looked through my eyes now, I was sure my face was black and hollow. I doubled over from the pain of having absorbed such an overload of negative energy. It was worse than I could have ever imagined.

Lily pulled me back to her and kissed me again, wrapping herself around me as if she meant to protect me from the world. Our bodies twisted into one, like two trees that had grown too close together. She said my name over and over like the chorus to a song. Her hands were in my hair . . . and she was filling me again, but this time with something that buoyed me back up to the living.

Her thoughts were a whisper, as if she had no idea of the chaos that was happening around us. *What did you do to me?*

"I saved you," I gasped. *"It was my turn."*

Lily released me and smiled for just a second when I lifted my head. But then something else caught her attention, reminding her of where we were.

Maris and Pavati circled each other, their tails lashing back and forth.

"What are they saying?" I asked. *"What are they fighting over?"*

"Danny," she said.

My relief at my mother's safety outweighed any concern I had for Daniel Catron. He, at least, had chosen his fate. My mom hadn't chosen danger. I'd put her in that position. *"Then my mom's still safe in the boat."*

Lily turned to me in horror when she realized whom her prey had been.

Before I could confirm the question in her eyes, we both turned in panic at the coppery smell of blood in the water.

"Danny!" Lily cried as Daniel's body went limp and slowly sank deeper, his arms raising to his sides and then up over his head.

Pavati chased after him, a streak of blue, then there was a loud crack and a burning smell in the water.

"Oh, man," I whispered.

"Danny," Lily whispered, as he raced away with Pavati, hand in hand, matching blue tails bending and arcing through the water, a trail of silver bubbles in their wake.

Maris, in her fury, charged the boat again. She would pacify herself with a victim, any victim, one way or another.

Lily screamed, *"Help!"*

"What do you need?" I asked.

"Not you," she said. *"Nadia. She owes me."*

I would have protested, but before I could speak, Lily gripped the pendant in her fist and closed her eyes.

"I did my part," she said, but she wasn't talking to me. *"Maris is not keeping her promise to you. If you want your family—what's left of it—to be together, you need to step in. You still have time. You still have time."* Lily was practically chanting now. *"There's still time to intervene."*

I reached out for her. She must have been delirious if she thought Nadia was going to come to anyone's rescue.

My fingers, however, were not met by her hand. Instead, they found an electricity surrounding Lily like a force field. It pulsed from the pendant like a heartbeat, throbbing, then pounding, then beating with a deafening noise. I covered my ears and closed my eyes as we all rose to the surface.

40

LILY

It started with a trembling. A thin layer of silver water vibrated on the surface of the dark lake like rain on a snare drum. Taut. Tense. Bouncing. A tremor of electricity raced through my veins, and instinctively I surfaced to search the sky. Storm clouds tumbled over one another like wrestling children, but no sign of lightning, no sound of thunder. Oh, God, what had I done now?

I dropped my gaze just in time to see a stampede of droplets skitter across the surface like tiny beads of mercury, rolling, then racing, all bound for one central point. Maris retreated a few strokes and stared. I could hear Calder breathing heavily behind me, and my mouth fell open.

"Lily, do you know what you're doing?" he asked.

Of course not. When did I ever? I'd always gone with my gut and things rarely turned out the way I planned. Still, it was the only way I knew how to do anything.

At the point where the beads of water joined, they leapt from the lake like rain in reverse, then a small fountain shot upward, collapsed, then shot higher. A geyser in Lake Superior. I was hyperaware of everything around me.

Gabby screamed and scuttled backward, falling onto the floor of the boat. Mrs. Boyd held Adrian with one arm and wrapped the other protectively around Sophie, who declined the comfort and went to stand at the rail. Maris cowered behind me and Calder.

We were all pinned in place–spellbound–by what took shape in the geyser: a head, a slender neck, beautiful shoulders, and the suggestion of arms. The geyser collapsed, followed by a terrifying hush, then shot up again in a roaring rush of sound, towering over us by twenty feet, this time holding its form.

"Holy hell," Calder mumbled.

"Nadia," I said.

Then came the voice. It was just as in my dreams, but deeper and farther away, as if she were speaking through a tunnel, or from a grave.

"You're not all here," she said, her voice tumbling. "Where's Pavati? And Tallulah?"

Calder grabbed my hand and pulled me behind him as

if he'd forgotten I was the one who'd summoned her. What would we say? How could I explain all that had happened?

"It's my fault," Maris said.

"Maris?" Nadia asked.

"I failed you."

"Who called me?" Nadia asked.

A small whimper escaped my lips, and Nadia spotted the pendant around my neck.

"My daughter," Dad said, swimming up behind me. I could sense his irritation at having found me missing from my room. "Your granddaughter."

Nadia's face softened at the first sight of her grown son—if softening was possible in the watery mask—and I swear I could see the love there. She rushed at my dad, making a giant wave and engulfing him in an embrace that took him under.

The lake fell quiet. Then Dad resurfaced behind Maris, his face shocked but exuberant, as the geyser shot up again.

"You came home," she said to my dad. Then she looked at me and Calder. "Did you find the Thin Woman? McElroy?"

"I did," Calder said, gesturing at the boat.

The pillar of water twisted like a cyclone and found Mrs. Boyd, who still held Adrian tight. She stood alongside Sophie and Gabby at the rail. Her mouth hung open in awe.

Nadia twisted again, finding me. "You did well."

I beamed with pride, and Maris let out a howl of betrayal. She flung herself from the water, arching into a back dive that marked her angry retreat.

Calder lunged and grabbed her arm, catching her. He

yanked her to his side and forcibly turned her chin to face Nadia. "Oh, no you don't," Calder said through gritted teeth. "Stand and face the music, Maris."

"There is no music to face, sweetheart," Nadia said to Maris, but based on the beautiful sound of her watery voice, that matter was up for debate.

The pillar that was Nadia curved and bent toward her oldest daughter. "Don't be ashamed, Maris. It was wrong of me to put so much responsibility on one so young."

Maris couldn't look at her mother. She closed her eyes and, still held tightly in Calder's hands, wrenched her head back and forth.

"I'm better off on my own," Maris spit through a locked jaw. She clawed at Calder's hands, trying to pull herself free. "I don't want to be a family with the likes of these. How do you expect me to look at them and not remember how they hurt you?"

"I'm not asking you to forget," Nadia said. "I'm asking you to forgive. To forgive them, to forgive me, and to forgive yourself."

Maris shrieked and sent a shock wave of pain through the water. Calder's hands flew back. I heard myself yell "No!" And with a flash of white light, Maris made her escape.

41

CALDER

Nadia melted away into the lake, finally laid to rest, her promise to Mrs. Boyd fulfilled. Lily held the pendant in her fingers, looking at it anew. "She's gone," she said, but she didn't have to tell me. I could feel her go. We could all sense Nadia's relief. The lake stilled to a glassy calm, warmer than it had been all season.

As soon as the water went quiet, Jason raced back home to tend to Mrs. H. He had revived her, just as I had done for the kayaker, but there had never been a proper reinvigoration. None of us knew whether the shock that had killed her would also change the course of the disease. I had my doubts, but only time would tell.

Sophie captained the Pettits' Sun Sport back to shore with Adrian slung over her shoulder, while Gabby and my mother huddled on the floor of the boat, in shock over what they'd seen. Honestly, I was no less in shock. We would try to explain everything to them later.

Maris was gone for good. We knew that as soon as Pavati and Daniel returned to check on their child, and Pavati said she could no longer hear Maris in the lake—the mental thread that bound them finally cut.

I wondered at the tenuous reunification of our family. Jason's promise to join Maris meant nothing now that she had severed the familial ties, and I had to admit that Pavati's actions in the lake made me more inclined to trust her as our new matriarch. The future looked brighter than it ever had.

For now, though, I could barely take my eyes off Lily, as she lay on top of the water, entirely peaceful, basking in the spot where the pillar of water had dissolved. I imagined Lily could still feel the love there.

Shards of pink light radiated from her tail, nearly blinding me. The way I felt brought Lily's poets back to memory. I was tempted to quote them—something about loving her to the depth and breadth and height my soul could reach. But the words didn't sound like enough, so I didn't ruin her moment.

She was the most amazing creature I'd ever seen. Because of her, I was more than I'd ever been before. I had a family. A real family. And it was bigger and better than anything I could have hoped for. I had a past. I had an identity. I was Patrick McElroy. My evolution was complete.

I gave Lily one more look–memorizing the image–before heading to shore.

Later that night, as we sat around the fireplace in the Hancocks' cozy living room, I watched the light flicker across all the faces I loved: Jason's, Carolyn's, Sophie's, and Lily's most of all. Mrs. Boyd sat silently, wrapped in a blanket, recovering from the day, holding Adrian.

Lily couldn't say sorry enough, but Mrs. Boyd . . . *Mom* (that was going to be hard to get used to) would have none of it. Seemed she was having trouble connecting her former employee with the memory of the sea monster who had nearly killed her.

After Mom left, making me promise to come see her in the morning, and after Sophie fell asleep, Lily stood up and pulled me outside and onto the front porch.

She rose on the balls of her feet. "Patrick," she said, kissing me once. "I guess I could get used to calling you that."

I wrapped my arms around her and laced my fingers behind her back. "It doesn't matter what you call me, so long as you let me stay."

"Don't be stupid," she said, wrinkling her nose.

"Oh, I think I'm entitled."

She bowed her head, gently bumping her forehead against my chest three times. "You know I was right to send you away. How could you doubt how I felt about you?"

"Chalk it up to a lifetime of insecurity. But you're right. I should never have doubted you. From the first time I met you I knew you were something special. You've proved that to me over and over again. I guess, when you told me Nadia was talking to you, I was just too scared to believe it."

"Well, you don't have a monopoly on fear, but . . . I think that part is over for now."

Lily led me off the porch to our hammock. She had me get in first before crawling in, curling her body to mine.

"So," she said.

"So?" I asked, running my fingers up and down her spine. She shivered and pulled herself closer to me, which was, of course, the desired effect.

"Maybe we can get back to that conversation we were having?" she suggested.

"Which conversation was that?"

She tipped her head back and looked at me with a serious expression. "The one that was so rudely interrupted." Her silvery eyes shone in the moonlight, and I sucked in my breath at their intensity.

I tangled my fingers in her long hair and reveled in the return of the happy pink light that shimmered from her shoulders, the tip of her nose, the curve of her ears. Even though I knew what she was talking about, I played dumb. "You lost me."

Lily blushed and looked out toward the lake. "You know the one. The one about our future."

A small laugh rumbled low in my chest. "Oh, that. Well, I had plenty of time to think about that while I was out on my own. It was probably a stupid idea. Just the result of an impulsive moment–"

351

"Calder!" she said, slapping my chest with her palms.

I grabbed her wrists and held both her hands between our bodies. "But . . . ," I hedged. "I'm known to be impulsive. I'm sure the moment will hit again someti–"

"If you won't do it, then I will."

"No . . . wait . . . I think I feel something coming on. . . ." I released her hands and reached into my pocket. With only a second of hesitation, I took out the circle of braided copper and slipped it on her waiting finger. The polished surface of the banded agate shone in the lights from the kitchen window. "I'm not perfect," I said.

She kept her eyes on her hand.

"But I'll try really hard to be that perfect Tennyson merman you've always wanted."

"Maybe I'd believe that," she teased, "if you could say it in rhyme."

I wrapped my arms around her and pulled her as close as I could without crushing her. "Now you're pushing your luck."

We lay there quietly, listening to the muffled voices of Lily's parents in the house, waves crashing on the shore, pine boughs groaning overhead, the occasional *pop* of an errant firecracker going off at a faraway campfire. . . .

"So you forgive me?" she asked.

"Let's see . . . for sending me away to find my mother, only so you could try to kill her the first chance you got?"

I could see Lily pale in the darkness.

"I'm sorry," I said. "That wasn't funny. You have to know I could never live without you. I need you with me."

"Need?" she asked. "Or want?"

"Is there a difference?" I asked.

"Slight," she said. "After what happened on the water yesterday"–she swallowed hard, remembering–"I understand what you mean by *need*, but it's not very romantic somehow."

"Then I *want* you, Lily Hancock. Always. Forever."

She smiled, and I could feel our heartbeats quicken in perfect synchronicity.

"And about the other thing?" she prompted.

"And yes, I forgive you for everything that happened. I was just as much to blame."

She sighed, and the light spiraling out of her mixed with the electricity in me. Together, it hummed like an aurora borealis light show between our two bodies, starting with our locked gazes and traveling across our collarbones, then down our arms and tangled legs.

"What's that thing you told me the first time we lay in this hammock?" I asked.

"Forgiveness," she said. "It's the thing that frees the heart."

ACKNOWLEDGMENTS

Whew. We've come to the end, and I've been so humbled by the experience. When I woke up in the middle of the night with Calder White's voice in my head saying, "I hadn't killed anyone all winter, and I have to say, I felt pretty good about that," I had no idea where that one line would take us. This series would not have been possible without the enthusiasm of readers, librarians, teachers, and bookstores. Thank you! I also have to thank, in no particular order, Françoise Bui, Rebecca Short, Paul Samuelson, Sonia Nash, and Random Buzzers; my wonderful agent, Jacqueline Flynn; Beta Readers Heather Anastasiu, Lauren Peck, David Nunez, Li Boyd, Carolyn Hall, Nina Badzin, and Kristen Simmons; and the Apocalypsies, Michelle Krys, the helpful staff of the Thunder Bay Public Library, my parents, and all the talented and inspiring kids at SAHS and SJHS. Finally, thank you to Sammy, Matt, Sophie, and Greg. Fire up the grill. It's time to celebrate!

ANNE GREENWOOD BROWN is the author of *Lies Beneath, Deep Betrayal,* and *Promise Bound.* She is terrified of high places, deep places, falling from high places into deep places, and fish of all sorts. Other than that, she's game for anything. You can find her here: annegreenwoodbrown.com; and here: facebook.com/annegreenwoodbrown; and sometimes here: @AnneGBrown; but most often with her nose in a book.